Love & Friendship

NANCY ROSS

POOLBEG

Published 2004
by Poolbeg Press Ltd
123 Grange Hill, Baldoyle
Dublin 13, Ireland
E-mail: poolbeg@poolbeg.com

© Nancy Ross 2004

The moral right of the author has been asserted.

Typesetting, layout, design © Poolbeg Press Ltd.

13 5 7 9 10 8 6 4 2

A catalogue record for this book is available from the British Library.

ISBN 1-84223-145-6

Typeset by Patricia Hope in Palatino 10/14.5
Printed by
Nørhaven A/S, Viborg,
Denmark

www.poolbeg.com

F126,029
E 9

About the Author

Nancy Ross is the only child of the well-known musician and songwriter, BC Hilliam. After a career in the WRNS, followed by several high-powered secretarial jobs, two marriages and three children, she started out on yet another career – writing.

Her previous novels, *Still Waters Run Deep* and *The Enchanted Island* were also published by Poolbeg.

Acknowledgements

British VC's of World War 2 A Study in Heroism by John Laffin, Sutton Publishing

The Battle of Arnhem – the Betrayal Myth Refuted by Cornelis Bauer on information supplied by Lt.Col Theodoor Boeree

The quotation from 'Abide with Me' by Henry Francis Lyte 1793 – 1847

To my grandchildren,
Cosmo, Carlos, Skye and Jimmy

Swift to its close ebbs out life's little day;
Earth's joys grow dim, its glories pass away.

HENRY FRANCIS LYTE

Chapter 1

"Come on, boy," I say, "it's time to do your stuff."

I open the hatchback of the car, there is a scuffle and I slam it shut. He is panting to be of service, eager to please, to grovel, to assume the soulful expression so much admired, even to lie on his back with his legs in the air if that is required of him. Of course, I can see his attraction; he is a delectable creature, my golden cocker spaniel named Flush. He is named for a very famous dog that belonged to Elizabeth Barrett Browning, the Victorian poetess. The original Flush was stolen three times by dog thieves who haunted an area of London called Shoreditch. My Flush has had no such escapades; the nearest he has got to a real adventure was in pursuit of a Labrador bitch on heat, a lady too tall and stately for him, but that did not deter him. He stationed himself outside her house, a lovesick swain, and the owner took note of the telephone number on the tag of his collar (Flush would never think of growling at a stranger) and telephoned us, asking for him to be collected as soon as possible.

A friend suggested the Pat-a Dog-Scheme, and said that Flush's charm and amiable nature was tailor-made for it. Rather foolishly, I put his name down. Now I feel we are involved for life, Flush's life that is.

There is an inevitable sadness about the old, and I have inflicted this upon myself twice weekly. Some of the men and women we visit are touchingly sweet, some are not, but Flush treats them all the same; they are human beings to him, like Dan and me and the boys, though he realises not so special. To him they are not victims of circumstances and old age. His tufted head is patted over and over again; biscuits are produced but politely refused by me as they are against the rules.

We visit two retirement homes: Dene Park, run by the Council, where the residents are all addressed by their Christian names, and Riverbank, a private home and completely different. Here I am introduced to Mrs This or Lady That, one by one, and Flush and I pass from private room to private room. The rooms are luxurious and hideously expensive; they have adjoining bathrooms and kitchenettes and are furnished with a cherished desk or table or the occupant's own chair.

The ladies who superintend these homes are very different too. Moira who sits behind the desk in the entrance hall of Riverbank is a tinted blonde with red lacquered nails. She is efficient and a little brusque, whereas Shirley, the superintendent of Dene Park is short and chubby and endlessly helpful.

Monday is Dene Park day, so we trail after Shirley. The residents are sitting in a communal room, clustered around a television set that is not turned off when we arrive. There are so many deaf people here that, in any case, Shirley has to shout to be heard.

"Peggy!" she screeches, leaning down. "Here's Flush to see you."

Peggy's eyes swivel from the screen and she looks genuinely pleased to see us. Here is a diversion and she welcomes it. A shaky hand emerges and Flush obligingly puts his wet nose into it. "The dear . . ." she says, giving me a grateful smile. There is no doubt the scheme does a great deal of good. The other residents gather around, the television forgotten for the moment, and Flush thumps his tail in delight at so much attention.

On Thursday we go to Riverbank. "We have a new guest today," Moira tells me. "Mrs Bailey. Her husband, Mr Theodore Bailey, has been with us for a year, and now his wife has joined him."

I say: "I have not met Mr Bailey."

Moira explains. "He is a very quiet gentleman, not quite with us, if you know what I mean. I don't think Flush would be helpful to him."

We visit most of the rooms, and it is nearly time to leave the occupants to their strange disembodied existence consisting of meals, television and the slow

3

passage of time leading to an inevitable conclusion. I heave a sigh of relief that it will soon be over. I confess I find there is something spurious about Riverbank that I do not like. It lacks the cosy good humour of Dene Park; at least there they have achieved what they set out to do, run a no-nonsense, no-frills establishment to cater for the old and infirm. Riverbank tries to emulate a five-star hotel while at the same time providing the comforts of an elegant home. In my view, it fails miserably on both counts, especially the last one; a few personal belongings squeezed into a small room do not constitute a home.

Mrs Bailey is our last call. I look at my watch because soon I must collect my elder son from school. I look forward to seeing his face, a young face, mingling with all the other young faces and hurtling bodies as they stream out of the classrooms.

The room I enter is not as overcrowded with furniture as the others. She has contented herself with a small rosewood desk, a table and a soft leather armchair with a footstool. There are no photographs to be seen, and I notice this at once because it is unusual. In every other room Flush and I have visited this afternoon there have been numerous photographs, mostly in silver frames. Photographs of children, no doubt children no longer, and of grandchildren and sometimes great-grandchildren. I know all about them because I have expressed an interest on many occasions; the family provides a good topic of conversation and I have resorted to it often. Here there are none, but I notice shelves have been put along one wall, no doubt on the lady's instructions, and they are packed with books. Of course there is the television supplied by the management, but I suspect the bed belongs to her: it is larger than the narrow beds in the other rooms. The other walls are bare save for one picture, a drawing of a girl wearing a turban. I glance at it quickly and see it bears the signature of Augustus John. Not an original, surely?

This thought is darting through my brain as I approach the old woman sitting in the armchair, and I push Flush towards her.

"I don't want to pet the bloody dog, darling," she says.

I am startled. "Don't you like dogs?" I ask.

"Oh, yes, I like dogs all right. When I . . . well, my husband, Theo, gave me a little dog of my own and I took him everywhere with me. He was called Bobby and he jumped out of a taxi window, right into the middle of the traffic."

"Oh, dear," I say. "Was he killed?"

"Not him," she responds cheerfully. "The taxi driver and I managed to catch him, running this way and that way between the cars and the buses. He lived until he was sixteen."

Her hand flutters over Flush's head as if she might relent and stroke him, but she does not; instead she reaches for the biscuit tin on an exquisite small antique table by her side.

"No," I say hastily, "he is not allowed biscuits. Too fattening."

She takes no notice and I wonder if she is deaf. The biscuit is gone in one delighted gulp.

"He enjoyed that," she says with satisfaction.

Later I will discover that she likes getting her own way. Now, she gives me a little conspiratorial smile, and I look into her face for the first time. I see an old woman with faded blue eyes, and they are staring at me with the guilelessness of a child, and it is a child's face I look into, a child's face grown grotesquely old without losing any of its childish qualities. Her hair is soft and white and almost curly. I think she must have been very beautiful at some time, and the beauty is still there, in the smooth skin and the line of her eyebrows. The fine symmetry of her features is not masked by old age.

"You are a newcomer here?" I ask.

"I arrived a week ago," she replies, and her mouth turns down a little as if the memory is not pleasing. "I had a succession of ladies looking after me. Some of them I liked and some of them I didn't, but it made no difference because the ones I grew to like were gone before we could become friends. Before I knew it they were instructing the next one about the house, where everything was kept, my little idiosyncrasies, what I liked for breakfast, and so on, and, when I was out of earshot, no doubt saying I was a selfish old bat. It could not go on, all that coming and going, endless changes, having to get used to new faces all the time; eventually

I decided to pack up and leave my home and join Theo at this place."

"It is surely better that you are together," I say reasonably, complacently prepared to pass judgement on something I know nothing about. With my thoughts on the time and getting away it seems the ideal solution; two married people should be together in their last years.

"You are right, darling," she says, and then, "Poor Theo."

I get to my feet, and so does Flush.

"You are not going?" She sounds almost desperate.

"Well, I thought . . ."

"You have no idea how lonely it is here," she says, sitting up a little in her chair as if to emphasise the point. "My only visitor is Father Donovan who says he will come to see me every Wednesday."

"Ah!" I say, still standing. "You are Irish, I thought I detected it in your voice but I couldn't be sure."

"Yes," she replies, "I am a good Catholic girl." And then she giggles. There is no other way to describe the laughter that comes from her mouth: it is a deep-throated giggle, like that of a naughty child who has been caught doing something outrageous. Coming from a rather dignified lady it is as unexpected as it is refreshing.

"Sit down, dear, for a few minutes more," she pleads.

I sit down on the edge of my chair and Flush, after

glancing at me, flops down again with his nose on his front paws.

"It must be only a few minutes," I tell her. "I have to pick up my son from school."

She nods. "I understand." She delays me by asking questions. How many children have I? What are their ages? What does my husband do for a living?

I reply politely to all her questions. I have two boys, Hugh aged six and Neil aged four. It is Hugh I have to collect from school as Neil only attends in the morning. My husband, Dan, is an architect and at present is engaged in designing one-bedroom flats for first-time buyers, young married couples and career men and women who do not want to share accommodation. I tell her there are a lot of bureaucratic obstacles to overcome in this scheme and he is very busy.

"I really must go," I say getting to my feet again, and Flush gets up too.

"Of course, you must, darling," she says. "You must not be late for Hugh or he will start getting fussed. Shall I see you tomorrow?"

Tomorrow? I can't believe my ears. In view of her rebuttal of Flush's advances I was not intending to call on her on my next visit to Riverbank.

"I'm afraid I can't come tomorrow," I say firmly.

"Well, come the day after then," she replies graciously, as if she is doing me a favour, "and bring the dog with you."

"That would be during the weekend and impossible

for me. Anyway, I thought you were not keen on Flush?"

"Oh, no, I love him. It's the petting thing I don't like. It makes me feel like all the old fogies in this place, just existing for a tiny change in their routine, like the arrival of a dog for them to pet. It's pathetic."

"It's not pathetic," I say hotly. "Maybe you don't need a bit of cheer in your day but there are others who do. I take Flush to another retirement home where conditions are not so luxurious as they are here, and I am always amazed at the happiness he brings into the lives of those people, if only for a few moments."

She looks distressed. "Oh, darling, I did not mean to upset you. I am a disagreeable old woman, but I am so old you must forgive me."

"How old are you?" I snap, remembering the oldest resident in Dene Park is over a hundred years old.

"Ninety-six . . ."

"Good heavens! I had no idea . . ." I relent. "You don't look it," I say sincerely.

It is the stock answer when one of them tells you his or her age: an exclamation of surprise followed by the words 'You don't look it'. In this case, it is true; her face is almost unlined compared to others of her age and her hair has a youthful vitality about it. She has not moved from her chair so I don't know how good she is on her pins.

"My husband, Theo, is nearly one hundred," she says. "Men live to a great age when they have no sex. Sex shortens their lives."

"Really?" I am already at the door, my fingers on the handle. "I'll come and see you on Tuesday of next week" I open the door quickly so I do not have to pursue the matter of Theo's sex life. "Goodbye, Mrs Bailey."

"Please call me Maeve," she says.

On the way out I am further delayed by Moira who asks me: "What do you make of Mrs Bailey?"

"Interesting," I reply hurriedly. "Marvellous for her age. She doesn't look ninety-six."

An expression of irritation passes over Moira's face. "She isn't," she says shortly. "She's ninety-two. I have documents to prove it. It really annoys me the way old people lie about their age."

I laugh. "She probably made herself younger than she really was for years, then when she got older she reversed the procedure to make herself more interesting."

"It's lying, whatever way you look at it. It beats me why someone of ninety-two would want to add four years to her age."

"I must fly. I'm coming to see Mrs Bailey early next week."

"I'm glad," says Moira as I make for the door. "She doesn't fit in well with the other residents, and I think she's lonely."

Chapter 2

Maeve delaying me from leaving and my being waylaid by Moira makes me ten minutes late. Hugh is standing outside the school gates and, as I drive up, I see that he is accompanied by one of the teachers who has stayed with him until I turn up. It is nice of her.

"I'm so sorry," I say, thinking that it is the first time I have been late.

"That's quite all right, Mrs Maitland," she says, faintly disapproving.

Hugh, clambering into the car, is crosser than her. "Where were you?" he demands.

I feel admonished by both of them, as if I had committed a criminal act during the afternoon.

"It was Pat-a-Dog day at Riverbank," I tell him, "and a bossy old lady would not let me go." As I speak Flush is jumping up and down in the hatchback section

11

of the car, trying in that small space to convey to Hugh how pleased he is to see him.

"Did he behave himself?" Hugh asks, already forgiving me for being late.

"Flush was a star," I tell him, "as always."

"He doesn't know they are old," he says. "To him they are just people."

"Yes, I was thinking the same thing myself. People who want to feed him titbits. Today was his lucky day; he got a biscuit from one of the ladies. I couldn't stop her."

"Are they all sad?" he asks, as if elderly people hail from another planet. I regret, not for the first time, that neither Dan nor I have living parents, so our children have no experience of grandparents. I think that is the reason Hugh made that observation; he puts old people in a special category, remote from the world that he and his brother, from a different generation, inhabit. Children should grow up knowing old people, and learn to understand their vulnerability and tolerate their eccentricities. What my children do not know, because they have no experience of it, is that grandparents have time to listen. I try to be a good listener but sometimes it is hard. I am too tired or too busy to concentrate on their problems. To give me my due, however, I only disregard trivial problems; if it's something important I'm there for them.

Neil recounts long convoluted stories about events at school (school being new and interesting) or

Thunderbird adventures he watches on video. At these times I find my concentration slipping, and Dan is hopeless. He is good when it comes to a game of cricket in the garden, but an impatient listener.

Neil is sitting at the kitchen table eating fish fingers and baked beans prepared by the baby-sitter, Ruby, who comes to look after Neil on the Pat-a-Dog days. She is clearly put out by my lateness and I mumble half-hearted apologies and rummage in my bag for her money.

"Has anything happened?" I ask. "Any calls?"

"Dan phoned to say he would be late tonight."

I have noticed that these days everyone, young and old alike, address us by our Christian names. Mr and Mrs are designations that are hardly ever used except in shops. There is no respect for married status any more, and I wonder why so many young people still bother with it. Perhaps it is the wedding that appeals to them.

"He said not to bother with a meal for him," says Ruby.

Nothing changes. The boys regard me seriously.

"Why isn't Daddy coming home?" Hugh asks.

"He's got a big project on at the moment."

Ruby has pocketed the money and is now packing up her things, anxious to be off. She brings her schoolwork with her, and she carries a heavy bag. The boys chorus their goodbyes; they accept her but they are not close to her. I suppose the age gap is too small. Ruby is old enough and capable enough to look after them, but young enough to resent being in charge of two small children. A middle-aged woman would make more of an effort, join in their games, but middle-aged babysitters are hard to find. I am thinking this as I see her to the door, and it is a continuation of my earlier reflections about the absence of grandparents.

Hugh has his evening meal and then settles down to his homework. As he is so young it is not very taxing, but he takes it seriously. Neil is not old enough yet to have any and for some reason, hard to understand, he thinks this is unfair. Then I allow them to watch a video, *The Jungle Book*, for about the hundredth time.

As usual, bath time is a protracted pleasure, with much splashing, laughing and fighting. I sit on a stool and watch them abstractedly, my arms full of towels. I remember that when they were much smaller this time of the evening was an enchantment that Dan liked to share, adjusting his day so that he could see his two little sons splashing in water.

I read them a story before they go to sleep. They sit up in their twin beds, blond wet hair flattened to their heads, smelling sweetly of soap and the body-scent peculiar to small boys. I think they are the most beautiful creatures that ever existed. When the book has been closed, I kiss them goodnight. "I love you," I say to each of them in turn, and they assure me they love me too.

I empty the water from the bath, gather up all the toys and put them in a basket. Then I go to the kitchen, prepare a salad with two slices of cold ham on the top, and pour myself a glass of red wine.

I eat and drink with a tray on my lap. I watch a soap on the television, and when it is finished I carry the tray back into the kitchen, mindful of the fact that my husband disapproves of the practice of eating in the sitting-room. I pour myself another glass of wine.

After the News I change from one channel to another, discarding programmes about hospitals, vets and wild life. I settle on an old movie, but it does not grab my attention and I find myself nodding off from time to time, another thing that Dan finds very irritating. When I wake with a start I have a feeling of guilt before I realise he is not with me.

Eventually, I let Flush out for his last run, and then I trail off to bed leaving him lying on his big cushion in the corner of the hall. I have a bath and spend time tidying the bedroom, trying to stay up until Dan's return. When I hear the clock downstairs strike eleven times I get into bed but, even then, I lie in the dark, eyes open, listening intently for the sound of his key in the lock of the front door.

When I hear it, and other sounds as well, I feel my back stiffen. The opening and shutting of doors, lights clicking on and then off again, Flush's welcome which is hastily subdued with the whispered words: "Back to your bed!" I know the process so well, the familiar process of my husband returning home. His feet are on the stairs. Halfway up one of them creaks.

When he enters the room, for some reason I do not understand myself, I feign sleep. He pads around the room, moving quietly so as not to disturb me. The mattress sinks on one side as he gets into bed. I do not move a muscle. I hear him give a little sigh and then he turns his broad back away from me. There is a cold space in the bed, between where our bodies are lying. His breathing settles into the rhythm of sleep. I lie motionless beside him, listening, as the breathing turns to gentle snoring punctuated by disturbing gaps. I am very used to the sleeping noises made by Dan. I have even found them endearing over the years and we have laughed together about them. It is not as if it is a full-blown snore like some men do; it is moderate, almost comforting and cannot be heard in the rest of the house. It is confined to this bed, this area where we exist as man and wife. I know that tonight it will keep me awake.

Breakfast is a hurried stressful affair. Dan and I always leave in two cars, he to his office, I to take the children to school. On the way I pick up another child, Amy, the daughter of my great friend, Jane. Amy is the same age as Neil and attends morning school only. I will pick them both up at half past twelve. Jane has been having a course of chemotherapy that is nearing completion, and she has given up doing the school run because of it. I park the car outside her gate, and Amy runs down the path. I get out and open the door for her, and she climbs into the back seat beside the boys.

"How is Mummy?"

"She's fine."

I look out of the window and see that Jane, in her dressing-gown, has come to her front door. And she waves cheerfully in my direction, and calls out: "Thank you. I'll telephone you."

"No, it's my turn. I'll call you."

I get round to doing it three hours later, and Jane tells me that the treatment has been diabolical. "They tell me I caught it in time," she says. "I did not waste a moment." My heart goes out to her and I wonder, faced with a similar situation, would I react as she did? Or would I wait and hope it would go away so that I would not have to face an outcome I dreaded? Was I, at this moment, evading an issue that I should be facing with courage? These questions attack me like a host of avenging bats all the time I am speaking to Jane.

"You're wonderful," I hear myself saying. "I'm so proud of you." At the same time I make a resolution to talk to Dan about the state of our marriage.

I met him at a dinner party given by a rich man who had just moved into an interesting house designed by Dan. The invitation lacked tact: "Come to dinner and meet my architect. He's single."

I felt a tiny twinge of resentment because I was not in the mood for a new relationship or any reminder that the old one no longer existed. I had been living, on and off, for five years with a married man who baulked at

17

divorcing his wife. Finally, the lack of future, lack of prospect of having children, influenced me into giving him up. It was a brave move and the wounds still hurt. I felt alone and very vulnerable and conscious of rapidly approaching the dreaded thirty benchmark, with nothing settled in my life except a career in publishing.

As soon as I saw Dan, I knew this was the man I wanted to marry. Later, much later, he said he felt the same way and I hoped it was true. I was not expecting any conquest that evening. I was emotionally drained after heated recriminations and accusations. All I wanted was to be left in peace. Then across the dining-table I looked into the craggy face of my beloved and I knew where I belonged.

It was so simple and uncomplicated. He was thirty-five and looking for stability in his life. Afterwards, he told me he was weary of meaningless relationships, tired of his lonely existence in the market town of Melford where he worked. He was conventional, not in his work but in the way he wanted to live, and he embraced the idea of marriage. We would have children, he decreed. No reservations such as 'let's wait two years' – that was not Dan's way. Once he had decided on matrimony and a family there must be no delays.

I did not have any doubts about the course I wanted to take. Without hesitation I gave up my rented flat in London and walked out of my well-paid job. There was no one of importance in my life to tell me I was behaving in a foolish precipitous way by falling in with the schemes of a man I had known for a very short time. Only my sister, Monica, intervened and telephoned to tell me I was mad, but I did not listen to her.

Dan's mother had died six months earlier and he could not face a church ceremony without her being there. He was apologetic, convinced that it was every girl's dream to have a big wedding with a choir and bridesmaids. I told him I preferred a registry office. Having been a man's mistress for five years I thought it would be hypocritical to walk down the aisle in a virginal white dress.

"Although I know everyone does it," I said.

"You could always wear a scarlet petticoat," Dan said.

Only four people witnessed our marriage, my sister Monica, five years my senior and unmarried, and Peter, Dan's best friend. Our two elderly fathers were present, one still grieving for the loss of his wife (Dan's father) and one recovering from the collapse of his third marriage (my father). Both of them would die within two years. Afterwards we went to an upmarket pub for lunch, and Peter insisted on getting to his feet and making a shortened best man's speech, much to our embarrassment and the interest of the people sitting at tables nearby. He was rather sweet, talking about Dan when he was at school and the scrapes they got into together, very proper and sincere in a toe-curling way. I tried not to look at Monica. I knew full well what her expression would be: one of pitying disdain that was

19

the expression she usually adopted when she was with me. I had to admit she looked terrific, she always did, hair and make-up perfect and her clothes impeccable and suitable for the occasion – and, as I alone knew, a little resentment gnawing inside her that it was I who was getting married and not her.

The fathers were not much better – Dan's father had too much to drink and soon lapsed into a silent world of his own of gloom and despondency from which none of us could rouse him. My father, on the other hand, was overbearingly cheerful, anecdotal, like Peter, and flirting with the rather pretty girl who brought us our food.

I was thankful when it was over.

Dan and I were unbelievably happy. I was aware that I must grasp every moment before it eluded me, for complete happiness brings with it a terrible fear. I felt the cycle would turn, our contented little existence would change, but miraculously it remained the same. After a time I began to relax and accept that we had something that would last us for the rest of our lives.

With the future in mind we started looking for somewhere to live. We were in Dan's rented flat in Melford, very small and cramped, and I was pregnant so we thought it was time for a move. Every weekend was spent looking at houses. Big houses, small houses, damp houses, cluttered houses, we saw them all, and then when we were beginning to feel desperate about the whole thing we saw *our* house.

It was an old farmhouse surrounded by a neglected garden, sheltered at the back with a line of trees and its own field beyond. A short drive, riddled with potholes, led to the front door. At one time there must have been more land but this had been sold, and all that remained was the garden and one field and a scattering of rundown barns. The house was empty and our feet echoed on the bare boards as we tramped from room to room. From the old-fashioned sash windows (we were sure they would stick if we tried to open them) we could see miles and miles of open countryside. There were beams but Dan did not have to lower his head, as the ceilings were high (over seven feet he informed me in a whisper). All the rooms were light and airy and, although it was forsaken, the house embraced us. We spoke to each other of its many faults; it needed a great deal of attention; it probably had every sort of dry or wet rot. How could we be sure that someone would not build on the land surrounding it? It was a much bigger house than we had planned to buy and, when we heard the price, it was over our budget.

We bought it, or rather Dan did, for I brought little money into the marriage, and we had decided I should give up the job I had taken in Melford soon after we knew about the baby. Our first big expenditure was putting in central heating. We had looked at the house in July and had not appreciated how freezing it would be in the winter. During the last months of my pregnancy I painted the walls of each room, finishing with the nursery. Dan devoted every weekend to doing jobs around the house. He made the kitchen cupboards, built a wardrobe in our bedroom and laid carpets in the sitting-room and dining-room. Our first child, Hugh, was born, named for my father who was living in Spain and did not keep in touch. Eighteen months later I gave birth to Neil. Life for us was centred on ourselves, our babies and our house, and we were completely satisfied with this existence because we knew we could not afford anything else. We immersed ourselves in country life, I laboured to bring the garden to life, and a small puppy, Flush, became part of our family. Neil was three years old when Dan started to be recognised as an architect and to earn real money that meant we were able to go on a family holiday, the first we had since our marriage.

Dan was with me for the birth of both our sons; we shared everything and we were as one person. *'Bone of his bone and flesh of his flesh'* was how Jane Eyre described married bliss with Edward Rochester. In my closeness to Dan I could relate to this feeling; nothing was hidden from the other. I felt I knew every channel of his mind, I understood the things that hurt him and the things that pleased him. Sometimes when I telephoned him at work I found the number unobtainable because he was already ringing me. His eye would always be there for me to catch, either in amusement or indignation; we never differed in our reactions. Of course, people envied us; it is rare to find two people of like minds. Our friends did not understand how we managed to achieve such unity of thought, the joy of uncomplicated love. We were unique and we revelled in it. We watched the small clouds of discontent passing over the heads of our acquaintances and we rejoiced that we were not part of that scenario.

How did it change? How is it that I now lie beside my husband, apart from him and unable to sleep? Like the small lump in the breast of my friend, Jane, it needs investigation.

With guilt and revulsion I explore the pockets of his suit jackets. Ends of pencils are revealed, scraps of paper with addresses and telephone numbers that I know are to do with his work and a tattered half tube of peppermints. I look at the stubs in his cheque book but they are blank; he is careless about filling them in. I tell myself I am worrying about nothing. He is tired, that is the trouble. Perhaps I should suggest that we go away together for a few days. I could ask Monica to come and look after the boys. Surely she could get time off from her high-powered job to do that. She is constantly telling me that I should never have given up working; she does not approve of wives and mothers who stay at home. Like many unmarried women she has the answers to all of life's complexities that do not affect her. Her views are directly opposed to Dan's, and I have long given up the idea that they will ever hit it off. When I suggest we ask her to come and stay so that we can have a break, he says: "Poor boys. She is so bossy. They would have a horrible time."

"She's not as bad as all that."

"Anyway, I'm far too pressed at the moment. The environmental people are on my back – there is no way I can go away."

I decide not to mention it again.

Then on the day I have promised to go and see Mrs Bailey, Maeve as she has asked me to call her, there is the usual frenetic departure from the house, made worse this day because Dan has lost his set of keys. Logic tells us they must be in the house because he has used them to drive into the garage and enter the house the night before. We all search, the boys, excited by this unexpected change in the routine, in unlikely places such as the refrigerator and the dirty-clothes basket. Dan becomes frantic and I save the day by producing a duplicate set that I keep in a drawer for emergencies. He gives me a grateful look and swoops down to kiss my cheek before rushing from the house.

When I get home after delivering the children at school and doing the shopping at the supermarket, the first thing I see as I enter the hall are the keys. There they are, gleaming, half hidden by a pile of letters on the hall table. I don't know how we managed to miss them.

I hold them in my hand with a feeling of triumph, and then I notice there are three keys on the ring, the key to Dan's car, the key to our front door . . . and another. There are explanations to consider: it could be the key to his office, for instance, but I seem to remember there is some sort of code that gives entry to that establishment. The key to a client's house? Possibly, but rather unlikely.

I am thinking about the key when I go to see Maeve. She is not alone; an old man sits in a wheelchair, his chin on his chest. He does not look up when I enter. The wheelchair takes up a great deal of room and I find it hard to get around it. I am about to make an excuse and leave when Maeve says: "I'll ring for someone to come and take it away," as if she is talking about a tray of dirty cups and saucers. She is vigorously pressing the bell as she speaks.

A nurse appears and I detect from her attitude that she does not approve of Maeve's treatment of her husband. "What a short visit!" she says reprovingly.

"Long enough," says Maeve. Silently the old man is wheeled from the room.

"Poor Theo," she says, as I have heard her say before, "there is no quality in his life any more. What little there was is all gone forever. Death would be a blessing for him." Her voice is not harsh when she utters these words; it is soft and gentle and understanding of her husband's hopeless situation. She genuinely feels she would like him to be spared the nothingness of his present existence, and I agree with her.

A sort of melancholy settles on both of us, as if our minds are exercised by disturbing thoughts. She looks at me seriously and I feel a desire to talk to her, this woman I have only met for a few minutes. I hardly know her, and yet I wish I could kneel by her chair and tell her about the key.

Instead I say: "I am sorry I did not bring Flush. I was not certain he would be welcome here on a non-official basis. I'll have a word with Moira about it."

"Don't worry, darling," says Maeve, recovering her equanimity. "Sit yourself down. I'm very grateful to you for coming to see me. Would you like something . . . coffee or tea? I can ring for it."

"Not for me, unless you would like –"

"No," she says firmly, "I like a proper drink later on. They allow me one glass of wine at noon and a glass of sherry and a glass of wine in the evening. That's how they would like it to be, but I fool them by ordering the booze from a shop in the village. When the ladies from the agency were looking after me they were a mixed bag – some of them were only too eager to drink me under the table; others hid the bottles from me. Why do people think they can order you about just because you are older than they are? It's always the other way round until you are about ninety and then it suddenly changes."

She glanced towards the glass door of her room, the most expensive in the building, facing an immaculate stretch of lawn and the river beyond. "Shall we move our chairs so we can see the view?"

We do so. "It is so beautiful," she says with a sigh. "I

am a lucky woman to end my days with this. I know I should not grumble when there are so many old people worse off than I am, but I have a dissatisfied nature and I can't help thinking about the lovely home I lived in for so many years. I miss it so much."

"What happened to it?"

"Oh, sold, of course. There was no one to inherit it, and it was put on the market just before I moved here. Theo's solicitor arranged it all, and he put a lot of stuff into a big sale and the best furniture into a depository. God knows what happens to that – it just sits there for ever I suppose."

We sit, side by side, surveying the scene.

"You were born in Ireland?" I ask at last.

"Yes," she says, "I was the only child of a Protestant minister and a Catholic woman. Even in those days the marriage was frowned upon." She paused. "But you don't want to hear my life history."

"Well," I say, "perhaps we haven't time to go through it all today. You have had a very long life, but you could make a start." I add to encourage her, "I'm really interested." Sitting here, looking at the river, it seems a good diversion from all the things that are bothering me at present. For a while at least I can hear about another marriage, a long time ago, between two people of different faiths who had one child, a daughter.

Chapter 3

Maeve has a very indistinct memory of her father. His name was Dermot O'Shea, and she supposes he must have loved her mother at some time otherwise they would not have married against such parental opposition. Her mother once told her that they met at a dance in the village, one of those Irish gatherings of the past where the couples danced on a wooden dais, the sounds of heavy boots on planks making a great deal of noise. Why the young curate to the Protestant vicar attended this party is not known; perhaps he was just young and wanted to enjoy himself.

Like most people, Maeve finds it hard to imagine the feelings of her parents for each other, but I like to think there would have been a great love between them in the early years of their marriage. Why else would a young woman decide to share her life with a man with few prospects and hardly any money? They lived in County

Meath; by this time his curacy was ended and he was the rector of a village parish. The vicarage was a tumbledown dwelling just big enough to house the small family, and the church was a monument seeped in history and dampness, far too large for a dwindling congregation, for Maeve's father, though eloquent when lecturing his wife and little daughter, lost his fire when preaching from the pulpit. Contrary to all his aspirations the numbers attending church on Sundays grew less and less.

Perhaps this melancholy fact influenced his treatment of those nearest to him, and Maeve and her mother were made to suffer because of the lacklustre attitude of the few people who dragged themselves to church because of their principles. The red-blooded Irishmen scorned the vicar because of the limp hand that was presented to them when they filed past him after the service. "Loike a wet fish," was how they described it.

Maeve vaguely remembers the rows. Significantly she does not remember any happy times, so perhaps the marriage had begun to founder before she was at an understanding age. When they parted she was four years old.

The big argument – what was it about? She does not know, but she recalls vividly the outcome. It began when all three of them were in the church. At first her parents spoke quietly but she could tell by the tone that they were angry. Then her mother's voice rose, and no doubt her husband reminded her that she was in a holy place. The next thing she knew they were locked in the church, the heavy doors were slammed shut, the key was turned in the ancient lock. Perhaps she heard her father's footsteps walking away down the path leading from the church door. She does not remember but, strangely, she has an idea of the time, about four o'clock in the afternoon when she should have been going home for her tea. Childhood memories are often associated with food, the desire for it or lack of it.

At first they sat in one of the pews, close together to keep warm. Maeve's mother made light of what had happened. "'Tis all jocose," she said, meaning that her husband was just playing a joke on them. She assured her little daughter that very soon the door would be unlocked. Gradually, it became dark, and Maeve says: "If I try hard I can bring back the stale damp atmosphere of that awful place, my mother leaving me to look around the church for something to keep us warm, then returning with nothing. I was too young to know about spectres and ghosts but I was aware of a terrible fear of the unknown. My mother enveloped me in her arms and said: 'When we get out of here we are leaving.' I do not recall her words but she told me about them later."

She was as good as her word. At about seven o'clock in the morning the door was opened by Maeve's father and a shaft of sunlight fell upon the stone floor of the old building. They were free. She does not know what happened after that, the efforts her father must have made to prevent their departure. At the beginning of the twentieth century it was unusual for a wife to desert her husband, and this was a woman with an inherent Catholic belief that marriage was indissoluble.

That morning with a few items of clothing in one suitcase, they boarded the new train heading for a place called Castlerock and a terraced house, number thirteen in tree-lined Orchard Street, where lived the only relatives who were likely to help them. What were the thoughts of Maeve's mother at this time? She was taking a gigantic step and must have been apprehensive. She was at the mercy of her sister and her husband; if they could not, or would not take them in, there was no alternative but to return to a marriage that had become intolerable. Her own parents were too old and poor to take on responsibility and they had never forgiven her for marrying a Protestant. Everything depended on the goodwill of Minnie and her husband.

The sister of Maeve's mother was known to the little girl as Aunt Min and her husband was Franklyn O'Connor or Uncle Frank. He was a rent collector, which always seemed to Maeve to be a very prestigious job. They had identical twin daughters, Beryl and Brona, two years younger than Maeve and, in time, she was to regard them as her sisters. The girls shared a double bed in the second bedroom of the house, and when Maeve and her mother appeared on the scene they were moved to the attic so that Min's beloved sister could share the bed with her little girl. It was a big disruption to the household, the removal of two toddlers to a rather bleak room at the top of the house, but it was an indication of the sterling qualities of Aunt Min and Uncle Frank. Childlike, Maeve took their kindness for granted. Her mother gave piano lessons to help pay for their board and food. The piano stood in a room that was seldom used – the parlour. When her mother was instructing one of her pupils the door was kept shut, and closed again when the student had left.

Maeve was unaware of the constant anxiety shared by the adults in that house that Maeve's father would try and snatch his daughter away from them. She started school before the twins, and she does remember that when she came out of the school building Uncle Frank was always standing by the gates waiting for her. That old veteran of the early troubles had a gun in his pocket just in case there was a confrontation with the wicked vicar who had, by now, assumed the guise of a monster, half devil, half beast. He never appeared to claim his daughter, but somehow he managed to keep track of his lost family, and when his wife died a few years later he knew about it, and remarried and started another family. In the meantime, Maeve was instructed not to speak to any man she did not know, and she was shown a sepia-coloured photograph of her father on his wedding day so that she could be particularly wary of a tall gaunt man with mutton-chop whiskers.

Maeve was seven years old when her mother became ill. A family conference decided that she should move to the attic and share the bed with Beryl and

Brona. Perhaps she could be forgiven because of her youth but she recoiled from the rapidly changing face of her mother. She did not possess the wisdom or the strength to deal sensitively with the situation. Afterwards she could not forgive herself for missing out on those last precious moments of her mother's life. She remembered how they had shared everything, the strange isolation of their existence, dependent on the charity of others, the intimacy of sharing a bed for three years 'lying like spoons' as her mother described it. When kind Uncle Frank gently broke the news to her of her death Maeve felt she wanted to run away, to escape the fearful grief that overwhelmed her and her feelings of guilt. She did run away, but not until much later.

Maeve gets out of her chair, painfully it seems to me, and she goes to her bedside table and brings out an old photograph, a daguerreotype that will last for ever and not fade with time as our modern coloured snapshots do. She hands it to me as she sinks back into her chair.

"I see a likeness," I tell her. I can also detect sadness there; the face of a woman who did what she felt was right and suffered all the rest of her life for it. It must have been hard for her, and lonely despite the companionship of her little girl. For some reason, the yellowed photograph depresses me, and I hand it back to Maeve.

The three cousins moved downstairs to the room with

the double bed. Maeve first and then the twins celebrated their first communion. Both these events were great occasions in the family. Maeve attended Mass regularly and went to confession. She had no sins except little ones, like quarrelling with a girl at school or fancying one of the teachers.

In Castlerock there was (and still is) a convent called the Convent of Perpetual Adoration. A nun is always in the chapel praying, any time during the day and night, and the sisters have taken a vow of silence. One of them was Maeve's Uncle Frank's sister, and the girls referred to her as 'Auntie Nun'. They were allowed to visit her once a year. A high wall surrounded the convent, and a little door was opened for them to enter, single file. The sisters who were not on praying duty were permitted by special dispensation to talk on the day the three girls came to see someone in their midst. It must have been a tremendous relief to them because the result was they never stopped talking. All though that magical day they never drew breath; it was as if a flock of starlings had invaded that sacred place. The girls ate a vast amount of food. The nuns seemed to think they had the appetites of giants, and they had gone to a great deal of trouble to present them with food they thought they would enjoy. It was delicious and, after wolfing down slabs of chocolate cake, Maeve, Beryl and Brona, sated with chatter and rich fare, emerged, feeling sick, through the little door into the world outside where Franklyn was waiting for them.

That day was the high spot of their year. Nothing much happened in Castlerock and Maeve began to think there must be more to life. She was aware there was another world across the sea, and she longed to know more about it. The day-to-day monotony was broken by a distant relative, a young girl who had come to seek help from Uncle Frank who, in his capacity as rent collector (and therefore, importantly, working for the government) was considered to be the head of the family. The girl was taken into the parlour, a room seldom used except for special occasions, and the three girls, huddled together on the stairs, listened to the sounds of raised voices and then sobs. Presently Aunt Min and Uncle Frank appeared with the girl and, observing her daughters and Maeve, Aunt Min turned to the visitor and said: "Button up your coat, girl, and hide your shame."

Later, they asked her about the incident, but she would tell them nothing. Her mouth closed in a hard straight line, and "May God forgive her," was all she would say.

Maeve was growing up and conscious that she was better-looking than her cousins. Like all people who possess beauty she was aware it was an asset, something that could be used to her advantage. At this stage in her development she probably thought it was a gift from God; anyway, she was grateful to Him for giving it to her. Then something happened to interrupt the boredom of her life; a young man appeared in Castlerock. It was wartime then, 1918 and soon the bloodiest, most horrific war of all time was to come to a close. He was a subaltern in the Irish Guards, tall with red hair and named George Palmer. He was from England, visiting his aunt who was an acquaintance of Aunt Min's; in fact it was an acquaintanceship much valued by that lady. Maeve loved him at once. She had recently become aware of her own good looks, now she discovered how she could use them to attract a man. He and his aunt were invited to dinner, and the preparations seemed to go on forever, so anxious was Aunt Min to impress her friend. The table was covered with a pristine white Irish linen tablecloth and the best service was brought out for the occasion. Uncle Frank wore his Sunday suit and Aunt Min her silk dress, the twins had identical white frocks with different coloured sashes and Maeve wore her first grown-up dress, chosen by her aunt. She would have liked it better if she had been allowed to choose it herself. The three girls sat in silent adoration as George regaled them with stories of his exploits in the army.

He asked Aunt Min if he could take Maeve out, to tea or to the new cinematograph, but Aunt Min said her niece, at the age of sixteen, was too young to go out alone with a man. Craftily, he said he would be delighted to take the twins out as well, if they agreed, of course.

During that week of his leave when he was not being charming to his aunt (of whom he had expectations), he met the girls. They went for walks most days, into the country that was easily accessible from Orchard Street. There was not much conversation so he became quite bored. He whispered to Maeve that he would like her cousins to make themselves scarce, and he said that he would pay them to do so. They thought the world of him, so with much giggling and consultation between themselves they eventually agreed to his suggestion.

And so it was that Aunt Min would give them a basket containing a picnic and she would watch the little group walking away down the street, never suspecting that once they turned the corner and were out of sight they would separate. With money in their pockets Brona and Beryl could spend the day as they pleased, browsing around the shops or eating ice creams in the park.

"Oh," says Maeve, "I have talked too much. You must be tired of the sound of my voice."

"No," I reply truthfully, "I'm fascinated."

"Well, I'm going to stop now," she says decidedly, "and if it is true that you are interested, perhaps you will come back again soon to hear what happened next."

"That's a deal," I say, laughing.

"Bring the dog with you – that can't be against the rules, surely? Although, considering the amount I pay to stay in this place I wonder how they have the gall to impose any rules." She brightens. "Or, better still, bring the boys. I'd love that."

"Perhaps one day . . ." I say doubtfully. I can't imagine how Hugh and Neil would view the prospect of a visit to this old lady, but remembering their lack of grandparents I decide it might be beneficial.

On the way out, Moira, as usual behind her desk in the hall, stops me. "How did you find Mrs Bailey today?"

"Missing her old home?"

"It's her fault if she is lonely," Moira says. "She flatly refuses to go into the dining-room or to get to know the other residents. She stays in her room all day long and won't budge. No wonder she gets depressed. She won't even go on any of the outings we organise. It's a real problem."

"So all her meals are taken to her room?"

"Well, it's an option for them, of course. Sometimes if they are not feeling up to the mark they prefer it that way, but not every day. We've never before had someone who refuses to venture out of her room at all."

"She seems so chatty," I say, "full of stories."

"She has taken to you," says Moira, "so I'm hoping you will be able to make her see sense. She could make good friends in this place, and I'm sure that would make her a happier person."

Chapter 4

Dan comes home earlier than usual. The children have eaten, Hugh has done his homework and they are sitting on the floor watching television.

"Please turn that thing off," says their father as soon as he enters the room.

"Dad!"

"It's not good for you to watch such rubbish."

"*The Simpsons* are not rubbish," Hugh protests.

I suggest: "Perhaps as Daddy has come home early, just to see us, we could turn it off."

Hugh is an obedient child and he gets to his feet and presses the switch. Homer and Marge fade from our midst. Neil cannot repress a little groan.

"I must say you make me feel very welcome," says Dan.

Little Neil gets to his feet and puts his arms around

his father's waist. "You are *very* welcome, Daddy," he says.

I notice a change in my husband's attitude towards his children. For some time now I have noticed a change in his attitude towards me, but this is the first time I realise it is affecting the boys. I think they are aware that something is different but they do not understand. They kiss him and then go upstairs to have their bath, quietly, without speaking.

I sit on the low cane chair in the bathroom, clutching towels, thinking. Very soon Hugh and Neil have recovered their high spirits and are making a noise. I sit and watch them cavorting in the bath, splashing so much the water begins to soak the floor. It is against the rules, but I do not reprimand them because I am abstracted, my mind concerned with that unidentified key. The realisation comes to me that a change has taken place in my marriage, a change that I have been aware of for some time but have not been able to face.

The boys are in their beds and I am putting away the toys and emptying the bath. The reality of running a house and bringing up children is endless repetition. Every day is the same, and for that one must be thankful, and friends and the person who is sharing the adventure with you provide the only distractions. For the rearing of a family is an adventure, full of hazards and pitfalls and, one hopes, rewards in the future if one has managed to get it right.

Dan used to help me at bedtime, and then we would

have our supper together, talking companionably about the events of the day. I knew everything about his current projects; now they are mysteries to me except I am told they are the reason he comes home late and is always preoccupied. Tired and dispirited, I fold the towels and hang them on the rail. The boys are calling me, asking for a story.

I stand at the top of the stairs and shout: "Dan, will you come and read to the children?"

He comes and we pass on the stairs, not touching.

In the kitchen I pour myself a glass of wine and one for him. I have taken a lasagne from the freezer, home-cooked, and I put it in the microwave. I wonder, where have I gone wrong? What is happening? I pray that it is some fault of mine that I can put right, but a cold fear clutches my heart that there will not be such an easy solution.

He is down very quickly. "How did you manage to get away?" I ask.

"They were not very demanding," he says. "I'm afraid I skipped several pages but they did not notice."

I am setting the table and I look up and say: "I doubt that very much."

"What do you mean?"

"Just that they always notice."

I hand him his glass of wine. "I'll just go up and kiss them goodnight."

I run up the stairs because they are calling me: "Mummy, Mummy!"

I sit on the edge of Hugh's bed and he says: "Daddy didn't read us the whole story."

"He's had a busy day, darling."

"He missed out half," chimes in Neil from the other bed.

"Never mind," I say brightly, "you know it by heart anyway."

I bend over and kiss Hugh and then I move to Neil's bed and I kiss him too. "I love you both," I say.

"I love you, Mummy," they tell me in unison.

It is the same as always.

Dan and I sit silently eating the lasagne. It is delicious and a favourite with him, but he does not comment on it. There was a time when it would be greeted with a satisfied exclamation of delight, but not this evening. I glance sideways at his face and I see that his expression is composed but serious.

At last I say: "I found your keys."

His head is bent but I know that my words are like stones dropped into a pool of water. I sense the ripples and Dan's discomfort. He has had time to think about the significance of the lost keys.

He looks up quickly. "Oh, good, where were they?"

"Obvious, really. On the hall table, hiding under some letters."

"Thank goodness you had spares."

I try to speak casually, but my heart is hammering. "I noticed there is another key on the ring. What is the story of that?"

He retorts: "Why should there be a story? It is just a key."

"Whose door does it fit?"

"Does it matter?"

"I hope not," I say, my confidence dwindling to nothing. "I won't mention it again if you tell me I have nothing to fear."

He does not speak.

"Dan?"

"I'd rather not say."

I take a deep breath. "Are you having an affair?" I ask.

For the first time he raises his eyes and looks straight at me, a long searching look. Then he gets up and leaves the room. I hear him go into the little study across the hall and shut the door behind him.

I stare at the unfinished food on his plate, and I push my own plate away from me. I sit, with my head in my hands, feeling miserable and ashamed. Of course, he is angry with me for asking that question, more of an accusation than a question. An accusation, I now realise to my dismay, based on a false assumption. How could I have been suspicious about something as innocuous as a key? Of course there is a reasonable explanation, and Dan would be justified in not giving it to me.

Wearily, I gather up the dirty plates and carry them into the kitchen. I scrape the remains of the food into the bin. There is a terrible silence in our house only broken by the sonorous ticking of the kitchen clock. I sit down at the table and Flush comes and puts his nose on my knee. Absently, I stroke his velvet head.

Dan comes into the room and sits opposite me. We regard each other sadly because it is the first real altercation we have had in our married life, and I am convinced it is my fault.

The apologies spring to my lips but they are never uttered because he says: "I have to tell you . . ."

Then I feel fear, and I want to shout at him: 'Stop! Please leave it alone. I don't want to hear,' but my mouth is dry and I cannot speak.

"I am asking you for a divorce," he says, "because I want to marry someone else."

It is worse than I thought. Not just a casual affair, but something involving real love. It is so like Dan to be totally honest with me. Perhaps he has been saving me from being hurt by not telling me the truth before, but now I have asked the vital question he will spare me nothing. I sealed my fate when I said those words, "Are you having an affair?" Already I regret saying them, and I think there must be many women who have saved their marriages by just remaining quiet. Because Dan and I have always been so open with each other it is difficult for me to dissemble; I asked the question before I had time to think of the impact it would have. I picture my little boys sleeping sweetly upstairs, innocent of the upheaval that is about to happen in their lives.

Now I ask another question: "Who is this person?"

"It is no one you know," he tells me.

Knowing him so well, I sense his suffering, but there is an edge to my voice when I say: "Well, are you going to tell me about it?"

"I met her a year ago. She came to the office because she wanted me to design an extension to her house in Upper Bratby."

"So close," I say wonderingly. "Is she married?"

"No, and she never has been."

I am struggling, but determined. "If she lives in a house and can afford you as an architect she must have a lucrative career."

"That's true," he tells me. "She is a doctor. However, she is not working at present. In fact," he continues rather awkwardly, "she has not worked during the year I have known her. As for her house, her parents died within a few months of each other and left it to her, their only child. Her father was a GP in Upper Bratby."

"Why did she give up working?"

"Because she was ill. She had cancer, but has had treatment and is now in remission. She returns to work at the surgery next month."

Yes, I'm sure Dan would sympathise with someone in that tragic position. What chance have I got against such heart-rending stuff?

"Why a divorce?" I ask. "Isn't that rather a drastic step for you to take considering you are the father of two children?"

He explains: "She is thirty-six and desperately wants

a child. As you know, I think children need their parents to have the stability of marriage."

Perhaps because I have managed to remain relatively calm up to this moment he is lulled into thinking he can be completely outspoken with me. Before Dan made that observation I have been in a state of numbed bewilderment; now I am suddenly roused to a blinding rage. "How dare you say such a thing?" I shout. "Don't you think your own children need parents with a stable marriage? Are you prepared to sacrifice that for an unborn child?"

"Hugh and Neil have a father and mother who love them," Dan says. "I know I am doing a terrible thing to you, but I promise I will make it as easy as possible for our sons."

"How do you propose to tell them?"

"I'll come tomorrow evening and try and explain it to them."

"Does that mean you are going to leave now?"

"Yes," he says simply. "I think it is easier for both of us that way. I'm sorry."

He gets up hurriedly as if he is anxious to go. I can understand how he feels; this secret must have been a terrible burden to him over the last year. He is relieved that it is now in the open. No wonder I detected a difference in him, and I try to think back over the last twelve months and how our marriage has changed during that time. "A year," I say thoughtfully. "We made love many times during the course of a whole year. Not as many times as we used to, of course, but we did make love. I don't understand . . ."

"I know this may sound perverse to you," Dan says, "but I still love you. I always will. It is just that since meeting Andrea I have found something really special. And I do not seem able to give it up."

Andrea. At last he has said her name. I try to picture someone with that name, a person whom Dan loves with such intensity. I see her tall and fair, rather delicate because she has suffered a life-threatening illness.

He is at the door when I say: "Please don't go."

He turns and takes one step towards me, just one step. "It's better I do," he says, "for both of us. When you think about it you will agree with me."

He is being very practical, but I know it is a pretence. He knows perfectly well that when I say 'Please don't go' I mean please don't leave me *forever*. It is my last plea to him and he purposely misconstrues it.

Alone, I sit and listen to the sounds upstairs, the opening of the cupboard in our bedroom, the rattle of hangers as clothes are removed. Dan pads backwards and forwards between the bathroom and our bedroom, not quietly because he knows that nothing short of an explosion will rouse the boys once they are asleep.

Eventually he lumbers down the stairs, carrying two big suitcases. I hear him take his keys from the hall table, the original set because I have left them there for him. I wonder if he is going to leave me without saying anything. There is a pause while I listen intently.

He is standing in the doorway. "I'm off," he says, as if he is going on some routine mission, to a late meeting or for some last, minute supermarket shopping in Melford.

I cannot reply. I turn my head away so that he cannot see my face. I hear him take a sharp intake of breath, and then he is gone. The front door slams. There are noises outside and they register on my brain like discordant notes, the opening and shutting of the boot of his car, the starting up of the engine, the familiar sounds of backing and driving out on to the road. I walk to the window and part the curtains. Outside there is darkness and silence.

I wonder why I do not cry. My eyes are so dry it is as if there is sand in them, pricking my eyelids and holding back the tears. Everything has happened so quickly, I have to take it in, think about it before I allow myself to weep.

I go to the front door and lock it from the inside. I call Flush and let him out into the back garden for his last run. I stand, straining my eyes, staring into the darkness of the garden that Dan and I planned together. I can see the gleam of the silver disk on Flush's collar, darting this way and that way until I call him and he comes at once. I close the back door and lock it.

I pour myself another glass of wine. It is too early to go to bed, but what can I do? I contemplate the prospect of sitting for another two or three hours thinking about what has happened to me this evening. I picture Dan arriving at her home, putting his key in the lock. Now he is telling Andrea that he has left me. He is hers now. She is holding his lovely head in her hands and she is kissing him. She is careful to hide her triumph, but inwardly she feels incredibly happy and pleased.

I turn on the television but I have no idea what I am watching. From time to time I top up my glass. At last it is a reasonable hour for me to go to bed, to sleep, if that luxury is permitted to me. On the way to our bedroom I look in on the boys and, on impulse, I snatch Neil from his bed and put his soft sleeping form in the place his father should be.

Chapter 5

"Where is Daddy?" asks Hugh. When I do not reply at once Neil repeats the question: "Where is Daddy?"

"At work," I say shortly, putting little squares of eggy bread on their plates. "He had to go away last night."

They are perfectly satisfied with my explanation and are intent on getting dollops of tomato ketchup on to their breakfast, the plastic bottle passing from hand to hand. They are too young, too guileless, to suspect a sinister reason for Dan's absence. They are completely secure in their little world, and two things amaze me, the normality of everything and the fact that I slept soundly until seven o'clock. I decide that I must have drunk more than usual last night, or I would never have slept so well.

We drive to Jane's house to collect Amy. As usual Jane comes to the door in her dressing-gown, and I nearly say to her 'After I've left the children at school I'll come back here. I want to talk to you,' but I do not say anything because I think she looks strained. There is an air of defeat about her this morning, and I decide I cannot add to her problems by telling her of my own.

During the afternoon I feel impelled to leave the house, and I go into the town to look around the shops. It is not a good idea because so many times before I have wandered around the main department store in Melford, lightly touching the clothes, examining the handbags, breathing in the heady perfume of the cosmetics, but today is different. On previous occasions I have been free of the heavy burden I carry with me now. Lately, there has been a little anxiety niggling in my mind, lurking somewhere in my subconscious, telling me all is not as it was, but nothing like this; this is something else. The familiarity of the surroundings only makes me more aware of how things have changed in my life.

When I collect the children from school they are in a buoyant mood, shouting and jumping up and down in the back of the car. I am glad that the law insists that they wear seatbelts; even so I keep one eye on the road and the other on the car mirror.

"Can you calm down?" I ask.

Apparently not, and a jiggling squirmy Amy is catapulted into the arms of her mother, who is waiting on the steps. No longer in her dressing-gown, but dressed and looking more like her usual efficient

51

cheerful self. "Come in," she pleads. "I long for company. I'll provide the food."

I know that the children will eat in the kitchen and Jane and I will be alone in the sitting-room. There will be time and opportunity for me to talk to her, but I am not ready to tell anyone what has happened, so I make an excuse. "Dan is coming home early this evening and as it happens so seldom we want to be there for him."

All three children express their disappointment loudly and forcibly, and Jane says: "Of course. I understand perfectly. Give him my love." She takes Amy's hand and looks into the back of the car. "Goodbye, boys," she calls before we drive away.

Dan does come back early, and the children are eating when he arrives. He breezes into his home as if everything is normal.

"Do you want to be alone with them?" I ask icily. His cavalier attitude annoys me, and somehow it makes it easier when, for a moment, anger takes over from despair. I look at him curiously. He is my husband, and yet I feel I have moved away from him already. I am aware of the characteristics that first attracted me, the way his clothes hang loosely on his tall figure, the fact that he always looks as if he needs a shave, the uneven features of his face, the nose a little too long, the eyebrows thick and untidy beneath a high jutting brow. He is not handsome but I knew from the moment I saw him that women are drawn to him.

He replies to my question: "No, I would prefer you to be here."

He sits at the table and I sit opposite him.

He begins: "Hugh, Neil, there is something I want to talk to you about . . ."

But they are not listening. Normally, he would be cross with them for not paying attention but today he remains silent while they rattle on about going to a theme park during the weekend. It is something they have wanted to do for weeks and Dan and I have been making promises to take them on a Saturday when he can find the time.

"Can we go this Saturday, Daddy?" begs Neil.

"I don't see why not," Dan replies, looking at me. I nod my head. I don't see what I can do but acquiesce; I am put into an impossible position because to refuse would make me look like a killjoy. I wonder how much they will mind when they realise that I am not going to take part in this treat.

"We're going! We're going!" Hugh shouts.

"Yes, we're going," says Dan, "but before we talk about that I want you to be quiet and listen to me. Both of you, please, just for a few moments."

This time they obey him and they are silent, eating their supper and looking at him, wide-eyed.

"Mummy and I love you very much," begins Dan, and my heart sinks. What he says is so predictable, textbook stuff, and must have been said, in just this way, on so many occasions, before coming to the crunch.

Here it comes, the crunch, and I can predict the words before he utters them. "Mummy and Daddy are not going to live together any more. I have moved to another house and I am living with another lady. You will stay here with Mummy, but you will still see me very often, more often than you see me now as you are usually fast asleep before I get home."

I look closely at their faces and I see, with a twinge of surprise, that they are embarrassed. Their little faces have turned quite pink, and their eyes fall to their plates. I wonder which one of them will speak first and, as expected, it is Hugh. "Are we still going to the theme park on Saturday?"

I have already indicated my agreement to the arrangement but, even so, Dan looks in my direction. "We must ask Mummy first," he says. Perhaps I imagine that his voice hardens. "Are you happy with that?"

Again, I nod my head. I feel I am drowning, caught in a situation in which I have no blueprint as to how I should behave. Everything about the position I find myself in is new to me. I think my husband is dealing with it better than I am, and I feel he has made a resolution, before coming here, to be fair-minded but firm at the same time. Overnight he has gained strength.

"Please can we go and play now?" asks Hugh. They want to get away from this uneasy conversation. The few moments of silence are up.

"Yes, off you go," says Dan, who seems to have taken on the full parental role and is leaving me out of it.

They scurry away.

"I think that went well," he says.

"Oh, it was great. Congratulations. Now, please will you leave at once?"

He gets to his feet. "Shall we make arrangements for Saturday? Perhaps I could pick them up at eleven o'clock – if that suits you."

"Please bring them back by seven," I say.

"Of course."

He leaves, stopping on the way to call: "Hugh! Neil! I'll see you on Saturday."

I wonder if they will emerge from the playroom and try to stop him from leaving by wrapping their arms around his legs. It is the sort of exuberant behaviour he has experienced on many occasions when he has had to go to some meeting or other. It usually half-pleases, half-exasperates him, but tonight it does neither because they do not come out but call from the room: "Goodbye, Daddy!"

I reflect with mixed feelings of triumph and sadness that already he is beginning to miss out on the affectionate moments of family life.

I decide to tell Jane and, as expected, she is shocked, even sheds a tear that, so far, I have not managed to do.

"It is tragic," she says, "and so astonishing. Bill and

I always think you are the happiest couple we know. Like ourselves in that respect." Bill is her husband, heavy, balding and proud of his wife and little daughter. He has been a great support to her during her ordeal, but then I think Dan must have been supportive to Andrea in the aftermath of her illness.

Like all people receiving confidences she is quick with advice. "You must get a solicitor," she tells me decidedly.

"I don't want a solicitor."

"It's important," she insists, "to get the visits with the children sorted out, for one thing. And how do you know he won't change his Will and leave everything to this woman? If there is a child there will be further complications."

I say nothing. I am beginning to regret telling her.

"A woman would be best," Jane says, becoming quite animated, "and I know just the person. I was at school with her, and she's brilliant. Has an office in Melford."

She is already rooting in her desk for an address book. She writes down a name and address on the back of an envelope and hands it to me.

"Ring her," she says, looking at me sharply. "Promise me."

I take the envelope but I do not promise.

I stand there with the envelope in my hand, and suddenly Jane cannot meet my eyes. She looks at a space beyond my head and says brokenly: "I'm so sorry."

I realise that I have joined the army of wives who have been dumped by their husbands, and I don't want to be part of that army. I have met these women and I have felt sorry for them; it is such a lonely thing to happen to someone and sets that person apart as an object of pity. I don't want to be pitied.

"Don't feel sorry for me," I urge my friend Jane. "I'm all right."

But I'm not all right – in fact, I'm anything but all right. I sense my little boys regarding me anxiously. Not all the time, of course, but occasionally I get uneasy glances from them. I think Hugh understands perfectly what is happening because many of his six-year-old friends are in the same position. Neil is two years younger and a baby when it comes to comprehending strange adult behaviour, but I'm sure his brother has done his best to fill in the gaps in his knowledge. I am certain he has warned him not to mention Dan's absence.

They sleep in my bed at night, one on either side of me. I have read enough magazine articles to know that it is wrong, but I do not want to lie in the big bed with a cold area to my left and to my right. Hugh and Neil are delighted with the new arrangement; they do not seem to have any misgivings about abandoning their little beds.

I telephone Shirley and I tell her that I will not be taking part in the Pat-a-Dog Scheme any more.

Her voice is anxious. "Flush is not ill, is he?"

"No, no," I tell her, "Flush is fine. It is just that I am too busy . . ." Now I come to think of it, Flush seems to be the happiest member of our family at present; nothing disturbs his equilibrium.

"It is a shame," says Shirley. "The residents enjoy his visits so much." She is faintly reproving and makes me feel guilty. She is a nice well-meaning woman and I wish I could explain to her that it is not the fault of the old dears or the dog or my busy life that I can't go on with it.

Then I telephone Moira and say almost the same thing to her. She is not so concerned; I think she may secretly regard the Pat-a-Dog Scheme as a waste of time, and she does not look the sort of person who appreciates a dog invading her immaculate place of work. She always questions me about muddy paws before she allows him to walk on the carpets.

I finish the conversation by asking about Maeve. "Is she settling in?"

"I'd say she is resigned. Her husband died which was sad for her. She still refuses to join the other guests for meals. Will you be coming to see her sometime? I know she'd like that."

"I'll try," I promise.

On Saturday morning I stand in the bedroom Dan and I shared. I am half-hidden by the curtain as I watch him walk up the path to fetch the boys. I know they are sitting on the front doorstep, side by side, where I have instructed them to wait for their father's arrival. From my vantage point I can see Hugh and Neil rush to meet him, and the three of them walk together to the car. With a little stab of triumph I see Hugh glance up at the window where I am standing. I strain my eyes to see if there is anyone else in the car, but the seat next to the driver is empty. They drive away and I am left alone.

I don't know what to do. There are a dozen possible ways I could occupy myself during the day. I could take Flush for a walk, and I can imagine his joy as I take the lead from the hook in the porch, but the lead remains in its usual place and Flush lies patiently with his nose resting on his front paws. I could visit Jane, but then I remember it is the weekend and family time. From now on weekends will be different for me and I am just beginning to appreciate this fact. I used to look forward to those days so much, Dan at home and no school for the children, time to lie in for a while in the morning, leisurely meals and fun outings. In the future there will be no Dan to share the sense of freedom, and for part of the time, at least, the children will not be with me. The hours during this first Saturday on my own drag by, and I almost wish I had arranged to go and see Maeve. I find myself thinking of her quite often.

Eventually, I potter in the garden, pulling up weeds and putting them in a big bucket. The sky is a blue arc above me with a few fluffy clouds scudding across. I think this is the perfect day for the theme park. I wander into the house again and make myself a cup of tea; then I eat three chocolate biscuits in rapid succession.

At five minutes to seven I am back in the bedroom again, sitting on the edge of the bed this time, listening for the sound of Dan's key in the lock. To my relief he does not come into the house. I hear the boys clattering up the stairs. They fall on me, wrapping their arms around me, overpowering me with their arms and legs flailing in all directions. We all fall backwards on the bed, tangled up and laughing.

Later, after they have had their supper, I ask them about their day. They describe it in detail, interrupting each other and shouting to be heard. Obviously, it has been a great success.

I can't resist asking the question: "Who was there? Just Daddy and yourselves?"

"And Andrea," says Neil, and I observe Hugh gives him a little warning glance.

I try to make my voice sound casual. "What is she like? Do you like her?"

"She's nice," says Neil, too young to have learned to be diplomatic. The accusing look he gets from his brother is the most hurtful thing that has happened to me this day.

"She was not in the car," I say. I feel myself falling deeper and deeper into a pitfall of my own making, saying things, asking questions that I know are against the rules.

"We went back to the house to collect her," Hugh tells me. There is a note of defiance in his voice, as if willing me not to say anything more. He is six years old, too young to be placed in such a delicate position. I give him a hug and suggest we play Ghost Castle (their favourite game) before they go to bed.

Chapter 6

Our new life settles into a sort of routine. Every Saturday Dan comes to collect the boys and they spend the day with him and Andrea. So far he has not suggested they spend the night with him, and I am relieved about this, as I know it would lead to conflict. I know that he is probably in his rights to have them to stay with him, but I would resist it with every fibre in my being. It is hard enough for me to agree to them spending any time at all in the company of Andrea – in my mind I pronounce her name with venom – but I realise I have to fall in with this arrangement. Standing in my usual position behind the curtain, I notice that now when he comes to collect them she is sitting beside him in the car, a shadowy figure whose features I cannot discern from that distance. I suppose that as I am never in evidence they decided it was foolish of her to stay away, and it means that he does not have to go back to collect her before starting on their outing.

The boys look forward to going out with them, and when the car arrives they run out to greet it with shouts of delight. Sometimes Dan arrives in the early evening to watch them having their bath. On these occasions I stay in the bedroom with the door shut, and I do not come out until I hear his car drive away.

Hugh and Neil do not tell me about the time spent with their father, and they have not mentioned Andrea since that first time. I think Hugh has instructed his brother not to mention her name. I try, by devious means, to make them talk about her, but in their childish way they have put up a barrier, and they shut their mouths tightly and scamper away to play whenever the sensitive subject comes up.

I do not go and see the woman solicitor recommended by my friend, Jane, although she is always pressing me to telephone and arrange an appointment. Dan and I no longer have a joint account, but he puts money into my new account each month, plenty of money for us to live on, and he pays the school fees and any other incidental expenses that may arise. I have an account with the local garage where I buy petrol and he settles the bill. I cannot fault his generosity, and so far he has not mentioned again the question of divorce. I lose patience with Jane who has so many gloomy forebodings about what could happen in the future, and I say: "Please do not mention this to me again. I'll make up my own mind if I decide to see her."

She looks abashed, hurt. "I'm sorry," she says. "I don't mean to interfere."

She makes me feel ashamed, but lately I have been feeling ashamed when reason tells me I am the last person who should have that emotion. Dan is the person who should feel shame, not me. Yet the feeling persists, that I have somehow let him down or otherwise he would not have taken this terrible step, and I feel guilty too about my treatment of our sons. They must be suffering too, like me, but I am too concerned with my own misery to worry about their needs.

I have a strange disembodied existence these days, and after a month of it I decide to get in touch with Maeve. After all, I tell myself, I hardly know the woman so she is unlikely to ask me any awkward questions. I do not know her private number so I telephone Moira for it.

"Of course," she says brightly, and she tells me the number and I put it in my address book.

"Thank you," I say, "I'll give her a ring and perhaps come and see her."

"That would be kind," she says, and I think I detect a sympathetic timbre in her voice that makes me wonder if she has heard a rumour about me. This unfounded suspicion stops me from telephoning Maeve and another month goes by.

I have got into the habit of deciding upon something and then changing my mind. This indecision even extends to the household chores; I start polishing the furniture, then abandon the duster and start instead to put plates in the dishwasher. Nothing gets finished, and the house has a lost look – unmade beds, toys scattered on the floor – and the garden is neglected. Dan asks Hugh to give me a message, that he will come on Sunday to mow the lawn. I ignore the offer, and a few days later a young man arrives telling me that Mr Maitland has instructed him to cut the grass and clear the weeds.

Then one day Maeve telephones me. I recognise at once her distinctive voice with its underlying Irish accent. She asks me out to lunch and I accept.

"I'm afraid you will have to do the driving," she says.

"I'm happy to do that."

It is the first time I have been out for weeks, and I am determined to make an effort. I put on a grey flannel trouser suit that I wear with a crisp blue striped shirt. I make up my face carefully. There are dark smudges under my eyes and I try to disguise them with concealer. Maeve has organised everything very well. She has booked a table at the hotel in the village, and she too has made an effort with her appearance. She is a magnificent figure as she hobbles ahead of me, leaning heavily on her stick, a large lady wearing a loose-fitting garment in a soft expensive shade.

It is obvious that she is enjoying herself, and I will soon discover that going out to lunch is one of the greatest pleasures in her life. It would be cruel to cast gloom on her evident delight and I must admit to a frisson of excitement myself. I have been to this old coaching inn many times with Dan and, despite the circumstances, I am glad to be back, and it is reassuring to be recognised by the waiter who serves us. The food is good and Maeve orders a bottle of wine. I allow myself one glass only as I am driving, and she happily quaffs the rest.

"Moira told me about your husband," I say. "I'm so sorry. You must miss him very much."

"Oh, I suppose I do," she says casually, "or perhaps I should say I miss him as he used to be, a loving friend. I can't feel sorry about his death. He had absolutely nothing to live for, and it was time he went."

She goes on to describe his funeral, miles away in a church in the Shropshire village where they lived for so many years. "The local taxi driver took me and brought me back," she tells me. "I knew it would be too far for you." I am surprised that she even considered I might take on such a task. "The church was packed with people, and they all said how much they missed me and how glad they were to see me again. It was quite a reunion." She finishes inconsequently: "I'm not going in for all that stuff. I've decided I want a cremation."

We end the meal with ice cream. "Chocolate ice cream," she says, smacking her lips, "my favourite." She gives a big contented sigh. "It's so nice to get away from that place." She anticipates my words when she says: "Oh, I know, it's very beautiful, but you know, darling, you can't live on a view."

"I'm sorry you are not happy."

"I feel trapped. The days are so long."

I venture: "Moira thinks it would help if you joined the others in the dining-room occasionally, and I believe they open up the bar at six o'clock."

"I know what Moira thinks and, of course, she is right; it is very antisocial of me. But, darling, they are all so old. They just remind me of my own sad state. I did try going to lunch once, and the man sitting opposite dribbled into his napkin. It was too much to bear and I vowed, never again."

"Yes," I say thoughtfully, "I can see how that would put you off."

I wonder why she and Theo chose to live in a place so many miles away from their old home. It must restrict the amount of visitors she can hope to see, as most people are not prepared to travel a great distance to call upon an old lady.

"Theo wanted us to come to Riverbank," she tells me, as if divining my thoughts. "His brother was here and he thought the world of the place. I can't say I agree with him, but it's improving." She pats my hand. "Thanks to you, dear." Apparently I am forgiven for staying out of touch for so long, but I get the impression that I will not be allowed to lapse again.

"You and Theo did not have children?" I ask the question although I am sure of the answer. There are no indications of there being any sons or daughters in her life and she once told me the house where she and Theo lived had been sold because there was no one to inherit it.

She pauses. "No," she says, "Theo and I had no children. But, as a matter of fact, I had two children, and I lost them both."

She announces this fact so casually I can't find anything to say. An incongruous picture goes through my head, a young Maeve in the park with her two children whom she manages to mislay. Lady Bracknell's famous words come to mind: *"To lose one parent, Mr Worthing, may be regarded as a misfortune; but to lose both looks like carelessness."* Substitute the word 'parent' for 'child' and Maeve's statement becomes almost comical. I pull myself together. Of course, this must have been a tragedy of enormous proportion and not a reason for levity, even in one's innermost thoughts. My emotions are abnormally heightened at present, and those involving sudden weeping or silly laughter lie just below the surface.

"How awful," I murmur, trying to keep my mouth from twitching. I catch her eye, and I see that she is smiling broadly.

"Awful of me to lose them," she says cheerfully, "and it is all my fault that I am such a lonely old woman. I deserve to be. I'll tell you about it sometime."

I find myself smiling back at her, and I realise I have not smiled a truly genuine smile for a very long time.

She pays the bill and suggests that we have coffee in her room at Riverbank.

She gives Moira a wave of her stick as she passes the desk. "We have had a lovely time," she calls, and Moira replies: "I'm so glad."

There is a little kitchenette attached to her room, and I plug in the electric kettle. "You have everything you need here," I say, and I hear her big sigh as she lowers herself into her chair.

I find two mugs, superior mugs I notice, like everything else in the place, and I put a teaspoonful of instant coffee in each; I find a half carton of milk in the miniature fridge. I place the mugs on a little tray that I discover in a special place by the sink, and I carry it into the next room. In the centre is a low table with an unusual top, a square of needlework, gros point and petit point, exquisitely embroidered and set under a glass panel. "Theo's mother worked that," Maeve tells me. "I never knew her. His parents both died before I met him."

The room is bathed in sunshine and there are flowers everywhere, and when I remark on them, Maeve explains: "I love flowers. I order them from a shop in the village." Although she has been slow to integrate herself into the life of the community she has soon cottoned on to all the amenities the local shops can offer. The wine shop in the village, the florist and the hairdressers have all benefited by her patronage.

We sit opposite each other, the mugs warming our hands.

She regards me closely with a serious expression. "You have become thinner since the last time I saw you," she says.

I know it is true, but I thought she had not noticed. Old people are usually so intent on their struggle for survival they do not have time to observe changes in other people.

"My dear," she says, "you must tell me. What has happened?"

It is the suddenness and unexpectedness of the question that fazes me. To my horror I feel the tears gushing from my eyes. It is the first time I have wept since Dan went away, and now I have started I find I cannot stop. I bend my head and cover my face with my hands. The tears seep through my fingers. I am lost.

Maeve takes my two hands in hers. I feel the comfort of her old fingers, the softness of the loose skin against mine. She does not speak, but just sits and holds my hands. Eventually, I free one of them, and search around in my pocket for a handkerchief. When I find it, I mop my streaming face.

"I'm so sorry," I say.

"You mustn't be."

I owe her an explanation, so I tell her everything. Still holding one of my hands, she listens carefully and doesn't say a word. I don't miss out any of the details, the keys, the departure, the boys sleeping in my bed and I even describe to her how I hide behind the bedroom curtain when Dan comes to the house. "I haven't seen his face for weeks and weeks."

At last she speaks: "And the children, how are they taking it?"

"It's hard to tell. They don't say much; it is as if they have made a pact between them to ignore the situation. They go off very happily each Saturday to spend time with their father and Andrea. I have managed to get out of them that she is always there, but they avoid talking about her."

"Oh, my poor girl," says Maeve, "it is so difficult for you. Your husband has accepted the situation. It is his own doing and he has got what he wanted. Men are so clever at justifying their actions. By now he will have convinced himself it was the right thing for him to do."

"He does seem quite sanguine. I suppose my attitude worries him, but it does not detract from his own happiness."

It is a relief that Maeve, unlike Jane, has not called him a bastard. Sometimes, I listen to Jane railing against my husband and it makes me feel uncomfortable. Truthfully, I cannot agree with her – Dan has never been a bastard, and leaving me has not made him one.

"Do you feel better now?" Maeve asks gently.

I nod. I have recovered my composure. Quietly, we finish our coffee, and I say: "I must go soon, to collect Hugh from school . . ."

"Before you go . . ." She waves one hand in the air, as if trying to summon the words she wants to say.

I remain seated.

"I don't want you to think I'm an interfering old woman, but there is something I feel I must say to you."

"I don't think you are interfering," I tell her, "and I would like to hear what you have to say."

She takes a deep breath before she starts. "It is that I think you will have to see your husband. You must bite the bullet and adopt a friendly attitude towards him, whatever you may think in private. This is not for his sake or for your sake, but for the sake of your precious children. Imagine how they must be feeling – it is bewildering for them, and they are too young to cope with confusion and mixed loyalties. You are asking too much of them. It is up to you to make things as normal as possible, and if you manage to do that they will love you for it, and it will give you great power. It will be your greatest weapon against rival forces. If Andrea becomes an important person in their lives, you must go along with it, whatever it costs you and, if you do, you will find that they no longer isolate you from that other life of theirs. You are a woman, and curious, aren't you? It's human nature to want to know what's going on."

Of course, she is right. I'm bursting with curiosity. I long for them to tell me everything, about the house, how she and their father behave together, even about the food she gives them when they are there.

"Think of weddings," says Maeve. "When your boys get married if will be awkward if people are not on speaking terms."

I have to smile, a rather wintry little smile. The last thing on my mind at present is the future nuptials of Hugh and Neil.

"Time goes very quickly," Maeve assures me. She releases my hand and pats my cheek. "I don't mean to preach, darling, but I think this is so important, I must say it."

I am filled with a rush of gratitude towards this woman. She has pointed a way to me that I have been too blind, too full of my own self-pity and misery, to see. My tears have cleansed my mind and spirit, and I feel strong.

I lean forward to kiss her cheek. It is soft to the touch of my lips, and her skin smells sweetly of the scent she uses. In that moment I recognise it as *Je Reviens*, and it will always make me think of her.

"Thank you," I say.

She insists on walking slowly with me to the front door. She clutches her stick in one hand and holds tightly to my arm with the other. There is another cheery wave of the stick to Moira. Moira, no doubt imagining we have had a cosy little chat together, never dreaming of the small drama that has been enacted behind the closed door of Maeve's room.

Before I leave, she says: "Will you have lunch with me again, a week today, on Friday? I don't want to crowd you so I won't ask you to come and see me before then."

"Are you sure? It's a treat for me, of course, but expensive for you."

"I have lots of money," she says simply, "and no one to spend it on except myself."

"I'd love to come."

As I turn the car in the drive, I look behind and see her anxious face peering at me through the glass of the front door of Riverbank. I raise my hand, and she raises hers in return.

Chapter 7

In the evening Dan comes to the house because he wants to make arrangements for the following day, which is Saturday and the day he sees the boys. Usually, I listen for the sound of his car, and, when I hear it, I go upstairs to my room. By now Dan is used to making plans with Hugh, and he takes his time before leaving, sometimes sitting down to help with homework or just chatting to them. Not too long though because, just as I am sitting waiting above, Andrea is sitting waiting in the car.

Tonight is different because I am there to greet him, and he looks over the heads of the boys and I can see he is surprised to see me.

"Stay a while," I say. "Have a drink."

I am pleased to see that he is embarrassed. "I can't stay," he says.

The front door is still open, and I peer through it. "Is

Andrea in the car?" I say coolly. "Please ask her to come in. I'd like to meet her."

He is squirming now, and I rejoice in his discomfort.

"I think it would be upsetting for her," he says.

"It is upsetting for all of us," I tell him firmly, "but we have to meet sometime. Why not now?"

The boys stand and watch us both; their eyes are like saucers.

"While you are bringing her in," I say brightly, "Hugh and Neil will help me with the drinks, won't you, darlings?"

In the kitchen I find the glasses and put them on a tray. I am glad to see that my hands do not tremble. I open the bottle of wine and put it beside the glasses, and then I carry the tray into the sitting-room. I glance through the open front door and I see that Dan is standing by his car, talking through the window to someone sitting inside. I wonder if she will refuse to come and meet me. No, I think she can never do that. It is with a sense of relief that I watch them coming up the path towards our house.

I had imagined her fair and delicate and, as so often happens when one tries to pin a face on a person one has not yet met, I am completely wrong. She is a big girl, much taller than me, and rather plump. Bad legs, I note with satisfaction. She has a pretty open face, no make-up. She looks as if, under normal circumstances, she would be an easy person to talk to, and I can understand my children taking to her at once. I call her a girl because, although Dan has told me she is thirty-six years old, she appears younger than that, a girl in fact. There are no signs of her recent illness; she looks the picture of health.

There are no introductions – they would be ludicrous in the circumstances.

To cover the awkwardness I say to Hugh: "I'll pour out the wine, and you hand out the glasses."

He is pleased to be given such a responsibility, and his little brother looks at him with awe.

"Let's sit down," I say, and we all seat ourselves in armchairs. All eyes watch anxiously as the glass teeters in Andrea's direction. It arrives and she takes it from Hugh.

I put my arm around Neil's taut little waist. "In the kitchen there is a plate of cheese straws – on the table. Will you get them for me, darling?"

In a few moments the glasses are safely in the right hands, and the cheese straws repose on a plate on the low table between us.

"What a relief!" I exclaim.

I seem to be the only person in this strange little group capable of speech. Dan sits, looking at a patch of carpet beneath his feet. Andrea, beside him, is silent. The children cluster around my chair, leaning against me, watching closely but saying nothing. I begin to understand what Maeve meant when she talked of power. Temporarily, at least, I have power over these people.

I turn to Andrea: "Where is your house?" I ask, although I know already the answer to the question.

"In Upper Bratby," she replies. Her voice has a crack in it, which she remedies with a nervous cough. "It is a house that belonged to my parents, and when my mother died ten years ago it was left to me." She carries on bravely: "My father was a GP in the village and I am lucky enough to work in his old practice."

"That must be lovely for you," I say, "and Dan tells me you are back at work now you are well again."

Her face breaks into a smile. "Yes, it's wonderful to be back, and all that business is behind me."

"I'm so glad."

It is such an ordinary little conversation, and one that I might have with any of my acquaintances, except that, in this case, I am having it with a woman who has snatched my husband from me.

There is another pause. Perhaps Andrea and I are thinking the same thing. I look at my husband, and I speak to him in my mind, as I have done many times before, certain he will receive the message. I say: 'Come on; help me out here. Don't sit there like a big dope, incapable of saying anything.'

I speak directly to him: "What are your plans for tomorrow?"

At last he speaks: "I thought we'd go to the seaside, the weather is so good."

The boys come to life then and they hop around with glee. They demand details – where are they going, what time are they leaving?

"That seems to have gone down well," says Andrea. She seems to have gained confidence.

"I'd like to come a bit early," Dan tells me, "about ten o'clock – if that suits you, of course." His excessive politeness irritates me, but I understand it better when I hear his next words: "There are some things I'd like to pick up, books etc and my golf clubs."

"Do you play golf?" I ask Andrea.

"Not at present," she replies, "but Dan has promised to teach me."

"He tried to teach me," I say, laughing, "but it was a hopeless task and, in the end, he had to give up." I look at him and I make him look at me. "I was terrible, wasn't I?"

"You were not great," he admits.

"It was just that I could never hit the ball," I say. "I tried and tried, but the club and ball did not connect. After what seemed like hours of bashing away at it I decided to call it a day."

"I expect I'll do the same," Andrea says.

I do not let the subject drop. "Dan gave me some golf clubs, and they are still in the attic. I'll never use them, so why don't you have them?"

"Well, I don't know . . ."

"She hasn't even started playing yet," Dan interrupts irritably. "There's no need."

"You have them," I say with determination. "It's silly not to – take them tomorrow when you come."

The conversation seems to have dried up but the noisy chatter of the boys relieves the feeling of tension.

They are in a high state of excitement, 'over the top' Dan would have described it in the past and he would have instructed them sharply to calm down. As it is, he gets to his feet with, I am sure, a sigh of relief, and says: "We'll see you tomorrow."

"Yes, yes," they shout and, I'm glad to see, they are not hiding their enthusiasm from me.

From the window I watch Dan and Andrea walk to the car. Hugh and Neil accompany them to the gate, bobbing up and down and talking shrilly. With a little stab of pain I see Dan put his arm around Andrea's shoulder before she climbs into the car.

When the children reappear I say heartily: "Well, that went well, didn't it? And, Neil, you were quite right when you told me Andrea is very nice. Now, I think we should watch *Monsters Inc* before you go to bed."

We sit close to each other on the sofa, watching the video. I feel drained but triumphant at the same time. I have achieved something this evening, something that has given me more satisfaction than hiding behind the curtain. I wonder how Dan has taken my surprising new reaction. Knowing him as I do, I have a sudden picture of him driving home, thinking about the course the evening has taken, driving in silence, not saying a word to the companion by his side.

That night I suggest that Hugh and Neil sleep in their own beds again.

Of course, they protest. "We want to sleep in your bed."

"It was nice," I admit, "but it can't go on for ever. What a waste of your beds that would be. I would have to sell them or give them away if they were not used. No, I think you must sleep in them from now on, but I want you to promise *faithfully* that you will come into my bed as soon as you wake up in the morning."

They promise and, as I kiss them and tuck them in, I say: "You were both so helpful to me this evening. I was very proud of you."

Later that evening I telephone Maeve. "I enjoyed our lunch so much," I tell her. "Thank you."

Then I give her a graphic description of the evening, not leaving anything out because I know she will be interested to hear every detail. I can tell by her voice that I am right.

"What was she like?" she wants to know.

"Very pleasant. An ordinary nice person and, under normal circumstances, I think I would like her. It was weird."

"Well, you've got over a big hurdle this evening," she says, "and I hope things will be a little better from now on."

"I think they will, and I am grateful for your advice."

"Oh, darling," she says, "I only wish I could make everything right for you, but that's impossible."

I change the subject. "I intended calling you today to ask you about the end of the story. I got to the point when you met the handsome young man in the Irish Guards. I was going to ask you yesterday what happened next, but other things intervened."

"Next Friday," says Maeve, "next Friday I'll tell you. And I have a proposition to make to you as well that I hope will interest you."

"I can't imagine what that could be."

"Wait and see," she says mysteriously, the throaty chuckle in her voice. "Now go to bed, my darling, and have a good night's rest. You deserve it."

Chapter 8

Getting Maeve into the car is quite an achievement. There is the slow progress from her room to the front door or Riverbank, clutching my arm, dragging it down like a dead weight, and then the careful manipulation of the shallow steps and finally settling her ample form into the front seat of the car. She heaves a big sigh of relief, and so do I, for I am only too aware how important it is for old people not to suffer a fall. A bad fall can mean the difference between a precarious hold on life and no hold at all.

"Oh!" she says. "Getting old is so annoying." But she finishes the sentence on a note of satisfaction: "But I've got here, so where shall we go to today? Somewhere different, I say."

I do not start the engine as I think we should decide on our destination first.

"Do you know where your husband is living?" Maeve asks.

Of course, I do. I have looked up Andrea's name in the telephone book and found the address: Pollards, Upper Bratby. Many, many times I have contemplated driving the car to that address, but always my nerve has failed me.

Now, I look at Maeve. "Dare we?" I ask.

"Of course, darling. You want to see what it is like, don't you? I know I do. We can find something to eat at a pub nearby."

"Oh, no," I cry, "we might see them during their lunch hour, and they would know we've been snooping."

"I think it's unlikely," she says, "but, if you insist, we can find somewhere further afield."

We have no difficulty finding the house, the name 'Pollards' is on the gate. It stands alone, set back from a country lane. I am able to park the car in a place bordering the garden and we sit, looking at it, without speaking. It is a Victorian dwelling, perhaps Edwardian, red-brick solidarity. Standing erect and unassuming in grounds of about half an acre, it looks what it was, and still is, a doctor's house. Clinical, surrounded by a sterile laurel hedge, the flower borders unkempt, neglected by a professional owner too busy to attend to them.

I can tell that Maeve is not impressed, but she makes no comment at this juncture.

"You are lucky in one way," she says at last. "You do not have to sell your house to provide for two homes. That is the usual procedure, I believe."

I am glad I have seen it. Now I know where Dan lays his head each night. Like Andrea herself, it is not as I imagined. It looks rather big and uninviting for two people in a close and loving relationship, but I have always maintained in the past that Dan and I would be happy in a hovel. I thrust that thought aside as I put the car into motion. We drive for several miles before we find a pub where we can have lunch without fear of my husband and his lover interrupting us.

Over lunch and the usual bottle of wine Maeve outlines her plan. She wants me to write down her memories, not for anyone's benefit but herself. Will I take on this project?

"I've already told you the beginning," she says, "so you will have to write that down from memory. Then we can carry on from there."

I wonder, do I really want to be burdened with this?

"It will give you something to think about," Maeve insists, "and take your mind off other troublesome things. And also it will be a little money coming in that you have earned yourself." She tells me that she proposes to pay me two hundred pounds a week. "There's no hurry to get it done," she says. "You can take as long as you want."

"It's far too much money," I protest.

"No, it's not enough," she replies decidedly, "and if

you do anything extra I'll pay for it." Later, I have reason to remember those words. "I have lots of money, darling, as I have told you many times, and no one to spend it on. I have a bee in my bonnet about getting everything down on paper, and I'll be so grateful if you will do it for me."

There is a note of entreaty in her voice that I find hard to resist. I agree, reluctantly at first, and then with a sense of expectancy and interest. Maeve is right, it will give me a project, and already I am anticipating the purchase of paper and a notebook.

We take our time over lunch; perhaps we started rather late after our inspection of Andrea's house but suddenly I realise the time is approaching when I must collect the boys from school. Two boys now, as well as Amy, because Neil has just had his fifth birthday and is attending school all day instead of just the mornings.

On impulse I say: "Will you come with me when I fetch Hugh and Neil, and then come back to my house for a cup of tea?"

She is excited at the prospect.

"They won't be expecting you back at Riverbank?"

"I can do what I want," she tells me with dignity.

We join the line of cars outside the school gates, and Maeve watches with amazement the sight of dozens of children emerging and meeting up with their parents. My two, and Amy, are reduced to an unusual silence when confronted with a stranger. She sits stolidly beside me and makes no effort to talk to them, and it occurs to me that she may not feel at ease with children. Later, I realise the case is just the opposite: she approaches them from their own level, never talking down to them. She is just waiting to get to know them better before embarking on a conversation. It is what children do themselves, and is so sensible.

Jane comes out to greet us as Amy is handed over. I am glad to see she looks relaxed and happy, and I think perhaps she is over the worst. I introduce her to Maeve, and they respond to each other at once, two charismatic characters, chatting without restraint as if they have known each other for years. As we drive away I tell her about Jane's recent problems, and she sighs and says: "Oh, that poor child! Cancer is such a horror; like a thief in the night waiting to pounce and destroy people's lives."

We arrive at the house, and I help her out of the car. She stands and leans on her stick, and takes a good look. I feel a surge of pride as I imagine what she must be thinking. Dan and I, between us, have made it such a beautiful home. It always had potential, we knew that the moment we saw it, but we gave it back its birthright. We put light behind the empty windows, we trained a *banksiae* rose to climb the mellow walls and hang over the front door, we hacked away trees and untidy bushes so that the house could breathe again and be seen in all its loveliness. We rescued it and brought it to life again, and no amount of unhappiness during the last few months can alter that fact.

"Better than the house we saw earlier today," was Maeve's only comment.

Hugh and Neil stare fascinated as we make our way slowly and painfully into the house.

At last with a thunderous sigh she sinks into a comfortable armchair. "I've arrived," she assures an anxious-looking Hugh who has never seen a really infirm person before.

I order him: "Fetch her the footstool!" and he races off to get it, putting it in front of her, and I am amused to see him gently lift her feet, one after the other, and place them carefully on it.

I make a pot of tea for Maeve and put a slab of lemon cake on a plate. She sips her tea and munches the cake, from time to time giving pieces to Flush. The dog, knowingly, has taken up a position as close to her as possible.

"I'm going to get the children's supper," I say. "Will you be all right?"

"Of course," says Maeve.

"Shall we watch a video?" asks Neil hopefully.

"No," I say firmly because I think they must learn that a video is not allowed when we have a guest.

I have an idea. "Maeve, would you read them a story?"

Her face lights up. "I'd love to do that."

Neil runs off to get a book, and returns with '*A Bear Called Paddington*', and my heart sinks because it is a long book and requires skilful skipping. I wonder if Maeve is up to the task.

I hear the rumbling of her deep Irish voice while I am in the kitchen, and I realise that she is reading every word. I leave them to it, but then about twenty minutes later I peek through the door at the little group and I see the boys have crept closer to her. The next time I look they are snuggling up against her and little Neil's face is laid against her bosom. It is such an endearing picture that I get a catch in my throat.

That is the moment when Dan arrives. He is alone, and obviously amazed by the scene. Introductions are made. Hugh clings to Maeve's arm and Neil holds on to her hand. "Finish it!" they plead, but she says: "Not now. It will have to wait until next time."

Dan explains that he has come to fetch various things that he did not take away with him on his last visit. "The tools from the garage for a start," he says.

I say; "Leave me a few."

He glances at me sharply, and turns to go to the garage. We listen to him banging about in there. I settle the children around the table for their supper.

"Can we go and help Daddy?"

"No."

He reappears. "What exactly do you want in the way of tools?"

I have no idea. I say airily: "Just the ordinary day-to-day things I may need. A hammer? And shouldn't I have the Black and Decker? Isn't that an essential for any girl?"

He cannot hide his exasperation.

"Oh, never mind," I say, "I expect I'll have to buy everything new. Take what you want."

He puts all the tools in the boot of his car. I expect he has taken everything but, somehow, I am left feeling in the wrong.

He comes back to fetch the computer that is in the room he used to have as a study. He is about to dismantle it and take it away.

The boys eat their supper without speaking, and Maeve sits beside them, silently bonding with them, as uneasy as they are about what is going on; the removal of familiar items from a home, however necessary, cannot engender a feeling of security.

I find the courage to speak up. "I need the computer. I'd rather you left it, if you don't mind."

"What?"

"I shall be using the word processor," I say.

"You don't understand it," he retorts. By now he is really nettled, and I know that he is not showing himself in the best light with Maeve. Perversely, I am sorry about this because, for some reason, I want her to like him.

I try to speak coolly. "I admit I don't understand it now, but I can learn."

"And who is going to teach you?" His tone implies that no one is capable of such a feat, and I marvel at how much he has changed. There was a time when he would never have denigrated me in this way.

The sadness of it engulfs me, but I manage to ask him: "Perhaps you will take on the job?"

He doesn't reply and I say: "I'm sure Andrea will buy you a new one."

He looks at me in blank astonishment, and I continue unhurriedly: "Now, please, will you stay with the boys while I drive Mrs Bailey home. I'll only be gone for about half an hour. It will be a big help to me not having to take them along, and Hugh has to do his homework. I want it all finished by the time I get back, Hugh, and Daddy will help you if you need it."

In the darkness of the car on the way to Riverbank I hear Maeve's chuckle. "You told him!"

"I know, but it does not give me any satisfaction."

"He is attractive," she says, "and I couldn't help liking him despite the fact that he was behaving in the most maddening male way."

Safely, on the other side of the door at Riverbank, she clasps my hand.

"Thank you, darling," she says. "Today I have been completely happy."

Chapter 9

Maeve dreamed of the handsome redheaded lieutenant in the Irish Guards. She fell asleep at night thinking of him, and when she awoke in the morning he was still on her mind.

She was very young, barely sixteen years old and, by today's standards, very immature. What she did not realise was that he too was young, only twenty, and whereas she was thinking of love and marriage, a happy life ever after and, most importantly, escape from Castlerock, these considerations were far from his thoughts. He was just pleased that a tedious duty week spent with his aunt in a remote part of Ireland had been unexpectedly enlivened by the presence of a black-haired blue-eyed beauty who was clearly smitten with him.

Aunt Min and Uncle Frank approved of him. There was something so open and honest about him it would have been hard to find fault. And the aunt helped in his cause too; they had always been anxious to be in her favour. The aunt was a lady, as was Aunt Min, but the aunt had riches which Aunt Min did not possess.

Although very conscious of the extreme youth of their niece, whom they regarded as an adopted daughter, they were happy for her to go out with George Palmer in the company of Beryl and Brona, believing, erroneously as it happened, that there was safety in numbers.

George was enjoying his leave more than he anticipated. The idea of spending a week with an elderly spinster aunt had not appealed to him, but his mother had prevailed upon him to go, hinting that it could be beneficial to him in the future. She, a widow, knew, as everyone in the country knew, that the war would be over in a matter of weeks, and after that she would be able to see more of her son. After his spell in the army he would have to embark on a career, maybe university, and expectations from a rich aunt would not come amiss. George's mother had no money worries but, like many people in that happy position, she was not averse to the idea of more coming in the way of her precious only child. She knew the aunt had interests in many charities and she was anxious to divert those interests to her son, and it looked as if she had succeeded in her mission. The aunt was as captivated by George's charms as were Aunt Min and Uncle Frank, and she was glad that he had met three nice girls who would keep him amused during his stay in Ireland.

George felt pleased with himself for solving the tricky problem of Beryl and Brona. As soon as they were a safe distance from the house the transaction was made, and the sisters pocketed the money he gave them and went merrily on their way. Their mother had thoughtfully provided each girl and George with a picnic lunch, and the twins munched through theirs, sitting on a bench in the park at Castlerock. Then they had the rest of the day to do with as they chose, and they wandered around looking in the shop windows, spending the money at the fair or even abandoning the sunshine for the dark smoky atmosphere of the cinema. They were lucky they did not run into anyone they knew, for two nice young girls on their own was not a familiar sight, and would have been reported back to Aunt Min without delay.

That week was blessed with perfect weather, and the sun beat down on George and Maeve as they sat down, side by side, on the grass. They had found a special place, and they went to it each day. There was no one around to disturb them, and only a skylark soaring over their heads witnessed their actions. The intense heat, the hot blood racing through their veins and the beating of their hearts all contributed to an inevitable conclusion. Even in old age, Maeve remembers the hard earth beneath her body and the smell of the grass close to her face.

George was gentle with her. She was a child, and he

was aware of that fact. Mixed in with all his other emotions was a little pinprick of guilt, and he soon discovered that Aunt Min had not initiated her into the mysteries of sex. She believed, as did most of the women of her generation, that knowledge of that aspect of life would be learned on the wedding night, whether with joy or revulsion was in the lap of the gods. She had been lucky, and she prayed her niece would be lucky as well. Maeve was not prepared to wait; she was hugely interested and longed to know more about it. She was acquiescent when George's exploring hands wandered to the inside of her legs and undid the little rubber suspender on her stockings.

She wanted it to happen, and, of course, it did. The encumbrance of clothes took a great deal away from the moment and the whole experience disappointed and hurt her. George, hearing her little cry of surprise and pain, comforted her by saying it was her first time and enjoyment would come later.

Maeve, who thought him perfect in every way, believed him, and he was right because by the end of the week she was shameless in her desire for him. On their last day alone together, as she straightened her clothes, brushed her hair and tied it back from her flushed face, she could hardly bear the thought that he was going to leave her. When the time came for him to depart for England she was heartbroken. She did not know how she could face life without him. The sight of him in his uniform filled her with despair, and she clung to him, tears streaming down her face. He kissed her wet cheeks and her lips over and over again, and he promised he would write to her.

After he had gone, life went on as usual in the little household. Beryl and Brona, half understanding, half scornful of Maeve's evident grief, watched her with interest, wondering if she would manage to control her feelings.

During supper on the day George left Maeve broke down and sobbed. Uncle Frank, man-like, was perplexed by her strange behaviour but Aunt Min felt compassion for the girl, tinged with a terrible fear. Her two daughters were unable to suppress their laughter and their father ordered them from the room. If there was a suspicion in Aunt Min's mind that Maeve's despair was not the result of an innocent relationship, she did not reveal it to her husband. Frank thought the world of Maeve. He considered she had more sense in her head than his two girls put together.

George did not write. The war was over so Maeve did not worry for his safety. She has something else to worry about, a missed period. She knew the significance of that, and it made her very frightened.

"He told me he wanted me to meet his mother," Maeve confided to her aunt.

Aunt Min was sceptical. "His ma won't be wanting him to choose a little bog-Irish girl for a bride, that's for sure. She would have higher ambitions for him than that."

"His mother is Irish," Maeve pointed out. "They are an Irish family."

"But living in England," retorted Aunt Min, "and they are the worst."

The days turned into weeks and the weeks into months. Still there was no letter from George, and by now there was no doubt in Maeve's mind about what was happening to her. She was consumed with a terrible dread. It was the fashion at that time for girls to wear low-waisted dresses and the folds of material above hid the small protuberance.

Her poor mother had died leaving very little money. The whole estate amounted to her savings of three hundred pounds, and Uncle Frank was surprised that she had this money, hidden away in a drawer and found after her death. It was a secret that died with her – the money was an unexpected gift from her husband, no doubt sent in a moment of remorse at the way he had treated his wife and daughter. Frank put the money into Post Office Savings Account for Maeve, with strict instructions that it should not be touched until she was of age. Aunt Min thought different, and she attempted to withdraw a small amount for the dress and veil for Maeve's first communion. It seemed reasonable to her, but Mrs O'Rooney, behind the grille, told her that Maeve herself must sign for the money as no one else could do it. Maeve signed; it was easy then and it was easy now. She withdrew the sum of thirty pounds.

She left a note: 'I have gone to England to see George's mother. Don't worry about me.'

She took the bus to Dublin and the steamer to England. It was a terrible crossing with high winds and a turbulent Irish Sea. Of course, Maeve did not have a cabin, and she huddled with a lot of fellow passengers in an airless room. It was too rough to go on deck, and below the one lavatory was always occupied with someone being sick. Nearly everyone was sick, including Maeve who felt she had lost all her insides. When she stood on the deck in the early morning light and watched the shores of England getting closer and closer, she reflected that her night of vomiting must have resulted in the loss of the baby. She was convinced that nothing could survive such an onslaught and, when she pressed her hands to her stomach, she felt that there was a void there where once there had been something growing inside her. She breathed a sigh of relief when her fingers encountered only emptiness.

In England she began her journey to the village of Dering where George had told her his mother lived. It was a long way, and complicated for a young girl who had never travelled anywhere, let alone on her own. On the edge of tears she sought help from porters at the railway stations; they advised her to get a train to Reading and then a bus to Dering. By the time she arrived at that village she was exhausted, and she stopped a policeman and asked him the way to Mrs Palmer's house.

"Oh, I know that house, right enough, Miss," he said. "See those big gates over there? Go through them and follow the drive to the house." He warned: "It's a tidy way."

She walked slowly along the drive, her feet dragging from extreme fatigue. There was a canopy of leaves overhead and her feet scrunched on the gravel; otherwise it was very quiet and still. She turned a corner in the winding drive and, ahead of her, was a big house. George had spoken lovingly of his home but he had not mentioned grandeur and riches. Maeve ascended the steps leading to the front door and tugged at the bell pull.

An old lady came to the door. Maeve did not realise at first that she was a servant, although she knew that most of the young domestics had gone into munitions during the war.

"I'd like to see Mrs Palmer, please," she said.

The woman looked at the girl with distaste. She observed the shabby coat and the down-at-heel shoes, and there was a faint sour odour about her person. Maeve had not been able to wash herself after her night of seasickness.

"What is your business?"

"It's private."

"Wait here." She turned on her heel, leaving Maeve standing alone on the doorstep.

It was a humiliating moment, and one she would remember always. For the first time she realised who she was, Maeve O'Shea, a poor little Irish girl with a thick brogue and no airs and graces. Perhaps it was at that moment, standing forlornly on the step, she made up her mind to change.

Presently she heard steps on the wooden floor of the hall inside the half-opened door, and another woman stood in front of her, middle-aged, slim and erect with her hair done in the old-fashioned way, a bun at the nape of her neck.

"Please come in," she said.

She walked ahead of Maeve into a drawing-room, the most beautiful room the girl had ever seen. The sun slanted through the big windows, enhancing the shine on the highly polished antique furniture. The heavy velvet curtains and the covers on the sofas and armchairs were in muted soft shades of pink and green, and the carpet beneath her feet was of the same colours. It was an Aubusson but, of course, she did not know that. She only knew that she thought the place was like a palace, and the formidable faces looking down at her from the heavy gilt frames were like the faces of royalty, princes and princesses, dressed in glorious splendour.

"How can I help you?" asked the woman in a sad sweet voice.

She looked in perplexity at this strange young girl who had suddenly invaded her privacy. Like her servant, she noticed the threadbare clothes, but she also noticed the beautiful face. For Maeve, at the age of sixteen, was already showing the first signs of a great beauty, a fact which Aunt Min took great pains to hide from her. Uncle Frank may have noticed but he knew better than to comment on it.

"Are you George's mother?" Maeve asked.

The woman flinched as if she had been struck, then she appeared to pull herself together and nodded her head.

Maeve took a tremulous step forward. "Please will you tell me where he is?" she urged. "It's important that I see him."

Mrs Palmer put a shaking hand to her mouth. It was as if she could not speak. The words formed on her lips but she was unable to utter them.

Maeve watched her in stunned silence. "You know where he is?" she asked.

"Yes, I know." The words, spoken at last, were whispered. "He is dead."

It had been such a cruel blow, just when she felt sure he was safe. The war was over and he had his whole future before him; then came the devastating news that he had been killed in action. Surely the last bullet had been aimed at her son.

Of course, Maeve knew that hundreds of boys had died in the trenches; everyone in Ireland followed the progress of the war. If Uncle Frank had been younger he would have been there in the fray, he had said so over and over again, but somehow she had never imagined George would be in danger, her George.

Aunt Min always maintained that Maeve was like

her mother, a fainter. So many times she had staggered out of church, sitting on a gravestone in the churchyard with her head down, trying to stop the world spinning around her. Now she was about to prove Aunt Min right. To her dismay she felt the darkness closing around her, and so familiar was she to the sensation she knew that if she did not sit down at once she would collapse in a small heap on the beautiful carpet.

Mrs Palmer helped her to a chair. "Put your head down, dear," she said gently. She pulled a cord and a bell sounded in the house. The elderly servant appeared and her mistress ordered a glass of water. "Quickly, Martha."

As the swirling blackness settled, and Maeve could discern the features of the two people watching her anxiously, she saw that the elder woman looked less disapproving than she had when she first saw her standing on the doorstep.

"Are you feeling better, dear?" she asked, a comforting hand on Maeve's shoulder.

"Yes, thank you," said Maeve, pulling herself together. She knew that once everything had steadied she was safe.

George's mother sat in a chair opposite the young girl and asked: "When did you meet my son?"

"In Ireland, when he was on leave, staying with his auntie."

"Ah!" Into Mrs Palmer's tortured mind came a picture of the two young people, the shy Irish colleen and her hot-blooded son. What went on between them? She wondered, and rejoiced that perhaps George had found some sexual satisfaction in the days before his death. In her view that was the only crumb of comfort to emerge after the arrival of the dreaded telegram; she had thought so often of the virile young man cut down at the height of his powers. Such was Mrs Palmer's intense grief it could not encompass the possibility that there might be another aspect to this romantic idyll. She thought only of herself and her lost child.

She wanted to be alone with her thoughts. "I am sorry I can't help you, my dear," she said in a dismissive voice.

Maeve picked up the signal at once. She got wearily to her feet.

"Martha will give you something to eat and drink before you go, won't you, Martha?"

"Of course, madam."

Maeve followed the woman across the hall, through a baize-covered door and along a corridor until the reached a vast kitchen. There was a long table in the centre, a dresser on one side covered with blue and white china, and copper pans hung from hooks on the ceiling. She was told to sit down while Martha prepared a cheese sandwich for her and poured milk into a cup from a churn. Maeve was hungry and she ate and drank what was given to her but, all the time, she was conscious that she had been relegated to the kitchen. That's what Mrs Palmer thought of her – she was a servant like Martha.

"Where will you go?" Martha enquired. Perhaps her sharp eyes had registered something that her mistress had missed, perhaps she was just concerned for the pathetic creature that had appeared in their midst.

Maeve replied with as much dignity as she could muster. "Don't worry," she said. "I know my way home."

Chapter 10

The wind had dropped and the sea was tranquil on the journey back to Ireland. Maeve did not feel the slightest bit nauseated. She sat on a hard bench and thought about George being dead. It was hard to believe that the warm young body that had lain against hers under a blue sky had been shattered into nothingness. The sadness of it was tempered by her personal anxiety; there was no way he could help her now. She felt a twinge of resentment that he had got off so lightly, then, in the darkness, she crossed herself for having such a sinful thought.

During the time it took to cross the Irish Sea she came to the conclusion that she had been wrong to assume that her violent vomiting of the night before had rid her of the baby. Tentatively, she put her hand beneath her coat and laid it on her stomach that no longer felt empty. She knew it was still there, and she even felt a slight movement – not only was the child inside her but it was a living entity.

The bus winding its way to Castlerock seemed to take an eternity, and when it dropped her off at the end of Orchard Street the first signs of a new day were showing. It was beginning to get light and there was an early morning mist over the roofs of the houses. Her home was in darkness because everyone in it was asleep, but she felt it welcomed her; it was her only home since she had arrived there with her mother twelve years before. When she rang the bell, Uncle Frank opened the door to her. "God be praised," he said when he saw who it was.

Maeve entered the dingy hall, smelling faintly of Aunt Min's cooking, and she went into the small sitting-room. Presently her aunt appeared, and behind her the twins, both in their long white nightgowns, curiosity having got the better of their desire to stay asleep.

Aunt Min did not embrace her but the relief was evident in her face. "We were wondering if we should call the Garda," she said, "but the Blessed Mary has brought you home to us." After this flight of fancy she adopted a more practical approach. "Why did you want to see George's mother?" she asked. During Maeve's absence a little nagging thought had invaded her consciousness, now she knew the moment had come when she must bring her suspicions into the open.

It was too much for the exhausted girl. All she wanted to do at that moment was to climb into bed with Beryl and Brona and sleep. She did not know how to answer her aunt's question, and she lowered her head and sobbed. Uncle Frank helped her to a chair.

"Are you carrying his child?" Aunt Min demanded. It was more a statement than a question.

Maeve nodded her head.

Uncle Frank ordered his daughters from the room. He turned on Maeve and shouted: "You have brought sin to this house!" Then he too left the room, slamming the door behind him.

Aunt Min looked at her sorrowfully. Unlike her husband, her mind did not dwell on the sin. She remembered clearly a hot summer in a village in Tipperary where she had been brought up, and a boy, eighteen years old like herself, who was the son of a neighbouring farmer. She thought she understood the sin part although, as a devout Catholic, she had been taught to live in dread of the word, such a little word encompassing so much fear. It was not the sin that bothered her now, but shame. She and Frank had always been poor but they had pride, and she knew full well how the neighbours would react when the news got around that Maeve was expecting a love child. That would be hard to live down; the disgrace of a baby born out of wedlock was a terrible thing,

Maeve was moved from the big bed she once shared with her mother to the attic room at the top of the house. The ceiling sloped to the floor, and there was a very small window overlooking the street. In the summer the room became unbearably hot and in the winter as now, it was impossible to keep warm. Cold draughts came from every direction, from the badly fitted windows and from the gaps in the floorboards. Uncle Frank, relenting of his invective against Maeve, carried up a Valor stove, but Aunt Min, quite rightly, decided it was a fire hazard in such an enclosed wooden space, and forbade the girl to light it. Instead she produced woollen garments and blankets for her to wrap around her shivering form.

There was only one sink and tap in the house and that was in the kitchen. Maeve was allowed to use it when everyone in the family had finished his or her ablutions. She crept downstairs and filled the jug standing on the washstand in her room, and carried it up the two flights of stairs. The weekly bath in front of the fire, a family ritual, was denied her. The lavatory was outside and she hurried outside to it, in all weathers, making sure that no one was around to see her. In the attic room she spent the last months of her confinement, mostly sitting on a chair, almost watching her stomach swell as the weeks and months went by. If this treatment was meant to make her repent of her bad behaviour, it worked, but that was not the objective. She was locked away at the top of the house so that prying neighbours would not guess what was going on. Aunt Min brought her food on a tray and, like a patient in hospital who is not too ill, she welcomed this diversion in the monotony of her day. The other thing she greeted every night as a dear friend was sleep, kind compassionate sleep that for a few hours blotted out the fears of the day.

The only other visitor besides her aunt was the priest. He surveyed her with a pained expression and knelt by her chair and prayed for her. She pleaded with him to bring her books to read, and he did take pity on her in this respect. On his next visit he arrived with a bag of books, books he considered suitable for a person in her condition, mostly novels with a moral. She devoured them hungrily, particularly enjoying '*Wildfell Hall*' which seemed to demonstrate that good can triumph over evil. Her stay in the attic had one good result: Maeve began to read, and she loved books all the rest of her life. In that little dark room they were her salvation.

She never thought of escape. If she walked down the stairs and out through the front door, where would she go? She was not perceptive enough to realise that if she had blurted out her secret to Mrs Palmer her life would have been very different. That lady would not have locked her away; she would have been cared for with joy and expectation. Maeve had almost forgotten that the child within her was part of George; she had no feeling for her unborn baby, it was just a source of terrible unhappiness and regret for her. Neither did she feel hostility towards Aunt Min and Uncle Frank; she thought their treatment of her was justified. She had sinned against God and her family and now she was paying the price.

Then another person came to see her – Mary O'Brien, the local midwife. She was enormously fat and seemed to fill the little attic room. The window was blocked out by her bulk, and her movements were slow and ponderous. She lumbered from the washstand to the bed, and pummelled Maeve's stomach with her cold damp hands. The girl dreaded her coming, and when she came more frequently she realised it meant her time for giving birth was getting nearer. Maeve was terrified of childbirth, and she had many lonely hours to contemplate her fear.

One day, when the door of her room was ajar she heard Aunt Min and Uncle Frank talking together, standing on the landing below.

"Mary swears she will not breathe a word to a soul," Aunt Min was saying.

"Well, people will learn soon enough." This was Uncle Frank talking. "Don't imagine you can keep it a secret for long."

Despite all her fears, Maeve could never have imagined the sheer agony of bringing a child into the world. Her daughter took a long time to arrive, and both Maeve and Mary O'Brien were drenched in sweat when eventually the little red creature emerged. Maeve was to have a lasting memory of the midwife standing over her, the damp patches under the arms of the tight uniform she wore, shouting to Maeve to push harder when all she could do was to protest at the top of her voice. Aunt Min and Uncle Frank were nowhere to be seen. They had been sitting downstairs listening to the screams, hoping that no one else could hear them. The silence that ensued filled them with dread, and then came the thin wail of the infant. Aunt Min looked at her husband and saw that, like her, he had tears in his eyes.

Mary held the baby up for Maeve to see. She thought she had never seen anything so ugly in her life, and she turned her head away from the sight.

Later, when she peeped at her daughter lying in a Moses basket, she changed her mind. She looked very sweet, lying on her side with one tiny hand spread out near her face, and even Aunt Min, when she climbed the stairs to view her great-niece, pronounced her a beautiful baby. Nameless, for as yet no one had thought of a name for her, and only a handful of people knew of her existence.

Maeve thought she would be allowed downstairs after the birth, admitted to the family circle once more, sullied but forgiven. It was not the case; she and her daughter remained in the attic room. Aunt Min produced clothes for the baby, clothes that had once been worn by her own girls, and Maeve produced quantities of milk for her nourishment. Mother and child thrived in body, but not in spirit.

It was now early spring and Maeve, looking out of the attic window, could see the trees in Orchard Street were bursting out into green leaves. She longed for freedom, and she wondered how long her aunt and uncle intended to keep her and her child confined to one room.

Maeve stared long and hard at her baby lying asleep in the basket. In her heart she knew that they would not stay forever in the attic. There would come a time when they would have to be admitted into the household. She remembered that twelve years earlier Aunt Min and Uncle Frank had shown kindness to her mother when she arrived on their doorstep, a small girl clinging to her skirt. The difference between that situation and the present one was that Maeve's mother had been respectably married to a minister of the church, though the marriage had foundered because of the reprehensible behaviour of one of the parties. The fact that it was the Protestant preacher who had acted so dishonourably persuaded religious folk like Aunt Min and Uncle Frank that it was their duty to protect the victim.

Now, it was Maeve who was the victim, but she had succumbed to the sins of the flesh and there was no pity for her. She could imagine Aunt Min trying to explain what had happened to her neighbours, Mrs Finnigan at number eleven and Mrs Hartigan at number fifteen, and she knew what their reactions would be, a mixture of sympathy and blame that Aunt Min would find hard to take. Maeve decided that her aunt did not deserve such treatment.

One morning she got up at five o'clock and dressed in her warmest clothes. She fed the baby, leisurely, not hurrying in this intimate and closest of functions. With her finger she stroked the soft head as it lay near her breast, sucking with little murmurs of pure delight. Then Maeve carefully wrapped her in a shawl, like a cocoon as her aunt had taught her, and then laid her gently in the basket. The baby appeared to look at her for a few seconds, almost, the anguished girl thought, as if she was seeing her for the first time, then the transparent lids closed over her eyes and she slept, sated with milk and loving kindness.

Carrying the basket, Maeve tiptoed down two flights of stairs and out through the front door.

No one saw her scurrying along the street. The inhabitants of Orchard Street and, indeed, most of Castlerock were sound asleep behind drawn curtains. Maeve, with her precious burden, headed straight for the Convent of Perpetual Adoration, and she placed the basket on the step outside the narrow door in the tall wall surrounding the building.

There was a metal bell pull, and when she tugged it the sound echoed through the convent.

She ran and hid behind a tree. She watched, and presently she saw that the door was opened, and two hands appeared and picked up the basket. It was not uncommon for unwanted babies to be left at that place of sanctuary.

Then Maeve walked slowly back to Orchard Street and her home.

And it seemed to her that every bird in Ireland was singing on that early morning.

Chapter 11

When Maeve entered the house she heard a noise coming from the small kitchen, and she knew that it was Uncle Frank who was in the habit of getting up early and making a cup of tea for his wife.

He looked surprised to see her. "What are you doing downstairs?" he asked. "You must go back to your room." He did not say these words harshly, because he was sorry for the girl. She had got herself into an impossible position and he did not know what the outcome would be. No doubt, his wife, cleverer than he, about such matters, had thought of a solution to the problem but, as yet, she had not told him what it was, and he was beginning to wonder if she knew herself.

"No," said Maeve firmly, "I am not staying in the attic any longer. It is like a prison and you can't keep me there until the end of my days."

Uncle Frank looked at her sadly, and perhaps he was

thinking that his little pet had become a woman because of what had happened to her; the child that he had loved so much was gone forever.

Presently, Aunt Min wandered downstairs, clutching a moth-eaten dressing-gown to her spare form. Her eyes were heavy with sleep, but she had been roused by the sound of voices.

"Maeve?" Like her husband she was surprised to see her niece in the kitchen.

"I told her to go to her room," said Uncle Frank.

"I thought I heard the baby cry," said his wife.

"You did not, so," said Maeve, "for she is no longer here."

Aunt Min was wide-awake now. "Where have you taken her?" she asked, and there was fear in her voice.

"To the convent."

"You left her outside – in the cold?"

"I waited until a sister came to the door, and I saw her take her in."

Aunt Min crossed herself. "God forgive us!" she said.

Uncle Frank, the old brown teapot in his hand, stood as if transfixed, staring at his two women. Then he put the teapot down on the tray and said: "What will be, will be."

Aunt Min said: "The sisters will see that she goes to a good home."

It was as if they were talking about a cat that had become a nuisance to them, but they still felt responsible for – and they seemed to have forgotten about Maeve, the mother of the abandoned child. She wondered if they credited her with any feelings at all.

"It's for the best," said Aunt Min decidedly.

Maeve experienced a sense of bitter disappointment. She had expected them to act differently; she had envisaged them making immediate arrangements to get the baby back. Her uncle would be despatched to the convent to explain to the sisters that a terrible mistake had been made. Already, she was beginning to doubt her decision, to realise the extent of her loss. In a short while her breasts would be heavy with milk, and she thought of her baby waking in new surroundings, and crying because there was no comfort for her.

Gradually, the rest of the household assembled in the kitchen. Beryl and Brona stared at the little group, guessing that there had been a new development in the drama that had been unfolding for months in their home. They had been sworn to secrecy about the existence of the baby, and they had not uttered a word to anyone at school. They were good at keeping secrets. Now their mother told them that the sisters at the convent had taken the baby. "She will be adopted," she explained to her daughters. "We have no room for a baby in this house."

That was the nub of the matter, thought Maeve, no room for a baby; room for a deserted relation and her child, but no room for a defenceless little mite. For the first time in many months Maeve felt resentful. Too late came the realisation that she had been unjustly treated, that these people she loved so much were hypocritical and behind the times in their views. Surely, the Virgin Mary, whom they worshipped, a mother herself, would not have condoned their actions. They're ignorant, that's what they are, she thought, and she felt almost sorry for them.

"You can come down and sleep with the girls again," said Aunt Min generously.

"Oh, no," cried the twins in unison, for they had become accustomed to sharing the big bed, without Maeve. Beryl reasoned: "It is a bed made for two people, not three."

"There is no need for me to move," said Maeve, "for I will not be here. I am going to England to get a job." In a flash of enlightenment she knew that was the only course for her to take.

"What sort of a job?" asked Uncle Frank.

"I don't know," she replied, but she had already made up her mind.

She would go on the stage. The war had ended and theatres were re-opening in London again. The bright lights would attract people who had suffered the deprivations of war for four years. It was a good time for young hopefuls. Maeve did not tell her aunt or uncle of her plan because she knew they would disapprove of it. They would point out that she had no particular talent and no experience of the stage.

"You will easily get a job as a domestic," said Aunt

Min. "I hear they are crying out for servants in England."

But Maeve had no intention of being a domestic. She aspired to better things – money and a beautiful house like she had glimpsed when she went to see George's mother. Her ambitions did not include marriage – the idea of a man touching her filled her with disgust and horror. The heady bliss of her sexual encounters with George Palmer, the warm sensation in her limbs as he penetrated her soft body, these feelings had taken on the substance of a dream. The long confinement in the attic room and the searing pain of childbirth had replaced the ecstatic moments. She remembered them, but she was content to think of George as the love of her life, a love that had been cruelly taken from her. It was best to leave it like that.

Aunt Min told Maeve that she intended to buy her a coat before she set out on her big adventure. The girl had told her about the horrendous journey to England when she went to seek out George's mother, and her aunt was determined that this time she would be properly clad. With Uncle Frank's blessing and a purse crammed with notes, saved over months of hard work and sacrifice, they set out for the shops. Maeve was not allowed to choose her own coat, and she hated the one Aunt Min chose for her. It was heavy grey tweed, like the uniform of a schoolgirl or a nursemaid. 'Serviceable' was how her aunt described it. Maeve resolved that she would not wear it after she left Orchard Street. As soon as her aunt and uncle and their daughters were out of sight she would take it off, and never put it on again. This did not happen because it was cold on the crossing, and cold too when she stepped on to English soil. She was glad of the coat.

Maeve decided the first thing she would do when she got to London was to find somewhere to live. She had taken every penny of the money her mother had left her and closed the post office account and, after paying for her fare on the boat, she still had the princely sum of two hundred pounds, which she had changed into English money. She knew that she could live on that for some time until she managed to get a job in the theatre.

She did not know anything about London and the city bewildered her. She walked and walked, gazing into the brilliantly lit shop windows. When she began to tire and, after her recent experience of childbirth, she still tired easily, she got on to one of the red buses that kept passing by. She allowed it to take her out of the West End and into the poorer parts where the houses and streets reminded her of Orchard Street. She had given the conductor four pennies and he sidled up to her and said: "Getting out here, love?" which she took as a hint that it was time for her to get off. She thought she had reached her destination because she found herself in an area where she could afford to live until she found employment.

She walked the length of a street called Primrose Road. Like Orchard Street in Castlerock it did not live up to its name. It was a road devoid of charm, not a tree to be seen and litter lying on the pavement and in the gutter. At least Orchard Street had a line of trees bordering it, as Maeve had witnessed, looking through the attic window and seeing the first green leaves of spring.

Maeve observed that there were notices in several of the windows announcing that there were vacancies. Apparently most of the houses in this road had rooms to rent, and at the end of the street Maeve retraced her steps and chose one of the dingy terraced houses, number nineteen, where the notice was displayed in the window in front of a drab lace curtain.

A woman answered the door when she rang the bell, and Maeve had no way of knowing that this woman would play a big part in her life. She saw a small dumpy figure wearing a floral overall. Later she was to discover the disgruntled expression was a permanent feature of the lady, who demanded: "Well?"

"Have you a room to rent, please?"

The woman mentioned the cost of the room. Was she prepared to pay that? She looked at Maeve doubtfully.

"Yes, of course."

"Are you able to put down a deposit?"

"Yes."

She followed the woman into the hall, dark brown shiny walls and smelling of stewed cabbage. Maeve had imagined that when she left Orchard Street she would never smell that particular pervasive odour again, but here it was turning up in a London lodging house, many miles from Castlerock.

She followed the woman up narrow stairs covered in dusty red carpet that ended when they reached the first landing, and was replaced by bare boards that continued up to the top of the house. "My name is Mrs Deacon," explained the landlady, pausing at the top of the first flight of stairs. "Me and my hubby live in the basement. My son has the flat at the top of the house. He works for the government." She pointed to a door ahead of them. "Mr Langridge lives there – he has an important job in the City," she said proudly. "The bathroom is on this floor. My husband and I have our own bathroom, of course, and likewise our son, but you share this with the other tenants."

Two other doors were indicated on the next floor, belonging to Miss Shaw, a hairdresser, and Mr Baines, a postman. On the top floor was the room that was to be Maeve's, and directly opposite it a flight of stairs leading to the closed door of the son's flat in the attic. The creation of the staircase had made a space where another bedroom must have been; consequently the landing on this floor was more spacious than the ones below, and a table had been placed against the wall upon which someone had placed a potted fern.

"If you take this room," said Mrs Deacon, pausing for breath, "you will have two keys, one for the front door and the other for your room. I like you to be in by midnight, and I don't permit gentlemen guests. If I catch you with a man in your room, you'll be out. The same rule applies to black people – no black people in my house, please."

It sounded very formidable, strict rules that Uncle Frank would have approved of – and Maeve had imagined she was escaping a life full of restrictions and prohibitions.

The room was big and furnished with a metal bed, a washstand with a basin and jug sitting on top of it, a worn but comfortable-looking armchair and a capacious wardrobe. A little shaft of sunshine slanted through the window and gave Maeve a glimmer of hope. Mrs Deacon drew back a curtain and revealed a spindly table covered with a sheet of oilcloth on which there was a small gas ring and a kettle, a box of matches by the side. She said: "No elaborate cooking, but you can brew yourself a cup of tea with that."

Hands on hips, she surveyed the girl with a stern look: "Well?"

"I'll take it," Maeve said.

"The sheets are changed once a fortnight. Put them and your towel outside your door, two weeks from today, on a Monday."

"Thank you."

Mrs Deacon felt in the pocket of her overall and handed over two keys on the same ring. "I'll have the deposit, please." She paused, as if thinking. "Ten pounds."

It seemed a vast amount of money, but Maeve did

not hesitate. She rummaged around in her bag for the money that was taken and pocketed with alacrity.

Suddenly, she found herself alone in the room, her room and her home for the unforeseeable future. It was all very exciting, if a little daunting, and she was relieved she had found somewhere to live so soon after arriving in London.

She unpacked her suitcase and hung her few clothes on hangers in the wardrobe. She put a sepia photograph of her mother on a small table by the bed. It was of a woman dressed in the cumbersome clothes of the era, standing by a pedestal that the photographer used for all his portraits, looking straight ahead of her with a defiant expression. It was a strong face, but an unsettling picture because Maeve was only too aware that her mother had never achieved any of her ambitions (except, perhaps, the one that involved giving birth to her) and her defiance had fallen on waste ground.

She went down two flights of stairs to explore the bathroom. It was not up to Aunt Min's standard of cleanliness; the linoleum floor was greasy with black patches and the paintwork on the walls was flaking. There was an Ascot boiler, a terrifying potential hazard, poised over a bath with claw feet. The lavatory was adjacent to the bathroom and smelled of smoke and other unpleasant odours. When Maeve returned to her room she understood why because there was a notice on the wall, saying *No Smoking*, but it did not concern her because she had never had a cigarette in her life, just as she had never had an alcoholic drink. George had once tried to persuade her to have a glass of wine, but she had refused – she had been brought up to regard drinking of alcohol as a sin.

She realised she was very hungry, and so she ventured down the three flights of narrow staircase and through the front door in a quest to find something to eat. She hurried along Primrose Road and found there was a group of shops at the end of it. It was beginning to get dark and the streets lights and the lights in the houses and shops were brightening up the gloom. She was frightened when a leering man staggered towards her and muttered; "Come and have a drink with me, love." She did not remember such a thing ever happening to her in Ireland, and she felt she had entered a dangerous world. She quickened her steps into the grocer's shop, and the light inside was reassuring. Maeve purchased cold ham, cut from a big joint, a packet of tea, a lettuce, tomatoes, a loaf of bread, a bottle of milk and a packet of butter. Then she remembered about breakfast, so she bought a pot of honey. The cheerful man behind the counter put all her purchases into a brown paper bag, and gave her a friendly smile as he put the money into the till. "You'll enjoy that, love," he said. Evidently, people in London called one 'love' – she had first noticed it in the bus.

Back in her room, she warily lit the gas ring and boiled the kettle. There was water in it already, and

Maeve supposed that when it was empty she would have to refill it from the bathroom tap below. She enjoyed the cup of tea and the little picnic in her room. She was very weary and, kettle in one hand and her sponge bag in the other, she descended to the bathroom. She decided she would not brave the Ascot boiler on her first night so she washed herself carefully and brushed her teeth. On the way upstairs she met a middle-aged woman coming down. They smiled at each other tentatively. It must be Miss Shaw, the hairdresser, thought Maeve.

As she had done every night since she could remember she knelt beside the bed, hands together, and prayed for her family; her poor dead mother came first followed by Uncle Frank, Aunt Min and the two girls. Then she prayed for her baby. "Please God," she whispered, "let her have a happy life with people who love her, and forgive me for not looking after her myself."

The sheets were clean and there were two rough blankets and a lumpy eiderdown. A glow from the streetlight outside penetrated the flimsy curtains and she thought it would keep her awake, but she was wrong. Sleep came easily to her almost as soon as her head touched the hard pillow, and her last thought was that she had never asked Mrs Deacon whether the amount for the rent she had mentioned was for a week or for a month. How could she have been so foolish? What must the woman think of her? If she, an ignorant little Irish girl, were to make any progress in the great city of London she would have to do better than that!

Maeve did not wake until the little alarm clock by her bed (a parting gift from Uncle Frank) proclaimed it was eight o'clock in the morning.

Chapter 12

After breakfast of tea, bread and honey, Maeve set out to look for a job. In the dark hall her landlady accosted her.

"Everything all right?" demanded Mrs Deacon. There was a curious gleam in her eye and Maeve realised that every movement she made would be, where possible, under close scrutiny.

"'Tis grand, thank you," said Maeve.

"You are Irish?"

"Yes."

"You seem young to be so far away from home."

Maeve did not want to start exchanging confidences and she changed the subject by asking boldly: "When do I pay you the rent?"

The woman was surprised and suspicious. Nervously, she fingered the month's deposit already paid, still in her overall pocket. "Once a week, I'll tell you when it is due. Is there a problem?"

"No, of course not. I wonder, too, if you would be so kind as to explain the boiler to me. I don't want to make a mistake."

"It's simple enough, but if it worries you I'll get my son to explain it to you."

"Thank you."

As Maeve slipped through the front door she felt the woman's eyes boring into her back. She was glad that she had put all her worldly wealth in her bag clutched in her hand; she was convinced that Mrs Deacon would examine her room closely after she had left the house.

She got on a red bus and it transported her to theatreland: Shaftesbury Avenue and the Haymarket lay before her for her to discover. She wandered from one theatre to the next, studying the faces of the actors and actresses portrayed behind the glass frames. Their names meant nothing to her. She thought her feet had led her away from theatreland when she suddenly faced a building and saw a placard posted by the lane leading to the stage door. It read: *Auditions in Progress*. Her heart quickened because she had heard of the word 'audition' and knew that it was an entry to a part in a stage production. At that moment she knew she had to be brave, a faint heart at this juncture would get her nowhere.

She walked boldly through the door and along a dark passage, and suddenly she found herself in an auditorium full of people. There, a harassed looking man waylaid her.

"What do you want, Miss?"

"I've come for an audition," she faltered. Nothing ventured, nothing gained.

"Have you a card?"

"No."

"You have to have a card. Sorry."

She turned away with mixed feelings of disappointment and relief, disappointment because she had been rejected and relief because she had no idea what was expected of her in an audition. She remembered her mother sitting at the piano in the parlour of the house in Orchard Street, singing sweet Irish ballads to her sister, Uncle Frank and the three little girls. Maeve had learnt these songs and she supposed she could sing one of them. She had been told many times that she had a lovely voice. Or she could recite one of the poems she had memorised at school – she loved the opening lines: '*Kathleen Mavourneen! The grey dawn is breaking, the horn of the hunter is heard on the hill . . .*' she felt sure she could inject drama and pathos into those lines, as she had done at school. But . . . there was a little niggling doubt at the back of her mind that the shadowy figures in the front row of the stalls might not think it appropriate, or appreciate a soulful Irish ditty for that matter. The idea of stepping on to that stage was very frightening, and she was almost glad that she did not have a card.

Maeve was leaving when a girl detached herself

from a group of chattering females, and caught her by the arm. She said hurriedly: "Wait for me outside. I can help you."

Maeve stood outside the stage door in an alley flanked on either side by a high brick wall. A bitter wind whistled through the narrow turning, and she clutched the grey tweed coat to her shivering body. Time went slowly, and she was beginning to think it was foolish to wait any longer when suddenly the girl appeared.

"Oh, how cold it is out here," she said. "Shall we go and have a cup of coffee somewhere? I know a place near here."

Maeve nodded, and the girl set off at a brisk pace, Maeve trotting behind her. Her new acquaintance was tall and walked with an easy grace. She had a mane of auburn hair that bobbed up and down as she walked. Maeve noticed with envy that she was wearing a soft woollen coat with a big fur collar. When they were seated in the warm café, she slipped out of the coat and left it hanging carelessly over the back of the chair. She was wearing a black silk dress, very tight and clinging to her beautiful figure. Maeve thought her very elegant, and she wondered whether she should keep her coat on, or take it off – thus displaying the dowdy clothes beneath.

"I think you should take your coat off – it's so hot in here." said the girl, as if reading her thoughts. "My name is Jenny Graham."

"My name is Maeve O'Shea."

"And you are from Ireland. I recognised that lovely accent at once. I don't want to be nosey but I can't help wondering why you were at that audition. What are you?"

Maeve was bewildered. "I don't know what you mean."

"Are you a soprano? That's what they were looking for this morning."

"I don't know," Maeve confessed. "I can sing in tune."

"Well, you would certainly have to sing in tune for that audition," said Jenny with an amused look, then seeing Maeve's blank expression she explained: "The audition was for the D'Oyly Carte Opera Company. That was the Savoy Theatre."

"I had no idea," said Maeve, and she gave a self-conscious little giggle. "I saw a notice saying 'Auditions in Progress'- so I thought I'd try." She glanced at her new friend and asked: "How did you do?"

"I lost my nerve and came away," said Jenny. "I knew I did not have a chance. The chorus of a musical is more my line, and I imagine it could be yours as well."

Cups of steaming coffee were put in front of them and, while they were sipping them, Maeve was able to observe her companion more closely. She thought her very attractive: pale slightly freckled skin and strange greenish eyes with long lashes. Her hair, luxuriant and vibrant, fell over her shoulders.

She could not guess that Jenny was equally admiring of the black hair and blue eyes of a typically Irish beauty. She noted that now the hideous coat had been removed a shapely figure was revealed. She knew only too well that the eyes of the men who passed judgement paid particular attention to breasts and legs. She had already seen the legs in this case would pass muster – a girl with thick ankles could whistle for a job in the chorus.

"You look very young," said Jenny.

"I'm seventeen," Maeve told her. It was true she had just had her seventeenth birthday.

"I'm two years older," Jenny said. She regarded Maeve as a naïve country girl, and she would have been surprised to learn that she had so recently given birth. It was this fact that was partly responsible for the girl's generous curves. Her breasts were painfully engorged with milk, and pads protected her nipples from leakages that still persisted to remind her of what she had lost.

Jenny questioned her about her presence in London, so far away from home, and Maeve told her that she had arrived the day before and although she had money to last her for a while it was essential that she get a job.

"Have you a routine prepared for an audition?"

"No." She did not like to mention the Irish ballad or 'Kathleen Mavourneen'.

"Oh, God!" exclaimed Jenny. "We'll have to do

something about that. Have you enough money to last you for, say, a week?"

"Yes."

"It will take all of a week to get you ready. If you will let me, I think I can help you, and then we can both try and get into the chorus of a musical. Does that appeal to you?"

"It does," said Maeve, "but do you want to wait a week? Can you manage without earnings for that time?"

"I can," Jenny assured her. "My parents pay me an allowance. They were not keen on my going on the stage but it was the only thing I ever wanted to do."

She took Maeve back to her lodgings that were a slight improvement on Mrs Deacon's house. The bathroom was adjacent to Jenny's room and was quite clean. Maeve told her about the lavatory that reeked of smoke, and Jenny's reply was that she hoped Maeve did not dislike the smell of smoke too much because she was dying for a cigarette. Would Maeve like one as well?

"I don't smoke," said Maeve primly.

"Have you ever tried?"

"No."

"I think you should try one, just to see if you like it or not. You should try everything once in life – that's my philosophy."

It was a philosophy that resulted in Maeve being a heavy smoker for over twenty years of her life.

On this first occasion she allowed herself to be given

a cigarette, and she gingerly put it into her mouth and Jenny lit it for her. One nervous puff made her decide she did not like it, but she persevered until she had smoked half, and then thankfully stubbed it out in an ashtray. Jenny produced a pot of tea and cakes, and after they had drunk and eaten Maeve tried another cigarette, and this time it did not seem so bad. By the third she was beginning to enjoy the experience, and it made her feel more sophisticated and ready to embark on the new life she hoped was ahead of her.

On the bus journey back to Primrose Road she began to feel rather sick. It was a relief when she reached the door of her room and knew that soon she would be able to lay her aching head on the pillow. As she inserted the key in the lock she heard heavy footsteps clumping down the stairs from the attic.

"I'm Jack Deacon," said a young man, "Mum told me you want me to explain about the boiler."

It was the last thing she wanted to do but she followed him down the two flights of stairs, noting as she went his tall figure and mop of fair hair.

He told her how to turn on the gas so that with a small explosion a blue flame appeared.

"Is it safe?" she asked nervously. Compared to the washing facilities at the house in Orchard Street it was a modern contraption. There the three girls took it in turns to bathe in a tin bath filled with buckets of hot water, carried laboriously by Uncle Frank. This was a weekly treat, and one that, as far as she knew, was never experienced by either her uncle or her aunt. Modesty forbade them to indulge in such a luxury.

"It's safe, right enough," said Jack. He looked at her closely. "Are you all right? You look a bit green."

"I'm quite all right, thank you," said Maeve with dignity. She perched on the edge of the bath because the room was not quite steady.

"Have you been drinking?"

"Of course not." She felt an explanation was necessary so she said: "I've been smoking."

"Ah!" he said. "The first ones always make you feel a bit funny. I'm a smoker myself and I wish I'd never started. My advice is – give it up now while you still can. It's a filthy habit." As he was speaking the water was gushing into the bath. "A good soak will do you good before you go to sleep," he said. "You run upstairs and get your things and I'll keep an eye on this."

She did as he said, but she wondered what would happen next. She need not have worried because by the time she returned to the bathroom she found that he had already gone. The bath was full and the taps were turned off. She locked the door. He was right – it was comforting lying in the warm water, feeling her limbs relax.

Kneeling beside her bed that night she felt the first pain of real loneliness; it came to her how far away she was from anyone who really knew her. When it came to the prayer for the baby she added a sad little postscript: "Please God, look after her and arrange for us to be reunited one day."

Later, lying in bed, she thought of the two friends she had made that day. Jenny, who had been so helpful, and now Jack. She decided he was a thoughtful young man with a nice open face. Not handsome, like George, but pleasant and kind.

She still felt slightly unwell, and the light from the streetlight outside seemed to be moving slightly. Jack had asked her if she had been drinking, and she supposed this was what it felt like – not quite in command of the senses. She and Jenny had not drunk any alcohol that day, only endless cups of tea and, of course, cigarettes. When she closed her tired eyes everything settled down, and her last thought before she fell asleep was that it had been quite a day.

Chapter 13

From the first time they met the two girls were friends, and it was a friendship that was to last many years. There are some people you love all your life, and nothing can alter that except death. That was how it was with Maeve and Jenny; they cared deeply about each other until the end. Of course, at the beginning of their friendship, when they were young, they did not think of the future; the present was all important to them, full of promise and untold adventures but, even then, they both recognised there was something special about their feelings for each other.

Jenny, as well as being older than Maeve, came from a very different background. Her father was a country GP who had distinguished himself during the war and her mother was a sweet-tempered educated woman who, like her husband, nurtured great hopes for their daughter, a much-loved only child. Both were disappointed when she expressed a desire to go on the stage. It was still not thought a suitable occupation for a well brought-up young lady,

When Maeve met her, Jenny had already been in the chorus of a musical called *High Heels* which came off after a run of six months. Now she was looking for another job. She told Maeve that being in the chorus was fun. "Although there's a lot of bitchiness," she said. It was the first time Maeve had heard someone use that word. Then Jenny went on to tell her about the friendly banter and humour between the girls, complicated by feelings of jealousy and envy because they all hoped to be made an understudy to one of the principals and, having acquired that position, prayed that a broken ankle or a sore throat would give them the chance of fame.

Maeve took Jenny to see her room, and the first thing she said, when she saw it was: "How much are you paying for this dump?" Maeve told her, and Jenny said: "You've been conned by that old cow downstairs. We'll have to find you somewhere else to live, but first let's get the matter of the job settled." Maeve's life had been taken over, and she could not have been happier.

It was tacitly decided between them that it was preferable to meet in Jenny's room. Maeve sat on a cushion on the floor, her back against the one armchair, and Jenny sprawled on the bed.

"Before we do anything else we must get you some new clothes," said Jenny. "How much can you afford to spend?"

Maeve replied to the question by emptying her purse on to the floor, and the two girls knelt down and counted the money. It never occurred to Maeve that this new friend might not be all that she seemed, that she might be stringing her along so that she could rob her of every penny she had. It never occurred to her, which was just as well because nothing could have been further from the truth. She had arrived in London with about two hundred pounds that seemed to her a princely sum. Some of it had gone on the deposit for her room, her purchases at the grocer's shop and her bus fares; still, in the early twenties it was a sizable amount of money.

"I hate my coat," said Maeve. "My Aunt Min chose it for me. She meant well, and it's beautifully warm, but it's so boring." With a pang of conscience she remembered her aunt clutching the purse full of notes she had saved over many months. "Coats are expensive," she said, "and I don't know whether I should spend any of my money on a new one."

"Perhaps you don't need to," said Jenny. She got to her feet and took the coat that Maeve had flung carelessly on to the bed. When she put it on it immediately acquired something extra, not smartness but a certain style. "The tweed is good," said Jenny, "and the shape isn't bad, nice and simple." She walked up and down the room in it, back straight and head back, like a mannequin. "A fur collar would transform it," she said. "A grey fox – perfect!"

"I could never afford that," protested Maeve.

"We'll look in the second-hand shops," Jenny said. "We'll find something there. They always have bits of fur to sell. Then I think we should buy you a really lovely dress, expensive and in a bright colour to contrast with the grey coat, then with new shoes, silk stockings and a hat the same colour as the dress you will be all set. Not quite set though because you must have your hair done. It is such pretty hair but it will look even better when it is bobbed."

"Do you mean shorter than yours?" asked Maeve doubtfully.

"Much shorter," replied Jenny decidedly. "I'd have mine the same but I know it would not suit me."

This sort of talk was very exciting for Maeve, and she could not help wondering what Aunt Min's reaction would be when she wrote and told her about the bobbed hair.

"When do we start?" she asked.

"This afternoon," Jenny told her. "We can't afford to waste time. We'll go to the shops and get your hair done as well but, before that, we'll have lunch. My treat."

The dress the girls chose was emerald green. Maeve never forgot that emerald green light wool dress. She guarded it like a precious jewel, hung it on the hanger as soon as she took it off, brushed it, sponged it and borrowed Mrs Deacon's flat iron to press it if she found the smallest wrinkle in its soft folds. It was her only dress. The hat that went with it was the same colour, a cloche framing her heart-shaped face. Her hair was now short and the hat hid it, except that there was a curl on each cheek – the trick was to sculpt the curls with spit on a finger. For the first time in her life Maeve used lipstick; she had a natural cupid's bow on her upper lip and this was considered very beautiful and was enhanced by the lipstick. Her profile, the small retroussé nose and the high cheekbone with the kiss curl was entrancing, and later a society photographer was to take a picture of her looking like that and it appeared in *The Tatler* with the caption *Miss Maeve O'Shea* – when that happened, Maeve felt she had truly arrived. But that was in the future, and for the present she had one emerald dress, an emerald hat, silk stockings and buckled shoes, a grey coat with a fox-fur collar, and no job.

The girls met every day; sometimes they sat in the park eating sandwiches and talking, talking all the time, or they went to Jenny's room and drank cups of tea and smoked cigarettes, which were very cheap.

Jenny took her to meet a young man who lived in a very smart flat. The main room was furnished entirely in black and white – black table and chairs, white walls and a white piano. His name was Roddy and Maeve never did discover his surname.

He agreed to teach Maeve how to dance and he would also advise her about the song she should sing at an audition. He was tall and thin, with sleek hair and expressive hands. He smoked endlessly, putting one cigarette after another into a long jade holder. Maeve thought he was absolutely wonderful, and he made the memory of George shadow into insignificance.

"Is he your boy?" she asked Jenny. She noticed they called each other 'darling'.

"Good God, no," said Jenny, "he's queer."

He did not seem at all queer to Maeve, and she wondered what Jenny found odd about him. "He seems very gay to me," she commented. "'Gay' was a word that had become very popular and Jenny used it a lot. It denoted someone or something happy and carefree, and it was not until many years later that it acquired another meaning. Maeve was experimenting with the use of it.

Roddy rolled back the shaggy white rug in his flat and proceeded to teach both girls new dance steps. While one was having a lesson the other took on the duty of turning the handle of the black gramophone. Maeve thought he was being very kind to take so much trouble; she did not guess that Jenny was paying for the instruction.

Maeve was a quick learner and she loved dancing. Her mother had been musical and her daughter had inherited her talents and perhaps – who knows? – her father's as well; after all, Maeve's parents had met on a dance floor of sorts. Then Roddy sat at the white piano and played a few notes to test her singing ability. She had a good voice, if a little thin. He encouraged her to breathe deeply and sing out loudly. Surprisingly, he was in favour of her singing an Irish ballad, and he produced a very sentimental Irish song for her to learn. He liked the idea of the girl in the emerald dress singing a song about the beauty of the Emerald Isle.

The other thing that Roddy did for Maeve was to introduce her to a new-fangled drink called a cocktail. It seemed to Maeve to be made mostly of orange juice and was not very big, so she decided it was not sinful.

They visited Roddy every evening and sometimes in the afternoon as well, and they practised the dance steps and sang popular songs to his accompaniment on the piano. Although the objective was serious it was such fun they almost forgot the reason for it.

Maeve received a letter from Aunt Min written in answer to a letter she had sent soon after her arrival in London. The letter had been written laboriously with a stub of pencil, and Maeve could imagine her aunt sitting down at the kitchen table with the lined pad of writing paper, and Uncle Frank, huddled over the stove, filling the room with the fumes from his smelly pipe.

"I hope you are going to Mass," wrote Aunt Min. *"Please do not let your faith lapse while you are carving out a career for yourself and meeting new people . . . '*

She need not have worried. Every Sunday Maeve went to church, and she continued to do so for many months to come. At this stage in her life, her religion meant a great deal to her.

The time came when Jenny decided to introduce Maeve

to a theatrical agent. He lived in the Charing Cross area and Jenny had been to see him before and had, in fact, obtained her last job in the chorus through him. They were on first-name terms. "Bert," she said, "I want you to meet my friend, Maeve O'Shea. She is from Ireland, and we both want a job in the chorus of *Buddies*." This was a show that had been on Broadway and was coming to the English stage in a few weeks' time; everyone with aspirations to be in a musical wanted to be part of it.

Bert Short sat behind his desk, a florid sweaty man, seemingly endlessly anxious to get on with the next item on his busy agenda. His impatience was conveyed to other people, so that everyone in his presence felt a sense of urgency.

"Stand over there," he ordered Maeve. Obediently she moved to the other side of the room. "Lift up your skirt!" he barked. The skirt was quite short already but she did as she was told, and he noted her shapely legs without comment. "What are you going to do at your audition?" he asked.

She explained about the dance she had practised and the Irish ballad.

"Roddy thinks she has a good voice," interrupted Jenny, "and she was quick picking up the dance routine."

The name Roddy seemed to work like magic. The two girls sailed out of Bert's office clutching the cards that would gain them entry to the audition, bypassing the queue already forming outside Drury Lane Theatre.

The group of girls standing at the side of the stage were trembling with nerves. One by one, with beating hearts, they stepped on to the stage. Their adjudicators were sitting in the stalls on the other side of the footlights. Their faces were indiscernible in the darkness; it was like performing before an unknown quantity and this made it even more intimidating.

Jenny was before Maeve and, as she left the stage, she glided by and whispered: "I'm in!"

This made Maeve even more certain that she would fail. Her mouth was dry and she did not think she would be able to sing a note. In her striking green dress she managed the steps that Roddy had taught her and sang the plaintive melody without faltering. She stood in the centre of the stage, in a pool of light, waiting for the verdict.

"Be here at nine o'clock on Monday morning," boomed a voice from the darkness.

The girls were jubilant. Their excitement was intense, and all that weekend they thought and talked of nothing but Monday morning. Predictions were that *Buddies* would be the show to end all shows.

After the audition Jenny had insisted on buying a bottle of wine.

Maeve was doubtful. "Are you sure?" she asked. It was all very well drinking the innocuous cocktails but wine was another matter. Uncle Frank always considered wine to be an indulgence of the idle rich.

"Oh, come on," said Jenny, "we have to celebrate." If she had her way she would have celebrated with champagne, but it was too expensive. "One day we'll find a couple of nice rich men who will give us champagne!"

And so they celebrated their success in Jenny's room with a strange mixture: fish and chips in newspaper, and a bottle of cheap wine accompanied by many cigarettes. They did not realise it at the time, but they were perhaps happier than they would ever be in their lives, for there were no rich men to complicate things, no members of the family to tell them how they should behave and, with the optimism of the young, they felt the world was opening up, ready for them to grasp and enjoy every glorious future moment.

Maeve's joy about their success was tempered by thoughts of her child: they were always there to trouble her mind, at times stronger than others, but always present to remind her of her shame and loss. When she got back to her room that night she found the milk in her breasts had dried up and she was able to throw away the pads. She felt as if she had lost the last link with her daughter.

Chapter 14

The people who forecast a success for *Buddies* were right, the tickets became like gold dust and everyone wanted to see it. Maeve and Jenny were lucky to have got jobs in the chorus and they basked in the glory of it. Their photographs appeared in glossy magazines and queues of excited fans waited every night for them to emerge through the stage door. The big dressing-room, shared by all the members of the chorus, was full of flowers. And the theatre messenger boys were kept busy carrying invitations from the admirers to have supper after the show.

Being in the chorus was an eye-opener for Maeve. The chatter of the girls revealed a world and a way of life she did not know existed. They respected her, and sometimes curbed their bad language in her presence. They thought her an innocent little Catholic girl and, like Jenny, they would have been surprised to learn she had given birth to a child. Although Jenny was her dearest friend, Maeve baulked at the idea of telling her this secret. It was a secret that disturbed her dreams from time to time so that she awoke feeling guilty, and the guilt would stay with her throughout the following day, making her more determined than ever to attend Mass on Sunday. Her dream was recurrent: she was hiding behind a tree near the convent when hands came through the door in the wall and snatched the basket. Up to that moment the dream was just as it had happened, that early morning months before, but the dream continued and in it she hammered on the door, crying out for her baby to be returned to her. Each time her crying awoke her from sleep, and she lay in the darkness, the tears on her cheeks, wishing she could erase the memory from her mind forever yet knowing, at the same time, she never could.

Now that Maeve was earning there was no difficulty about paying the rent and she was able to buy new clothes. The emerald dress, although still her favourite, was squashed between numerous filmy dresses, short pleated skirts and blouses. The shelf in the cupboard was covered with hats of all descriptions and colours, and her shoes were lined neatly against the wall. In the middle of all this frantic expenditure she found time to think of Aunt Min and the girls, and once a week she put money into an envelope and sent it to them.

Jenny tried to persuade her to leave Primrose Road,

but Maeve had to decide whether her wardrobe or a better place to live was more important, and she opted for the former. She had got used to her room, had improved it with tasselled shawls flung over the bed and chair, and she had even mastered the quirks of the Ascot boiler and enjoyed a hot bath every evening before going to the theatre. She poured disinfectant into the lavatory bowl and, greatly daring, pinned a notice on the wall saying: *No Smoking Please* and it seemed to have worked. Maeve, herself a smoker, respected Mrs Deacon's wishes and did not smoke in her room, although she could not help noticing the smoking smells emanating from the basement flat when she passed it. Occasionally she caught a glimpse of Mr Deacon's unshaven face with a brown cigarette permanently hanging from his lips. The Deacons gave her the creeps, and she hurried past the door to the accompaniment of the parrot noises that came from a bird sitting on a perch in the room. Maeve thought that if a man had ever visited her room that bird would have warned the Deacons of his presence. It created an uproar when Jenny came to see her.

Except for Jack Deacon she did not get to know any of the other occupants of the house. She smiled at Miss Shaw when she met her on the stairs and sometimes she bumped into the moth-eaten Mr Langridge who supposedly worked in the City. Maeve suspected it was he who had been guilty of smoking in the lavatory. Mr Baines, the postman, left the house before anyone was up and no one ever saw him.

Jack was his mother's pride and joy, rightly so, in Maeve's opinion, as he was a cut above his parents and held down a respectable job in a government office. She could not imagine why he had not escaped from the house in Primrose Road but he seemed content with his flat below the roof. He had a bedroom, small sitting-room, kitchen and bathroom and he had done all the decorations himself and put in a new window so that it was light. He was proud of his work and he asked Maeve to come and inspect it, so one evening she mounted the flight of stairs preceded by his burly form. She was quick to praise but then, encouraged, he attempted to kiss her and she made a hasty retreat.

It was not as if she had not become used to such advances. She had been in the chorus of *Buddies* for nearly a year now and she had many admirers. She enjoyed the flowers and the boxes of chocolates, and the sight of the young men standing outside the stage door eager to talk to her, but she was frightened of anything more than that. She listened to the girls talking about abortions, illegal and dangerous, and she made up her mind that sex led to misery and pain. There was nothing to prevent an unwanted pregnancy and it was something that happened all too frequently. The girls talked about pills that fizzed inside you and creams that you applied before intercourse, but they had to admit none of them was reliable. It seemed to Maeve that having sex was too unpredictable, and she shied away from it like a young filly that has once been frightened and cannot be broken in as a result. Jenny, on the other hand, had a very healthy interest in the chase and the eventual admission. She enjoyed every aspect of it, and could not understand Maeve's attitude. It was the one thing on which they could never agree.

The dance that brought the house down in *Buddies* was called 'The Catherine Wheel' and it came near the end of the performance. The girls were all dressed in bright firework colours, and they danced in a circle, arms encircling waists, getting faster and faster as the music quickened. The overall picture was like a Catherine wheel whirling at a tremendous rate, culminating with the girls lying on the floor of the stage, their heads at the apex of the wheel, their beautiful legs radiating like the petals of a flower. The producer (nowadays he would be called a director) was a man called Adam Aster, famous in his day, and he was proud of the precision and perfect timing of the Catherine-wheel dance. He was there, standing in the wings every night, watching carefully for any flaws in the performance.

It was an exhausting dance, for the girls were in close proximity to each other and the atmosphere became hot and claustrophobic. There were replacements at the side of the stage in case anyone dropped out, but it seldom happened; the presence of Mr Aster spurred them on to complete the course. There was no familiarity with people in authority in those days; Adam Aster was always called Mr Aster and never just Adam. Maeve had no qualms, she was sure her fainting days were in the past and she knew every *minutia* of the routine. Because the dance was at the end of the show the dancers, their bright plumage soaked in perspiration and sticking to their bodies, were able to flop down in the dressing-room, heads down, and regain their equilibrium.

Buddies had been running in London for nearly a year when Maeve, dancing in the circle, her arms around the waist of the girl on either side of her, one of whom was Jenny, felt a sensation horribly familiar. Darkness settled over her eyes, like the lid of a box, and she found herself falling. The girls held on tightly to her flaccid body and managed, with almost superhuman strength, to eject her to the side of the stage, her place immediately being taken by a girl waiting in the wings. It was a manoeuvre achieved with great dexterity, and probably not noticed by many people in the audience. But Maeve was aware that Adam Aster would have observed every detail.

She recovered quickly, as she had always done, and sat on a chair in the dressing-room sipping a glass of water. Her friends gathered around her, concerned and full of sympathy.

Maeve thought she would be summoned to Adam's side to give an explanation. She expected any moment one of the theatre messenger boys would say to her: 'Mr Astor wants to see you in his office', and she was very frightened. But the days passed and nothing happened.

The incident was not mentioned, and she began to feel secure again.

At 19 Primrose Road life continued as usual with Jack Deacon continuing his pursuit of her. He had been to see *Buddies* three times, and he had managed to get photographs of the chorus, which he displayed in his flat. He was a likable fellow, and Maeve might have thought more of him had it not been for his parents. The shadowy figures of the Deacons, she, unsmiling, and out for every penny, and he with his brown-stained fingers, were not the material of future in-laws. Maeve appreciated that Jack had distanced himself from his family, although still living under the same roof, and he behaved honourably towards her. After the first rejection he did not approach her again in a romantic way, seeming happy to wait for better things.

Adam Astor noticed Jenny and he gave her a minor role when a soubrette left the cast. Jenny was over the moon. She sang a sentimental little number dressed as a maid in a very short black dress with a frilly apron. Maeve felt happy for her, and she watched with pride as Jenny stood centre stage for her brief moment of fame, in a circle of light, her beautiful hair cascading from the band of the cap on her head. She knew, in her heart, that Jenny possessed a charm and talent she did not have, and never would have. She was only human, and she did feel a pang of envy, but her love for her friend overcame the feeling and was short-lived. She resigned herself to being in the chorus of *Buddies* for the rest of its run.

It was not to be. She had been dancing in the Catherine Wheel for over a year when she suffered her second faint, and this time Adam Aster asked to see her after the show. She knew what he was going to say to her as, trembling, she made her way to his little office at the back of the theatre. He said he was sincerely sorry and he had decided to do nothing on the first occasion, but now he felt there was no alternative – she would have to go.

That evening when Jack called to see her in her room he found her in tears. He comforted her as best he could, saying that Mr Aster had made a big mistake that he would regret. She would find another job in no time. Maeve thought sadly that this time she would be on her own in her quest for employment – there would be no Jenny to encourage and help her.

Jenny herself arrived later that evening. She swept into Maeve's little room, dressed dramatically in a long velvet coat. She was accompanied by her latest conquest, a young viscount called Rupert Branden, whom she would later marry. It was quite common for members of the aristocracy to marry girls on the stage.

Their sympathy was not what Maeve wanted. She felt she had reverted to the ignorant little Irish girl who had come to make her fortune in London, and all that she had accomplished since her arrival had become like dust. She knew that Jenny was genuinely distressed for her, and if she had come on her own it might have been different. She thought wryly that Jack and Rupert were the only males that had ever been in her room, and she did not think that Mrs Deacon could complain about either of them. Rupert stood awkwardly mumbling words of commiseration, but Maeve was not deceived. She knew that his only desire was to be with Jenny. The quiet understanding of Jack was better suited to her present mood. She longed for them to leave, and sighed with relief when they did.

She went back to see the agent, Bert Short, but he offered her little hope of another job in the chorus. To be sacked from a show like *Buddies* did not enhance her chances. Maeve got the distinct impression that Bert was no longer interested in her and, without Jenny's support, she was a nonentity in his eyes.

"I'll let you know if anything turns up," were his last dismissive words.

The days that followed were very empty and depressing for Maeve. She did not write and tell Aunt Min and Uncle Frank that she was no longer working, although no doubt they guessed the truth because the weekly money was not forthcoming. Her problems were exacerbated by Mrs Deacon's constant demands for the rent owing. Maeve had not saved. As well as the clothes in the cheap wardrobe, the drawers in the dressing table were crammed with flimsy underclothing and the top was crowded with jars of cream, lipsticks and flacons of expensive perfumes. If she was going to appease her landlady by payment of the rent it was essential that she get a job.

In the years after the Great War there was much unemployment, and Maeve was lucky to obtain a position in one of the main department stores. It was her pretty face and smart appearance that appealed to the young man who interviewed her. It did not appeal to the woman in charge of the shoe department where Maeve was to work.

Miss Stock was middle-aged, unmarried and bitter and the last thing she wanted was a nubile young woman working under her. Maeve made mistakes, muddled up shoe sizes and Miss Stock was scathing in her criticism of her. She shamed the girl in front of customers by saying: "Oh, dear! I'd better take over from here, Miss Shea." For some reason, she never called Maeve by her proper name, perhaps it was a subtle method of intimidation, and Maeve was too frightened of her to correct her.

Maeve met Jenny during the lunch break, and Jenny was alone this time and she was able to pour out her troubles to her. Jenny, picking up the tab, listened sympathetically, but she did not know how to help her friend.

Maeve arrived back at the shoe department ten minutes late, flustered and apologetic. Stage people, like Jenny, do not worry about time during the day; it is only in the evening, before the curtain rises, that it concerns them. Jenny's chatter delayed Maeve from getting back to work on time. It was the first time she had broken the rules, and she was greeted with the words: "One hour is allowed for lunch, Miss Shea, not one hour and ten minutes. Please remember that."

"Yes, Miss Stock. I'm sorry."

When Maeve went to the Staff Ladies' Room she was told she had spent too much time in there. "It is just as well. Miss Shea, we are not all so vain or no work would be done." She was too pretty, that was the trouble – the older woman was consumed with jealousy. Maeve had no way of knowing this was the reason for the petty cruelty, and she was bewildered by it.

Then one day a fat old woman swept into the shoe department. She eased herself into the narrow seat and demanded to see the most expensive shoes. Maeve deduced she was rich from the mink coat she wore and the fact her plump hands were weighed down with diamonds. Maeve scurried backwards and forwards, collecting more and more shoes from the shelves in the area behind the shop, and the old woman forced her misshapen feet into them, one after the other. Miss Stock was not there (no doubt if she had been she would have taken over) and Maeve was aware it was her great opportunity to prove her worth and make a sale. Soon the floor was littered with white boxes and discarded shoes and she wondered, panic-stricken, whether she would ever be able to match them up again.

"Is that all you have?"

Maeve, kneeling in front of her, tried to stop the mist forming before her eyes. She forced herself to reject the blackness, to ignore the strange movements of her heart. She failed and fell forward, her nose meeting the woman's fat foot poised on the footrest. The old woman let out a scream as if a wasp had stung her, but Maeve did not hear her.

When she recovered the customer had gone, having purchased nothing, and Miss Stock was regarding her with the glint of victory in her eyes. It was instant dismissal, and the only good thing about the unhappy episode was that Maeve was not asked to put the shoes back in the right boxes.

Back in her room, Maeve sat on the edge of the bed and wondered what she should do next. It seemed that her propensity to faint, inherited from her mother, had made her unemployable.

There was a rap on the door. Jack? He was always popping in with little gifts for her – something nice to eat or a bottle of wine. No, it was his mother standing in the doorway with the light of battle in her eyes, her mouth a thin straight line. She had come to collect the arrears in rent.

Maeve sobbed. She did not have the money. Mrs Deacon was unsympathetic; perhaps she had noticed her son's fondness for the girl and hoped for better things for him. She was quick to give a reason for her harshness; it was not her business that Maeve had lost two jobs in rapid succession. If she could not pay the rent she was out, and that was all there was to it. She left, slamming the door behind her.

Presently Jack appeared. He said his mother was out of order speaking to Maeve like that – he would talk to her about it. He was visibly distressed to see her tears, and said that she must not worry, she could move in with him and he would look after her.

"How can I do that?" Maeve asked. She felt trapped and at the end of her tether. She knew that her only solution was to borrow money for the fare from Jenny, and return to Ireland, but that was an admission of failure and she did not know how she could face that.

"We could get married," said Jack tentatively. "That would make it all right with your religion and that. I'm not a Catholic but I respect your beliefs. I love you, Maeve, and I want you to marry me."

In his sincere love for her he knelt on the floor, his face level with her silken knees. She put out a hand and touched the top of his head. His hair was soft to her fingers. She took a deep breath and accepted his offer of marriage.

At the time, it seemed the only thing to do.

Chapter 15

"Are we seeing Maeve today?" Hugh asks. It always astonishes me that my two sons want to see an old lady in her nineties. Mostly Maeve comes to our house, and they prefer that to visiting her at Riverbank. Moira tends to be excessively hearty in their presence, and it embarrasses them. In fact, the whole place makes them feel uncomfortable, and the occasional glimpse of people in the last stages of senile decay or decrepitude unnerves them. "Don't worry," Maeve says to them. "I don't like it either."

She loves coming to our house, and she is appreciative of everything, the food, the surroundings and the company. She still reads aloud to the boys, even though they have really grown out of this pleasure, not giving up until their eyes droop. She plays games with them and seems to be an expert at PlayStation, something I have never been able to master. In the summer she sits in a deckchair, a straw hat shading her face, and watches them play cricket on the lawn. I know she is itching to heave herself out of the seat and join in the game. Her cumbersome inactive body causes her much irritation. "I hate being old," she says.

She is good for me when sometimes I feel I cannot stand another moment of their bad behaviour or exuberant high spirits, and my hand instinctively moves to strike one of them or I find myself shouting like a fishwife. "For goodness sake, boys," she says, "give your poor mother a chance."

I produce the manuscript of her story, neatly typed and enclosed in a hard cover. I am pleased with it because it looks very professional. Perhaps she reads it when she is alone, but when she is with me she hardly glances at it. I can't help feeling disappointed that after all my hard work she appears so uninterested. She pays me two hundred pounds a week, and although, at first, I thought it was too much money, now I think I earn this sum because, in addition to my secretarial work, I see her every day. Most of those days she comes to my house and I feed her. One night when it was late I offered her a bed for the night, and she accepted gladly. I telephoned Moira to tell her that Maeve was staying with me, and when I drove her to Riverbank the following morning, Moira accosted me on my way out.

"Not a good idea, if you don't mind my saying, Mrs Maitland."

That nettled me. "Why do you say that?"

"It might make her dissatisfied with her life here."

"Does moving into a retirement home have to deprive you of any life outside that establishment?" I demand. "You are making Riverbank sound like a prison, except that the inmates are charged a lot of money for their sentences."

"That is not my intention," Moira replies with dignity, "and I prefer to call them guests, not inmates. It is just that should Mrs Bailey, in time, become unacceptable as a constant visitor to your home, it would make it sad for both of you. Believe me, I have observed the ravages of old age, and they can make terrible changes to a person. Sometimes, I think death is a blessing when deterioration is setting in, it is so destructive."

I have not realised before that Moira possesses such sensitivity. Of course I should have known it is an essential ingredient of her job. I feel humbled, and I say: "Of course, you are right. I hope Maeve escapes that indignity."

Moira's usually impassive countenance breaks into one of her rare smiles. "I don't think you need be concerned," she says kindly. "She's as bright as a button, that one."

As I walk slowly back to the car I think of Maeve on the previous night, sitting in my spare bed, a lot of pillows at her back, completely happy. The boys were asleep in the next room, and the house settled comfortably around her. "I'll leave the light on in the bathroom," was the last thing I said to her before I shut the door.

Maeve repays me a hundredfold for the small kindnesses I show to her. She takes me out to lunch, she forces presents on me, bottles of wine and treats she has ordered from the local grocer. She has discovered my liking for smoked salmon and she is always pressing a flat foil-wrapped package into my hands. One day she insists on buying me a new coat. She has her excuse ready: "You can't go around in that awful old thing." Nothing pleases her more than taking Hugh and Neil to the toyshop in the village where they are allowed to choose what they want. They take an eternity, but she never loses patience with them. She loves them and they return her love. My old regret about the children missing out on grandparents is past: she provides them with constant affection and tolerance – qualities I imagine good grandparents possess.

She never solicits their love; she keeps her distance from them and they veer towards her, snuggling up close to her soft ample body, holding her old liver-spotted hands. I have grown fond of her but I do not take such liberties.

Dan is a frequent visitor to the house, and the boys go to Pollards every other weekend and spend part of the holidays with him and Andrea. I don't remember how we came to this arrangement; it was just agreed between the three of us and it works as well as can be expected. He is used to seeing Maeve, sitting in her special chair, her legs on the footstool in front of her, and they get on well together. He usually arrives armed with a bottle of wine, and they sit drinking and talking amicably together while I get the boys to bed. Occasionally, Andrea comes with him, and there is no constraint between us. All is harmony, and if there is any tension it emanates from me and, I hope, is not discernible. She and Dan have been living together now for two years; they are a working couple that meet for lunch, when they can, and in the evening when they go home. I observe them closely and I see real love between them. Perhaps they are not as careful as they previously were about hiding it from me. I catch my husband looking at her in a way that causes me so much pain I feel I can hardly breathe, but I know my suffering is partly my fault – I give the impression that I do not care any more.

There is no mention of divorce, and I think they are content to let matters stay as they are. While Dan and I are still married I can have my dream of him returning to me, telling me that it has all been a terrible mistake. When I am with them, I have to acknowledge that their love is stronger than ever, and my dream will never be reality.

Then one evening Dan comes to see me and tells me that Andrea is pregnant. It is one of the rare evenings when Maeve is not with us, a day in summer when darkness comes late, and the boys are playing in the garden. I suggest we take our drinks outside, and we sit, side by side, in chairs on the terrace. It is something we have done on similar summer evenings for many years in the past. Nothing has changed, the shadows falling across the lawn, the bats circling above our heads and the shouts of our two children.

"She must be very pleased," I say at last.

I know him so well that I immediately detect he is faintly gloomy, when he should be feeling ecstatic. He tries to hide his depression from me, but I know it is there.

"We both hope for a girl," he says.

Then he broaches the question of divorce. He explains that it has not been necessary before this, but now he and Andrea want to marry as soon as possible before the birth of the baby.

"I hope you understand . . ."

"Oh, yes, I understand."

The next day I rummage in my desk, and find the telephone number of the solicitor in Melford, given to me by Jane two years ago. I telephone and make an appointment. When I walk into her office I am a bit concerned to find a young child sitting on the floor in front of her desk, busily crayoning into a book. Nearby is a pram containing a sleeping infant.

The woman apologises. "The lady who looks after them let me down."

I sit in a chair opposite her and I explain the situation. "It all seems very civilised," she says. "I wish more people were like you."

Civilised. I think, that is what I have become, a civilised person, a person who is friendly towards her husband's lover, who accepts what has happened with good grace.

She goes through the financial arrangements with me. "Your husband seems a generous man," she says.

"Yes."

"And access?" She cannot believe that, between us, Dan and I have been so efficient in the break-up of our marriage. "I can't fault it," she says.

At this point the child squatting on the floor becomes bored with crayons and hurls them across the room with a penetrating scream. This wakes the baby in the pram and pandemonium ensues. I make a hasty retreat, wondering whether my bill will be reduced because of the interruptions. The harassed woman accompanies me to the door and, through the noise, manages to convey to me that arrangements will be put in motion for a speedy divorce.

"How do you feel now it is actually going to happen?" Jane asks me when I see her.

It is a hard question to answer. Resigned? No, I will never be resigned to Dan and me parting for good. Even after all this time, I still find it hard to believe. Strong? I hope so; my two little boys are two good reasons why I cannot allow myself to weaken. I have to be strong for them. I try to explain this to Jane, but I can tell she does not begin to understand. To her, a life alone, without a husband, is inconceivable, and she cannot imagine how I can bear such an existence. I think, you silly woman, you can bear anything if there is no alternative. Then I remember her courage during the time of her illness, and I feel ashamed of my thoughts. I love Jane, but it is a complicated relationship, and we are never completely straightforward with each other. With Maeve, on the other hand, I can say anything and I know she will understand at once.

It does not seem to matter that she is so much older than me.

"I suppose," I say, "you want me to try and find your daughter?"

"Only if you feel like it," she says. "I don't want to be a nuisance."

"The boys are going for a holiday in Portugal," I tell her, "with their father and Andrea. While they are away I could make a trip to Ireland."

"Oh, darling, would you really?"

I know that beguiling tone of voice, and I succumb to it every time.

"I wish I could come with you," she says.

The prospect of Maeve as a fellow traveller is too awful to contemplate. "I think I will do better without you."

"I must give you money for the trip."

"There is no need. You have paid me enough already."

She forces money on me, telling me, as she has told

me many times before, that she is a rich woman with no family commitments. "Perhaps you are about to find my family," she says.

"You may be disappointed," I warn her.

"Oh, I'm prepared for that," she says airily. "I'd just like to know that she's well and happy – that's all."

She tells me the name of a hotel in Castlerock. "It's not the Ritz but it's comfortable and the food is good. At least, it was many years ago – I expect it's still there. I want you to feel relaxed, darling. You deserve a rest, and I hope the change will do you good."

Chapter 16

I ought to be used to it by now but I always feel a sense of abandonment when the children depart for a holiday with Dan and Andrea. Hugh and Neil are so excited by the prospect that it would be cruel to dampen their spirits by my own gloom, so I try to put a good face on it when we are making all the preparations. Even after all this time, I am still conscious that they are watching me anxiously, looking for cracks in my apparent resignation about what has happened to our family. I try, for their sakes, not to show my despair with the endless arrangements that have to be made in order to keep everything running smoothly between the two establishments.

I count my blessings. I have two wonderful sons, and we have been able to continue living in the lovely house that Dan and I chose together, and altered and tweaked until it was just right for us. Every part of it holds memories for me because we did everything together, the choosing of the curtains and carpets, and one weekend when we painstakingly stripped the brown paint from the panels in the dining-room. It was a labour of love, love for the home we were in the process of creating, and love for each other. Now I have the home, at least, and I am grateful for that.

The moment of departure arrives, and Hugh and Neil climb into Dan's car, each with the usual little backward glance at me standing by the front door. Andrea, sitting in the front, gives a cheerful wave, and they are off. I wave back, thinking that thanks to Maeve's wise counsel I am not now hovering in the upstairs bedroom, hiding behind the curtain.

I give a little sigh of relief – they are gone and there is nothing I can do about it except hope they have a good time. Now I must get on with my own life. It is not very spectacular, a trip to Ireland on Maeve's behalf that will probably prove fruitless, but I have never been to Dublin before so that must be an interesting experience.

I take Flush to the kennels and he resists, showing his reluctance by making his legs into jelly, so that he has to be dragged by the lead. As always, he succeeds in making me feel guilty, but the girl who takes him away assures me that he will settle down as soon as I have gone. Teachers in the past have said the same thing to me, but then I have been able to question the child when I collect him from school. "What was it like?"

"Good."

With Flush I must take her word for it.

Slightly dejected, I make for home to pack for the journey. In my mind, I echo Dan's sentiments, also from the past – it's only a dog, for Christ's sake.

I fly from Heathrow to Dublin, a short trip of just over an hour. Then I get a train to Castlerock and a taxi to the hotel. As Maeve told me it is comfortable, the bed is inviting and I sleep for a long time. There is something about a hotel bedroom that gives a sense of freedom. There you are, alone, and no one is likely to interrupt your peace. It is as if for a space in your life you are on a desert island. I know that many people have felt at their lowest ebb in a hotel bedroom but, in my case, I have done my weeping in the confines of my home, now I just want to lie spread-eagled on the big double bed and rejoice in my solitude. My sleep is dreamless as if I have not got a care in the world.

Eventually I get up because soon it will be time to go downstairs and have dinner – I see from a notice on this wall that this starts at eight o'clock. I have a leisurely bath; there is a freebie of bath oil beside the bath and I use it. I am enjoying myself. I take time with my make-up and then slip into a dress that Maeve and I chose together. She wanted to buy it for me, but I managed to dissuade her. Later, on my own, I returned to the shop and bought it. There is nothing she likes better than to accompany me on a shopping trip, persuading me into buying clothes I would never consider in the normal way. This time I thought her judgement was correct, and anyway I felt like having something new. Maeve loves clothes, for herself and other people. I remember the cheap wardrobe in her room in Primrose Road, crammed with clothes that were the reason she could not come up with the rent she owed.

I am pleased when I look at myself in the mirror. For the first time in many months I feel good and I look good. I walk slowly down the wide stairs and into the dining-room. A waiter escorts me to a small table in the corner. I sit and eat a delicious meal, and gradually, insidiously, my mood changes. I think about my life, my two little sons, now parted from me, about Dan living a few miles away with Andrea and about Andrea, expecting his child. I feel incredibly alone. Being on my own had seemed quite pleasant in the room above but now it has become a threat. I imagine the room, the crumpled sheets and the emptiness – I dread returning to it.

After dinner I go into the lounge and help myself to coffee set out on a table. I sit on a chair and watch the people. I'm on holiday, I tell myself. Perhaps the fact that there are so few people makes this hard to believe: none of them shows any indication of being on holiday. They are a cheerless lot – a husband and wife with a small boy, unnaturally quiet, and elderly couple and a solitary man.

There are no sounds in the room except the crackling of a real fire in the hearth, the sonorous ticking of a clock on the mantle above the fireplace and the faint rustle of the man's newspaper as he turns a page.

Presently, the couple with the child get up and leave; it must be their son's bedtime Very soon after, the old people heave themselves to their feet and glide noiselessly from the room. There is just the man and I left now, and the silence is oppressive. When he lowers his newspaper for an instance I register that he looks nice, and I am sorry that convention forbids that we should strike up a conversation. I long for the sound of a friendly voice, and I realise that except for ordering from the waiter, I have not spoken out loud since checking in at the reception desk. I give a little experimental cough as if to prove to myself that I still have the power of speech.

I decide to go to my soulless room when I have finished my coffee. It is too early to go to sleep, and anyway I have slept so much I am no longer tired. I have a book, and I can read for an hour or so. I imagine the cool sheets of the bed caressing my body after I have wiped the make-up from my face and slipped out of the new dress.

I am lifting the cup to my lips when the silence is broken by the deafening sound of a loud bell. It is so obtrusively strident that my hand jerks and I nearly spill the coffee, and I observe the man's newspaper quiver in his hands. He lowers it and I see his face, frowning slightly, wondering, as I am, what is going on. Our eyes meet and we smile slightly at each other as the noise continues.

Eventually, he speaks: "It must be the fire alarm."

"Of course – that's what it is."

The waiter comes in looking agitated. "I'm afraid you must be leaving the building," he says.

"What is happening?" asks the man. "Is there a fire?"

It seems a reasonable question but the waiter ignores it. "Follow me, madam," he says to me and then to my companion: "Follow me, sir, please."

So we follow him obediently, across the deserted hall, through the big front door that he opens for us, and into the street outside. It is bitterly cold. I look around at the handful of people clustered on the pavement, shivering, and I notice they are all employees of the hotel. The man and I stand together, and the mystery of the whole event overcomes my usual hesitancy to speak to a total stranger, and I say: "Do you think I would be allowed to go inside and get my coat?"

He turns to the waiter who is clapping his hands together and stamping his feet in an effort to get warm. "We are freezing out here. Can we go and get something warm to put on?"

"I'm afraid not, sir."

The man looks faintly annoyed. He is middle-aged and looks like a prosperous businessman, used to getting his own way. "Have you any idea what this is all about?" he demands, an edge to his voice.

"I'm afraid not, sir," the waiter says again, and he moves away as if anxious to avoid any more awkward questions.

I ask: "What about the other guests – the old couple and the people with the child? Where are they? Are they, at this moment, frizzling in the fire?" I can make this rather flippant observation because it is obvious there is no fire. No smell of smoke, no signs of the fire brigade arriving on the scene.

The man leaves me and heads for the front door of the hotel. The thought occurs to me that he may want to get away from me, that he has no wish to get involved with a strange woman. I am almost relieved when he returns to my side. "We are locked out," he says shortly. I feel his frustration and anger.

"This could only happen in Ireland," he says. "Thank God that bloody bell has stopped at last."

I realise he is right. Perhaps now we will be allowed in again. I am so cold I feel I will never be warm again. My new dress is flimsy and has a low neckline. My ears, my feet, my hands have turned to ice.

He thrusts his hands in his pockets and says: "My name is Tom Byrne, by the way."

I introduce myself, and he removes one hand and we shake hands – two cold hands clasp and draw apart.

I can see he is concerned about me. "You'll get pneumonia standing out here in that dress," he says, "and I'm trying to think what we should do. My car is in the hotel car park; perhaps we should go and sit in that? Or walk along the street and find a pub where, at least, we'd be under cover."

I am considering these two options when, suddenly,

the door of the hotel is thrown open and we move back into the warmth of the empty lounge.

Tom Byrne turns to the waiter, hovering now, no doubt expecting an order. "What the hell was all that about?"

"Sorry, sir."

"You have not answered my question. I asked for an explanation."

The waiter looks blank. "Perhaps you would like a word with the manager, sir?"

"Yes, please."

The waiter is gone, returning in a moment with a young man who says: "I am the manager, sir. Is something wrong?"

"Yes, indeed, there is something wrong. This lady and I have been standing outside in the freezing cold for the last half an hour, and I would like to know why."

"It was a fire practice, sir. By law we are supposed to have one at least every six months."

"And what about the other guests? Why were they not involved?"

"They had gone to bed, sir, and it seemed unfair to disturb them. The hotel is very empty, sir, so it seemed a good night to have the practice. I'm sorry that it caused you discomfort, sir." He turned to me. "I'm very sorry, madam."

I can see that Tom Byrne is beginning to see the funny side of the whole episode. I like to see that he is softening towards these apologetic men. While he has been talking I have been studying him. He has a regular face, so unlike the craggy uneven features of my husband. This man is tall and has grey hair and he is dressed impeccably, unlike Dan whose clothes hang on him untidily and always look as if they are in need of a press.

The manager, with a little bow, and another word of apology, leaves us, but the waiter remains.

"I hope the bar is not closed," says my companion. "We could both do with a drink."

"Of course, sir."

"What about a brandy?" he asks me. "That ought to warm you up."

He draws two chairs close to the fire that is not as bright as before. There is a basket of logs by the hearth, and he bends down and throws logs on to the embers, one after another, then he adjusts them with a well-shod slender foot. I decide that I like men who wear expensive highly polished shoes and have good ankles.

The brandies arrive in balloon glasses. The warmth from the fire, and the warmth from the drink I hold between my hands, permeates my body. I stop shivering.

"Are you better now?" he asks anxiously. "You are not dressed for standing in the street in Arctic conditions."

"Much better," I assure him, "but you must let me pay for my drink."

He brushes that aside impatiently. "Please . . ."

I do not protest.

We sit in front of the fire and I feel sure we both have the same thought – that there is a great deal of talking to be done; the formalities have been dealt with and now there is so much information to be exchanged.

He tells me he is married and has two grown-up children, a son and a daughter. They are both married and have a child apiece.

"So you are a grandfather? It is hard to believe."

"My son is in his thirties and he works with me in the family firm."

"Which is . . . ?"

"Publishers in Dublin."

"Do you live in Dublin?"

"No, but not too far away, in a place called Kildalkey in County Meath.

I ask him what he is doing in Castlerock. It seems a strange place for a man like him to visit on his own – the hotel is so quiet and there are no indications of a conference taking place or, indeed, anything happening at all.

"I have been to a funeral," he tells me, "this afternoon. Believe it or not, my sister was the Mother Superior of the convent in this town. She joined the order when she was in her sixties. Up to that point she led a very colourful life and was a source of great anxiety to her poor husband who died fifteen years ago. I always wondered if, after she was widowed, she fell for a priest and he persuaded her to take this step. Whatever the reason, she was happier being a nun than she had ever been in her whole life. It seemed to give her peace of mind she never enjoyed before."

"This is so extraordinary," I say and I proceed to tell him about Maeve, not mentioning her name. "When she was a child she used to visit her 'Auntie Nun', as she called her, at the Convent of Perpetual Adoration, here in Castlerock. The sisters had a special dispensation and were allowed to speak on the day of her visit."

"That is exactly as it was this afternoon. They all talked ninety to the dozen at the wake afterwards, and the table was laden with food. There was a great deal of alcoholic liquor to be had too, and some of my sister's old friends from her previous existence had a bit too much to drink. Altogether, it was a bizarre affair, but oddly moving in its way. My wife felt she could not face it and my children made excuses, so it was left to me to represent the family. I loved my sister dearly, so it was a sad occasion for me, but it comforts me to know that she found real contentment in the last years of her life."

I say: "I suppose it would be an acceptable life for a woman of her age who was a believer and yet wanted to escape the world. But a young girl – what sort of future can life in a convent offer her?"

"There are many young women in the convent," he tells me, "and they all seem remarkably cheerful. Once they are behind that high wall they have no contact with life outside, except on an occasion like this afternoon. The good they do in the world is all through the power of prayer."

"I'm not a Catholic," I say, "and I find it difficult to understand."

"I am," he says, "and I too find it difficult." He pauses. "But I have reason to be grateful to the Sisters of the Convent of Perpetual Adoration. Five years ago my younger son died of leukaemia. He was only twenty-one and it was a bitter blow to my wife and me and to our other two children. None of us seemed able to deal with such a tragic situation. Eventually, in my despair, I turned to my sister, and I have to say the commitment of those women to my plight was a help to me, I felt that all their energies were focussed on trying to make me come to terms with what had happened."

I want to ask him if his marriage has become stronger because of the loss of his son, but I do not think I knew him well enough to pose such a question.

He laughs and I think perhaps he is slightly embarrassed, and maybe surprised, that he has told me so much about his personal life. "We have got on to religion very early in our friendship," he says. "It's something I seldom talk about in the usual way."

"It's because of the convent," I say, trying to reassure him. "I am going there tomorrow." And I tell him about my mission to trace Maeve's daughter.

"I expect you'll see the secretary. She is a lady who is permitted to speak whenever she pleases."

I anticipate he will want to know about my life so I tell him about Hugh and Neil. Then I swallow hard and admit that I am about to become a divorcee. "I am waiting for the papers to arrive."

"You feel sad about that?" he asks, looking at me closely. Our chairs are near to each other.

"Yes, I do." I cast my eyes down and hope I will not weep, as I am inclined to do even after all this time. After my outburst of grief in Maeve's presence, I find that tears are very near the surface. "It is not been easy for me," I say. "I have joined the regiment of women dumped by their husbands, and I suppose I cannot get used to the idea."

"I don't like the word 'dumped' associated with you," he says, frowning slightly. "It doesn't suit you at all."

"Thank you for saying that, but it happened to me and I can't deny the fact. It was just that it was so unexpected. I thought we were happy."

We are silent now, and we both put our empty glasses on a small table by my chair. He leans over in front of me to put his glass beside mine. Nothing is said, and it is the moment to get up and bid each other goodnight, but we do not. I am thinking about a time recently when Neil said to his father: "Don't you love Mummy any more?"

There was a little pause after this question, and then Dan said slowly: "I shall always love Mummy."

His answer annoyed me. It was so pat. An honest question had been asked and it did not receive the reply it deserved. I heard myself saying: "But you love Andrea more."

I was aware that my comment did not do me any favours. It made me look bitchy and bitter but, nevertheless, I was glad I made it.

I come back to the present and find Tom Byrne is regarding me seriously. "If you don't mind my saying," he says, "I think you are too sensitive. Sensitivity is a lovely attribute but, for your own sake, you will have to grow a thicker skin. I don't know anything about such a situation but I am certain of one thing, it will grow easier with time."

Maeve has said almost the same thing to me many times. She knows that I still nurture a forlorn hope that the affair with Andrea will end, and Dan will return to us. I think that when there is a divorce that hope will be gone forever.

"It's just that I am envious of people with happy marriages, and I blame myself that mine went so wrong."

"You must stop doing that. Marriage is a very precarious business. It appears to be running smoothly and then something happens that puts it into reverse."

I feel I can ask him the question now: "Did the loss of your son make your marriage stronger?"

"The opposite happened. We became so wrapped up in our personal grief it distanced us from each other. I had to go on working, of course, but my poor wife was left at home with more time to think. I can't bear to speculate how awful it must have been for her, but I was too engrossed in my own misery to pay attention to how she was feeling. Eventually, our doctor, a friend of the family, informed me that she was on the verge of a nervous breakdown. It was suggested that she find some outside interest, and so she involved herself in local affairs. In fact, she became so involved that, since then, I have felt almost an outsider in her life. Please don't think I am playing the misunderstood husband card; far from it, my wife and I are happy together and nothing can alter that. It is just that things are different since the tragedy in our family, and we are both dealing with it in our own way."

I try to imagine how I would feel if something happened to Hugh or Neil. All mothers have these thoughts from time to time, and they dispel them from their minds as quickly as possible because such thoughts cannot be borne.

"I am so sorry," I say. "You make me feel my sadness is very insignificant compared to yours."

"I'm sure it is of no interest to you," he says, "but I think your husband must be mad."

We look at each other without speaking. Something is happening here and we both know it. He takes my hand and holds it in his own. I do not withdraw the hand that feels secure and comfortable in his cool firm grasp.

Our reverie is interrupted by a weary-looking waiter who, rather noisily, removes the two empty glasses; the clattering of his tray is a heavy hint that it is time for us to leave. We make our way up the stairs, for there is no lift in this rather old-fashioned establishment. We laugh nervously when we discover our rooms are on the same floor and opposite each other.

"It's a very small hotel," he says. He accompanies me to the door of my room. I hand him my key and he puts it into the lock. When the door opens he turns to me, and I put my hand on his arm, restraining him. He takes me in his arms and kisses me. It is a long time since a man has kissed me, and I feel myself drowning in the pleasure of it.

He is aware of my response and says: "Do you want me to stay?" There is a note of pleading in his voice as if he knows, as I do, that this is our only chance.

I nod silently. We go into my room and he locks the door.

Chapter 17

He leaves me when the early morning light is edging the curtains. I lie on my back, wide-awake, one hand resting on the empty space where he has been so recently and the warmth of his body penetrates my fingers.

It is hard to believe what has happened, an impulsive act so alien to everything I have always held sacred. It was as if another woman took over from me and I was powerless to do anything about it. I remember, after watching him lock the door of the room, I started to shake, and I said, naïvely: "I suppose this is what they call a one-night stand?"

He looked at me very seriously and said: "I'm afraid it is, but I hope you will believe me when I say I have never done anything like this in my life."

I did believe him, and I knew that I only had to ask him to leave me and he would have done so at once. The sense of immediacy prevented me from doing that, and the knowledge that we would not get a second chance.

Now, lying in the big hotel bed, I have no regrets, only joy. I know it was right; I could never have believed that anything could be so right. We made love as if it was something we had perfected over many years together. I feel I know him better than anyone else in my life, and yet I am conscious of the fact that when I set off for Dublin on the previous day I did not know of his existence. I was desperate then, desperate after two long lonely years and, when we kissed, I felt his desperation too. I do not know the reason for that, although perhaps I was given a hint during our conversation that evening. I reflect, a little sadly, that there will be no time for me to find out why his loneliness matched my own.

I lie in bed for a long time, luxuriating in the miracle that has happened to me. Then I get up in a leisurely way, have a shower and get dressed. I make my way downstairs to the dining-room. I notice the couple with the child are seated at a table and the elderly pair at another. They must be the only people staying in the hotel. The waiter of the previous evening comes forward and escorts me to a small table by the window.

I wonder if I will see Tom Byrne again. I think, perhaps he has already left; he told me that he is returning to Dublin in the morning. The terrible thought crosses my mind that he does not want to see me again, that he is feeling guilty. As I pick up the menu, I pray, please God don't let him feel guilty!

I look up suddenly and I see him standing in the doorway. My heart starts to beat very fast as if I was a young girl in the throes of first love. My face breaks into a smile, and his does the same. Even then, I wonder if he will make his way to another table, but he does not. He comes straight to mine, and asks: "Do you mind if I sit here?" I nod, still smiling, and he sits opposite me.

"Darling . . . !"

He takes my hand under the tablecloth. "I love you," he says simply. "I can't bear the thought of not seeing you again."

The waiter comes to take our orders.

"I'm having the works," I say happily. "Everything there is, please."

He orders the same, and our plates arrive laden with sausages, tomatoes, bacon, scrambled egg and fried bread. A jug of aromatic coffee is place on the table. "It's the best thing about staying in a hotel," I say, "the breakfast."

"The best thing?"

"Well, not the best thing in unusual circumstances."

I watch him all the time. As he ploughs through his breakfast I watch him, and when he is spreading marmalade on a piece of toast, I am still watching him. Every moment, however, trivial, is precious to me.

He looks up and smiles. "I want to remember everything," I say.

"Do we have to part in this way? Perhaps we should be more gentle with ourselves."

The temptation is great, but I know I must be firm. "We have to be strong, not gentle."

"I know you are right," he says. "I could not bear to give my wife pain. She has had enough of that already, without my adding to it." He always refers to her as 'my wife' so I do not know her name. He is more loyal to her than Dan was to me, and I hope with all my heart that he will be able to disguise his feelings when he is with her. As I know only too well women have an uncanny gift of being able to detect when there is a subtle change in their marriage. I do not want to think about that aspect. It seems inevitable that we should be together, and I hope that what we feel for each other will not result in harm being done.

"Perhaps I could write to you?" he says.

I realise, wonderingly, that Tom cares deeply, and it occurs to me that this is how Dan must have felt about Andrea and, for the first time, I experience a vestige of sympathy for him.

"No, darling, I don't think that would be a good idea."

He sighs and says: "I suppose you are right."

We finish our breakfast and silently go to our rooms on opposite sides of the landing. I do my packing in a few minutes, and then I sit on the edge of the bed and gradually my feeling of contentment starts to diminish. It seems a very little time to be happy.

There is a tap on the door and when I open it he is standing there with an armful of flowers.

"I got them at the florist's up the road," he says almost apologetically. "I don't know what they are."

"They are stocks," I tell him, "and perfectly beautiful." I take them from him and bury my nose in them and take a great gulp of heady scent. "They smell wonderful. Thank you so much."

I know I shall not be allowed to take them on the aeroplane – he has not thought of that.

We look at each other sadly. We both know there is no point in prolonging his departure. We kiss, a long kiss, and we part. He has parked his car in the road outside the hotel; already he has paid his bill and put his suitcase in the boot. From the window I watch his tall figure striding towards it. He looks up briefly, and I wave. I see him get into his car and drive away.

I fill the basin in the bathroom with water, and I put his flowers in it. It was such a boyish impulsive gesture from a middle-aged businessman. I prop up the pillows and I lie on the top of the bed, thinking of him. I know I will think of him many times during the rest of my life. I indulge in a daydream that many years from this day I am in a public place, a theatre perhaps, and I see him amongst all the people. My imaginings become more melancholy when I think that, at a later stage in my existence, when I am old, I will learn of his death.

He is older than me, and women live longer than men, so it is likely that I will outlive him. I will see a notice in the Deaths column in *The Times*: 'Thomas Byrne, beloved husband of . . . ' I know, in my heightened state of emotion, I have made a true prediction for the future – it will happen that way. Through the years I know he will remember me, although the memory will become fainter with time. Men, although sometimes careless in their relationships, are not forgetful. Even Dan, I know, has not forgotten, his memories are set in stone and there is nothing Andrea can do to remove them forever.

I decide such foolish thoughts must stop, and I get up and put on my coat. It is time I paid a visit to the convent which I remind myself is my reason for coming to Castlerock.

I stop at the reception desk and ask the girl if it would matter if I do not leave before twelve o'clock as stipulated. I wonder if I shall have to pay for another night, but she informs me, as I already know, the hotel is almost empty. I can leave on that day at any time I want. I tell her that my plane takes off at eight o'clock, so I will collect my packed case from my room two hours before that time.

I ask her for directions to the convent.

"It is about twenty minutes walk from here," she says. "Do you want me to get you a taxi?"

No, I think I prefer to go on foot. I walk briskly because it is still cold, but not as cold as on the previous evening. The convent is easy to find because of the high wall surrounding it. I stand at the door and, as Maeve did many years before, I tug at the metal bell pull and, as she did, I hear the sound of the bell echoing in the building beyond.

Chapter 18

Somehow I feel a nun who is also a secretary is a bit incongruous, although I have been told that as a unique member of this particular order she is allowed to speak. The other sisters are silent. Dressed in her habit she sits behind a big desk, spectacles on the end of her nose. I notice a wisp of hair has escaped the tight coif that encircles her head, and I wonder if this too is an indication of her status in the community. I am sitting in her office but it is more like a private room than an office. There is no sign of a computer but I see there is a telephone on the desk, and on the wall behind her there are two big filing cabinets. On another wall there is a watercolour, a landscape, probably of somewhere in Ireland. The curtains at the narrow window are floral, and bright and cheerful. This nun has made the most of her special privileges.

In front of her is a file, and as she flicks through it I

get a glimpse of the letter I wrote to her asking for an interview.

"We have a record of when this baby came to us," she says. "It was the morning of April the fifth, nineteen hundred and nineteen." As she speaks I visualise that morning, as Maeve has described it to me, and the frightened girl hiding behind the tree, watching the hands come out and pick up the basket. At that moment the child's fate was sealed, whether for good or bad will no doubt be revealed.

"She was adopted by a childless couple here in Castlerock," went on the secretary nun. "Her father was the local undertaker."

"Oh!"

She looks up at me and gives a little smile. "The business was sold as there were no male heirs to take it on. Of course, you realise the person we are talking about is no longer young?"

"Yes, I know that. Her mother is ninety-four."

"She has lived in this town all her life," went on the secretary nun. "She went to school here, worked in the local library until she retired and, I think I am right in saying, she has never left this place. She has been brought up in the Catholic faith and is very devout – at one time it was thought she would be a nun but it did not happen. She has never married, and now both her parents are dead she has no relations close to her. I wrote to her after I received your letter, and she came to see me at once. She was very excited by the prospect of meeting her biological mother, and she is prepared to travel to England for that purpose. When I told her that you were coming to see me today, she wondered if you could find time to call on her before you return – is that possible? I know she would appreciate it very much. She is half expecting you."

"Of course, I shall be delighted to see her," I say.

The secretary hands me a slip of paper, obviously prepared in advance, on which is written, *Sheelagh Devane, 17, Caversham Street, Castlerock.*

"That is settled then," she says with satisfaction, and I realise it is my moment to depart. I follow her black rustling skirts across a wooden floor. Sisters glide noiselessly by and the silence is interrupted by the strident tolling of a bell calling them to prayer.

I slip through the door in the wall I have heard mentioned so many times, and suddenly I am out in the fresh air again. I had not realised until that moment that the air in the convent was so stale. The busy street, the sound of the children playing, the cars and the buses on the other side of the wall greet my ears as if I am a stranger returned from a different world. I walk slowly back to the hotel. I cannot find a taxi and I tell myself that the walk will clear my head. I feel so confused about everything that has happened to me during the last twenty-four hours and I am physically and emotionally exhausted.

I walk into the hotel dining-room and I find it is empty. I order a glass of white wine and a sandwich and I sit in solitary state at our table (in my mind I call it 'our table') until I decide to go up to my room. As soon as I enter it the flowers in the bathroom basin greet me with their delicious scent. I press my nose into them again and think of the person who gave them to me. I make up my mind they are too nice to be wasted, and I will present them to Sheelagh on my arrival at her house. The gesture will break the ice, and everyone loves to receive flowers. Carefully, I wrap wet tissue around the stems and wrap them in the paper they came in – holding them like a bride I descend the stairs and out into the street. This time I hail a taxi – I have no idea where Caversham Street is and I have walked enough during the morning.

It is quite a long distance from the hotel, and Sheelagh's house is a small terraced house in a row of identical houses. Most of her neighbours have chosen bright colours for their front doors but Sheelagh's door is a drab brown. I ring the doorbell and the door is opened at once; I get the impression she has been standing on the other side of it, awaiting my arrival.

I am a little taken aback by my first impression. She is an old lady, in appearance not much younger than Maeve.

"I'm so pleased to see you," she says and we shake hands in a formal way. I follow her plump rear view into a small sitting-room. It is sparsely furnished and without charm, and everywhere there are religious pictures and statuettes of the Virgin Mary. I can't help thinking the secretary's office at the convent was more up to date. I sit on an armchair covered in a loose brown cover and I see there is a tray on a small table with cups and saucers and, in the middle, a Victoria sponge.

"I'll just go into the kitchen and fetch the teapot," she says. She has a pleasant voice, a melodic Irish accent. When she returns I look more closely at her face and I see blue eyes – Maeve's eyes.

"You have your mother's eyes," I tell her.

Clearly I have said the right thing for I can see she is pleased, if a little flustered by my comment. "I wondered if you would spot a resemblance somewhere. This means so much to me. I can't tell you. . ."

I remember the flowers. "I brought these for you."

"Oh!" It is a little cry of gratitude, but at the same time she is disconcerted, and I think she has never had flowers given to her before, or bought them for herself.

"They are beautiful," she says, taking them from me but not putting them to her face as I have done.

"They have a nice smell," I say. For a moment I wish I had not given them to her, that I had left them behind in my hotel bedroom to die naturally, mine alone until the chambermaid tossed them in the bin.

I follow Sheelagh into a dark old-fashioned kitchen. Obviously she does not know what to with the flowers. "I have nothing to put them in," she says helplessly.

"What about a pail?"

"A pail?"

"Have you a bucket?"

She parts a curtain under the sink and removes a bucket. I take over and fill it with water from the kitchen tap and put the flowers into it. I know they will remain there in the kitchen until they wither and die, like the love I have lost this day.

I sense her relief at getting back to the tea and cake. These are things with which she is familiar, unlike the flowers that only cause her anxiety. With renewed confidence she pours me a cup of tea and cuts me a generous slab of cake – too generous and it presents a problem to me. I murmur about the sandwich so recently eaten, but she takes no notice.

"Please tell me about my mother," she says, perching on the edge of her chair.

"She is a very interesting lady," I tell her. "Ninety-four years old, but young for her age. Rather stout and not very mobile on her pins." Sheelagh looks confused so I explain: "She is arthritic so finds walking difficult. She possesses all her marbles and has a great sense of humour – a wonderful laugh."

I get the feeling that my description is not what she expects, but I plough on, determined to present her with the truth. "My two young sons love her," I continue, "and she seems to relate to young people. It is quite amazing, really, how well they get on with her."

"How old are your children?"

"Hugh is eight and Neil is six."

"You must be very proud of them," she says thoughtfully. "I'm afraid I have little experience of children. Working in the library I saw them when they came in to choose their books, but I never got to know any of them."

"I have been writing a sort of biography of Maeve's life," I tell her, "and, of course, you feature in it. She was sixteen when she became pregnant with you." I pause because I feel slightly embarrassed, although I know there is no reason for it. This old woman gives the impression of being set apart from the ordinary things of life, the love of a man for a woman, a child born out of wedlock; her faith has excluded her from the raw facts of our existence and, like the flowers I presented to her, she has no idea how to deal with them. I meet her innocent gaze and say: "In this day and age it is hard to understand the shame the pregnancy of a young unmarried girl could cause the people looking after her."

She nods sagely. She understands the shame. "Of course, it is a terrible disgrace." She speaks in the present tense and, in her mind, there has been no change of attitude. Sheelagh is like Aunt Min in another era.

I go on: "Maeve was living with her aunt and uncle and their two daughters, a respectable Catholic family. She was made to stay in an attic room, out of sight of the neighbours. When you were born she loved you but she did not know where to turn. You can imagine how difficult it was for a young girl, a child almost, and I think you can understand why she did what she did."

"In a way," says Sheelagh, "she did me a service. Wonderful God-fearing people adopted me and I had a happy life. Sadly, my parents are both dead, but I remember them in my prayers every day. Now I know about my real mother I will pray for her also." She looks at me quite sharply. "Of course, she is a Catholic?"

"Of course."

"It is a blessing that we have that in common."

I did not like to mention that Maeve is not a very good Catholic, but I remind myself that the priest visits her once a week, and surely that must count for something?

"I shall come to England to see her," says Sheelagh, and her determination makes me think of Maeve. "Next week – will that be all right?"

"She will be so pleased," I say, "and I shall be delighted to have you to stay with me during your visit."

"Thank you very much."

I have managed to finish the last crumb of cake on my plate, and now she presses me to have another slice. "No, no. I must leave you – I have a plane to catch back to England."

"I have never been on an aeroplane," she says. "This will be my first time."

"Maeve has given me money," I tell her, "and I know she would want to pay for your fare."

A faint spot of colour comes to her cheeks. "There is no need," she says with dignity. "My parents had no other children and left everything to me; in fact I am quite well off. I do not move from this house because I think God wants us to live as simply as possible."

"You are probably right," I say wearily. I am so utterly exhausted with this day of sad partings and strange encounters; I wonder how I can endure the journey back. Ahead of me lies the wait at the airport, the search for my car and the drive home, picking up an ecstatic Flush on the way.

I thank Sheelagh for the tea and she comes to the door to see me off. "If you walk to the end of the street you will come to a big road, and you can get a taxi there."

I notice that she is still wearing the apron that she put around her waist when she went to make the tea in the kitchen. Under it she wears a serviceable navy blue woollen skirt and a white blouse, and she has thick stockings and lace-up brown shoes. Her hair is scraped back in a bun, a knot of straggly grey hair with a faint reddish undertone, anchored by hairpins.

As I say goodbye I can't help wondering what Maeve will make of her.

Chapter 19

"Well?" says Maeve. "Tell me the worst."

I reply slowly, choosing my words carefully. "I don't know what you expect – perhaps your expectations are too high. For instance, do you know how old she is?"

"Of course, darling, I am quite capable of working out her age. She is in her seventies and I was cool when I was that age."

'Cool' is a word she has learnt from Hugh and she uses it quite often.

"Sheelagh is not cool."

She shifts uncomfortably in the wheelchair; walking has become a hardship for her and, reluctantly, she has resorted to being pushed around in a wheelchair that folds and fits into the boot of my car. At this moment we are trundling along the street on the way to a restaurant where we are going to have lunch. Maeve is a dead weight, and she has no idea how hard it is to shove the heavy contraption; every uneven patch on the pavement makes it harder. I am always out of breath by the time we reach our destination.

"Do you mind if we leave Sheelagh for a while?" I pant. "Talk about her when we get there?"

"All right," she says resignedly.

We are known at this place, and have a special table reserved for us. I am thankful when the dreaded wheelchair is whisked out of sight, and Maeve and I advance very slowly to our seats. At last, with a grunt of pleasure, she settles herself into the chair opposite me. She rewards me for my labours with a cherubic smile.

The waiter is attentive, she is a good tipper, and the first thing she orders is a bottle of wine. It is always the first thing she orders, and I have one glass from it and she polishes off the rest. The people at Riverbank try to restrict her drinking; in their view one glass of wine a day is sufficient for a woman of her age. I think that having got so far she might as well do as she likes.

After the waiter has taken our orders – we are both having fish – he leaves us, and she turns to me and says impatiently: "Come on, I'm longing to know about my daughter. I can tell by your expression you were not impressed."

"That is not fair," I reply. "She is a nice person, but she has lived in the same place all her life – Castlerock which, as you know, is not the most inspiring of places. As far as I know she has had a very happy life, and for that you must be thankful. She has never married but religion has taken the place of that."

"What does she look like?"

I do not know how to reply to her question. I have a sudden mental picture of a rather stout undistinguished-looking woman with her hair in an old-fashioned bun.

"I can see you are lost for words," says Maeve dryly.

"Not at all – it's just that sometimes it is difficult to describe a person. I remember her eyes – blue like yours. That similarity was one of the first things I noticed about her, and I mentioned it and she was very pleased."

"Is she like me in any other way?"

"Not really." I pause. "I'm sorry to be so hopeless. I think you must be patient and wait until you see her yourself."

There is a little pause while Maeve carefully breaks up a roll on her side plate. Then she looks up with a mischievous smile and says: "I can't wait to meet her."

I feel slightly aggrieved. After all, she was the one who was so keen to track her down. "If you are disappointed, you have brought it on yourself."

"I know that," she says, "and I am beginning to think we should never have embarked on this venture. Perhaps we should retreat now while we still can."

"No way," I say. "She is very excited about the prospect of meeting you. Can you imagine how she must be feeling – seeing her real mother after all these years? She has led a very simple life and at last something momentous has happened. It would be cruel to let her down at this stage. No, she is coming, and that's that – there is no turning back."

"Of course, you are right, darling," says Maeve, "and it is only for a visit, after all. We ought to be able to manage that between us."

"You make it sound like a punishment instead of a joy – you should be so happy about this."

I am," she says, "and it's what I have thought about for years. Now it has happened, thanks to you, I don't know why I should have so many misgivings."

The waiter arrives with out food, and Maeve starts to tuck in at once. Moira always says she has a hearty appetite, unusual in an old person, and in my house or in a restaurant she finishes every morsel.

"By the way," she says, "how was the holiday?"

"Holiday?" I am thinking of my short stay in Dublin.

"Portugal." She sounds amused.

In fact, today I sense amusement lurking in those blue eyes that look at me so closely. I cannot imagine what causes it but it pleases me to see her in such a good mood. Sometimes, Maeve in a grumpy frame of mind can be very trying, when she rails against advancing years, for instance, or complains about the residents of Riverbank.

"Of course, Portugal. They had a wonderful time."

I know she is always interested to hear every detail about my family so I tell her how they all arrived the day before, and how I had been anxiously awaiting their arrival. Dan and Andrea delivered the boys on the way back from the airport, and I was grateful for this, that they had not taken them to their home before bringing them to me. I have never been parted from Hugh and Neil for such a long time, and I missed them horribly.

I describe to Maeve the events of yesterday, how I stood in the doorway and I saw their little figures dashing up the path towards me, and I opened wide my arms to greet them, as an ill-fated princess once did to her two little sons when she saw them again after an absence. We three clung together, all tearful, and Dan and Andrea followed behind more slowly. She was walking in the way some pregnant women do, proudly. When I was pregnant I used to wear a loose shirt over comfortable trousers that had a hole for the bump. Nowadays, that is no longer the fashion, and Andrea was wearing a tight top, stretched to its limits. I averted my eyes from the extended stomach. During the last two years I have learnt to hide my feelings but I have not yet got used to the idea of Dan's child by another woman.

We went into the house and each child had brought me a small gift. From Hugh a little terracotta dish for olives and from Neil a silver-plated key. I turned it over wonderingly as it is obviously a symbol of the key to the door of life, a cheap trinket a girl might receive on her eighteenth or twenty-first birthday.

"It's a funny sort of present," said Hugh, apologising for his brother.

"He insisted on buying it for you," said Andrea.

"I love it." I bent down and kissed a beaming Neil.

I offered Dan and Andrea a drink but Dan refused for them both. They were anxious to get back to Pollards. At last, I was alone with my children and we indulged in more hugging and kissing. Between us we dragged their cases to their bedroom and started to unpack. Piles of dirty clothes were collected in the middle of the room and the sand from them was scattered on the carpet. They have been in a different world, apart from me, and however much they choose to tell me about the holiday I have not shared it with them. I told myself that we must share less and less as they grow older, but it does not mean we will grow apart. It seemed to me that they have accepted the changes in their lives with equanimity, and their voices were natural and casual when they spoke of Andrea.

"She is having a baby," Hugh told me, "and she will be our sister."

"Or brother," I said. I did not believe that Dan and Andrea know the sex of their child. I should have said 'half brother' but I restrained myself. The boys do not understand the complications of halves and steps; this baby will be a sister or brother and that's that.

As if understanding my feelings, the sensitive little Neil put his soft arms around my neck. "I love you, Mummy." He gave a sigh of pure contentment – he was glad to be home.

"I love you too," I said.

Maeve is now tucking into ice cream. "They are such wonderful children," she says. "You don't know how lucky you are."

"I think I do."

When we are both installed in the car and the wheelchair is safely stowed in the back, I ask: "Shall we both go and collect them from school? Then you can come back for an early supper. I know they have a little present for you."

"Have they really?" She is like a delighted child.

I park the car outside the school. I am early and there are a few minutes to wait until the little human dynamos are ejected from the building after the first day of a new term.

Maeve looks at me. "So what happened to you, darling?"

I knew that I would not be able to keep any secret from her for long. All though lunch I have been planning how to respond when she asks me that question. I feel the colour rising in my face. "Is it so obvious?"

"I'm afraid it is," she says. "You are positively glowing. You look as if you have been on an exotic holiday with someone special instead of whiling your time away waiting for the boys to return."

So I tell her about Tom Byrne – of course I always meant to tell her, I just didn't know how to begin. I hope I will not cheapen the story in the telling of it. I still find it hard to believe what happened that night and, remembering every moment, feel no sense of shame, only realisation that for one night at least I was loved. Maeve listens without interrupting; one of her most endearing qualities is that she such a wonderful listener. I know she will understand, and, of course, I am right.

"It is the best thing that could have happened to you at this time," she says, "but it is sad that it must be as short-lived as the flowers he gave you."

She is not the only one to be so perceptive. I tell her that as Dan and Andrea turn to leave the day before, he said to me: "Are you all right?"

"What do you mean?"

"You look different . . ."

"I am the same," I told him, on the defensive. "Perhaps a bit happier, that's all."

"I'm glad," he said.

I reflect on that short exchange of words between us, and I think that when two people have been as close as we have been, there is an invisible bond between them connecting their thoughts and feelings. I thought that bond had been snapped, but now I know it is still there, and nothing can sever it completely.

Dan arrives during the evening because he forgot on the previous day to give me the boys' passports. Despite the suntan after a holiday abroad he looks strained. This time he accepts the offer of a drink, and sits beside Maeve. His sons hover lovingly around him. She congratulates him on their forthcoming child and, watching closely his reaction, I see a shadow pass over his face, and it confirms my previous suspicion that he is not altogether happy about the prospect. He reiterates something he has said before: "We both hope for a girl."

"Why?" I ask. "When boys are so perfect?"

He looks at my sharply. "A girl would round off the family."

Maeve says comfortably: "I'm sure neither of you are worried about the sex of the baby as long as it is healthy."

"Of course, that's true," Dan says.

"But boys are perfect," interrupts Hugh, "so I hope we'll have a boy."

I am bored by this conversation, and it is a relief when Dan gets up to go. I wonder if he will offer to take Maeve back to Riverbank, but he does not. It means that we all have to pile into the car to take her, but the winter is nearly over and the days are getting longer so Hugh and Neil are allowed to go to bed later than usual. But they are tired after the first day of school and they both go to sleep in the back seat. I look at their drooping heads in the car mirror, and I groan. "I'll have to waken them when we get home, and they will be bad-tempered."

"I'm sorry," says Maeve. "I feel it is my fault."

"No, no," I say hastily. "Don't think that for an instant."

"You feel differently about him, don't you?" she says, turning to look at me. "It has happened at last, what I always hoped for, that you would be able to look at him without feeling breathless."

"You make me sound very pathetic."

"Not pathetic, but vulnerable. Feeling as you do now you will find yourself at a great advantage. Just liking him, rather than loving him with all your being, will make it easier for you to face what is ahead of you."

"Don't count on it," I say dryly.

I park the car outside Riverbank, as near to the front door as I can. The boys do not stir. Maeve has a set of keys so I am able to open the door, and I remove the wheelchair from the boot and trundle it into the hall. Then I return to the car to fetch Maeve. Slowly, very slowly, we make our way to her room. The place seems empty, not a soul to be seen. Moira must have left hours before and the members of staff are probably in the kitchen, gossiping over cups of tea or something stronger.

At the door of her room, I say anxiously: "Will you be all right?" My thoughts are with Hugh and Neil, asleep in the car.

"Of course, darling." She takes my face between her hands and kisses me. "You go back to your precious children."

As I turn to leave, she says: "It was nice of Dan to bring back the passports. Many fathers would have decided to keep them."

"I know," I say. "Dan has always tried to be fair."

Chapter 20

Sheelagh arrives the following week, and stays with me as we arranged in Ireland. I go to meet her at Heathrow and, as her plane arrives at a late hour, we decide to go straight to my house. She sits stolidly beside me in the car, capacious handbag clasped on her knees, her face inscrutable. I wonder what she can be thinking – it is a momentous experience that lies ahead of her, meeting someone who, up to now, has been a shadowy figure in her life.

"I thought we would go to Riverbank tomorrow." I say. "How was your first flight? Did you enjoy it?"

"It was all right."

"Maeve is looking forward to meeting you," I tell her encouragingly. "How do you feel about it? Are you nervous?" As always happens when conversation does not flow easily I am resorting to questions.

"Of course not," she says. "It's my mother I am going

to see, my own flesh and blood. There is no call for me to feel nervous."

It cannot be anything but a formal meeting between a mother and daughter who do not know each other. However close the relationship they will not fall into each other's arms. I think of the television programmes where this happens, and I am relieved I am not subjected to such a display of emotion. Instead they stare at each other for a few moments, without speaking, and then Maeve takes both of Sheelagh's hands in hers. It is a sweet gesture and Sheelagh is clearly overcome. I decide to leave them to it, and I get up quickly, not without noticing the look of panic on Maeve's face when she sees I am deserting her. Afterwards, Maeve tells me that within a few minutes they were talking like old friends and Sheelagh suggested she turn on the electric kettle for a cup of tea.

Sheelagh spends a few hours each day at Riverbank, and soon a routine is established. I leave her there at noon and collect her during the afternoon's school run. She is an easy guest, and there are no signs in the house of her presence. Her bedroom lacks the usual things women carry around with them, jars and bottles, even her hairbrush has been tucked away somewhere, out of sight. It is like a nun's room: the bed made without a crease, virginal, circumspect, and only a Bible and a prayer book on the bedside table.

She has lunch with Maeve in her room, and is appreciative of the food I give her in the evening; she eats small amounts, unlike her mother who ploughs into a meal with evident delight. She is so quiet that the boys, after the first introductions, hardly notice her. She asks them about school, and they answer her politely. I get the feeling that she is faintly disapproving of the way I am bringing them up, no grace said before meals and they do not kneel down to say their prayers before they go to sleep. I think Sheelagh notices these deficiencies and, of course, she is shocked by the imminent divorce. I had to explain the reason for Dan's visits to collect Hugh and Neil, and the fact that he does not live with us. She listened in silence when I told her, and she has not mentioned it since.

I do not think she and Maeve have much to say to each other; perhaps after that first meeting there is nothing left for them to talk about. When I go to collect her, Maeve is usually lying flat on her bed, staring in space, and Sheelagh is sitting in a chair near her, knitting. She is knitting a pair of gloves on four needles that she juggles dexterously between her fingers.

"Very clever," I say.

"They are for Mother," she tells me.

It is a surprise to me that she calls Maeve 'Mother' and, in fact, has done so since the first day. I am certain Maeve did not ask her to do this, and I wonder how she feels about it.

Sheelagh tells me, in confidence, that she hopes to persuade her mother not to drink so much. "You know, she orders bottles of wine from the village shop – she should not be allowed to do that. The people here should forbid it."

"Just because she is old does not mean that she can be ordered about; she can do as she pleases."

"It can't be good for her," says Sheelagh, determined to press her point.

"Does 'being good for her' really matter at this stage?" I argue. "Wouldn't it be kinder to let her do as she wants?"

I can see from Sheelagh's pursed lips that she does not agree with me.

"Mrs Bailey's daughter is very caring," says Moira to me one day. "She takes endless trouble over her mother. I must say I had no idea the old lady had a daughter. It came as a complete surprise to me – I was not told of her existence."

I have no wish to satisfy her curiosity, so I change the subject by saying: "How do you think Mrs Bailey is keeping? I know she can't get around much any more because of her knees but, generally, is she in good shape for her years?"

It is something I think of from time to time, the inevitable fact that Maeve will not be with us forever. There must be a time, in the not so distant future, when we will be forging ahead with our little lives, as before, and she will not be with us. Sometimes, I wonder if I should explain this foregone conclusion to the boys, but I do not because I think they understand how it will be.

"Well, she has a heart, of course," Moira tells me. I

can't help thinking of the absurdity of the English language. When she says Maeve 'has a heart' she means she has a heart condition, perhaps a dangerous one, whereas to have no heart would be fatal.

"I did not know that."

"Yes, she had a severe heart attack six months before she came to Riverbank. That is why she decided to join her husband here."

"Has she had any problems since?" Maeve has never mentioned to me that she has a bad heart.

"Well, there have been a few times when I felt I had to call the doctor. Just little scares, mostly after a late night and too much wine." She looks at me reprovingly.

"I'll try to remember," I say hastily.

After this conversation I walk into Maeve's room, and the usual scene confronts me. Sheelagh sitting in her chair knitting, and Maeve lying, fully clothed, on the bed eating a piece of cake. I have brought Flush with me so he immediately gets a bit of cake that is gone in one gulp. He puts his paws on the bed and licks Maeve's fingers.

"I don't think you should let him do that, Mother," says Sheelagh.

"He's a nice doggie," Maeve replies. "I love him and he loves me." I hope she speaks the truth, and it is not just the titbits that draw him to her side.

Sheelagh lays down her knitting and gets up. She walks over to Maeve and, with her hand, brushes crumbs off her bosom. Like most old people Maeve has a habit of dropping food down her front. She glares at Sheelagh. "Leave me alone," she growls.

"I'm only trying to keep you nice and tidy," says Sheelagh placidly.

Maeve turns to me. "Lunch tomorrow?" she says plaintively. I see desperation in her eyes, and I think she is at the end of her tether.

"That would be lovely."

"On our own," says Maeve firmly. "You don't mind, do you, Sheelagh?"

"Of course not, Mother dear. I have lots to do."

Over lunch at our usual table, I say: "She is kind, you know. Look at the way she trundles you around in your wheelchair." It's true; I often see her, red-faced, pushing the heavy wheelchair up and down the garden paths of the home, while Maeve sits, an immovable lump, chin on chest.

"Oh, come on, darling," she says now. "It's the least she can do."

"That chair is very heavy," I say with feeling. "You must give credit where credit is due. She has come a long way to see you. I hope my visit to Dublin was not a waste of time."

"Not in your case, darling," says Maeve. "I'm just happy that something worked out well. As for Sheelagh, let's forget her and enjoy our lunch. I'm sure she is very worthy." She could not have made a more damning assessment of her character.

I think about the young Maeve before she met

George Palmer and before she went to London to pursue a career on the stage; if she had stayed at Castlerock what would she have been like now? I remind Maeve of that girl, and she agrees: "Yes, I was an awful prude. Thank God I grew out of it."

"But if you had stayed with Aunt Min and Uncle Frank, might you not have grown old like Sheelagh?"

"Never!" she says cheerfully, quaffing her wine.

Obediently I turn the conversation away from Sheelagh. "You did not tell me you have a bad heart – I had to hear it from Moira." I am wondering whether I should suggest we have a half bottle instead of a whole bottle of wine in the future, thereby demolishing all my previous views that Maeve should do as she pleases.

"Everyone of my age has *something.* A wonky heart is the best because it is likely to carry you off if you have a stroke. In fact, the doctors discovered I always had a weak heart. Apparently, I was born with it, and it probably accounts for all the fainting I did when I was young."

"I wish you had told me," I say. "I don't like secrets."

"I'm sorry, darling. I promise, no more secrets."

I think I should have a word with Sheelagh. "I don't think Maeve likes you brushing off bits of food she spills down her front. My advice is just let them be. There are excellent facilities at Riverbank for washing and ironing her clothes."

Sheelagh ignores the point of my remarks. "It's disgraceful," she tells me, "what a mess they make of

Mother's lovely clothes. They washed some of her white underclothing with a red top and turned her bras and knickers pink! I have made arrangements with Moira that I wash her clothes by hand in future and do her ironing. That way I can be sure they don't lose their colour or shrink."

I give up. I tell myself she is leaving soon, the week is nearly up and, I must say, I am glad. Although she is so unassuming and quiet, the boys and I do not feel completely natural with her in the house.

She and Maeve part, and the finished gloves are accepted with apparent gratitude.

Maeve kisses her daughter, and Sheelagh is tearful. On the way to the airport she says: "I can't tell you how much this visit has meant to me. I had a happy life with wonderful parents and I thank God for blessing me, but I have always wondered about my real mother. It is only natural, isn't it? Now I have met her, she is everything to me. I thank you from the bottom of my heart for giving me the opportunity to get to know her. Sometimes I think I might never have seen her, and then I would have missed out on something so precious . . ." Her voice breaks.

I feel ashamed for some of the thoughts I have had about her during the past week.

"Never mind," I say reassuringly, "you can come again, you know."

"Oh, I'm doing that," she says brightly. "I have rented a cottage in the village so that I can be near Mother. I'm returning to Castlerock now to arrange about letting my own house while I'm away. I'm not selling it because one day I shall return to it when, I can't speak the words, when my dear mother is called to God's side."

"Does Maeve know about this?"

"I thought I'd write her a letter but, if you want to tell her my plans, please feel free to do so."

When I see Maeve again she is sitting on the edge of her bed trying to get into her shoes. "Sheelagh always insisted on doing this for me," she says, "and now I seem to have lost the art." She gives up, and sits with her stockinged feet planted firmly on the ground.

"She was sad to leave you," I tell her.

"I hope she will not feel sad for long," Maeve says. "I think she is better suited living in Castlerock than looking after an old woman here. After all it is her home, and it is always nice to go home."

Then I tell her. "She is returning. She has rented a cottage in the village."

I sit down beside her on the bed, and I take one of her veined old hands in mine. "She wants to be near you."

Maeve looks at me in blank amazement. Then we both see the funny side of the situation at the same time. We start to laugh, and we laugh until the tears run down our cheeks. I love to hear Maeve's deep-throated laugh, it is so unique to her. Clutching each other, we both fall back on the pillows on the bed, and we lie there, holding each other, laughing hysterically.

Chapter 21

The divorce papers arrive and I am summoned to attend court in London. "It doesn't seem fair," I say to my solicitor who, over the months, has become a close woman friend. "I have done nothing, and yet I have to go through this ordeal. Dan is let off the hook."

"In your case it is a very simple procedure," she reassures me, "and will be over quite quickly. There is no need for you to feel nervous about it."

It is the finality that fills me with fear. A few legal phrases will ensure that I am no longer Dan's wife, and yet I feel I shall always be his wife. I am doing the honourable thing by divorcing him so that he can marry the mother of his unborn child. I don't feel honourable, just foolish and hard done by. I tell myself, over and over again, that I knew this moment would come, and now it has, I must face it without flinching.

Because I have to go to London I ask my sister if I can spend the night with her after the hearing.

I anticipate the little note of doubt in her voice when she answers my request with the words: "Yes, of course." How could she say anything else? We are sisters, and at this crucial point in my life I ought to be able to rely on her support. She owns a very nice flat in Drayton Gardens and she has a fairly high-powered job. I suppose when we were young we must have got on and liked each other, and I don't know when that changed. Dan disliked her from the start, but I can't blame him for the dislocation of the relationship between us; it happened before he met her. I always have the feeling that she bears a grudge against me, but I don't understand why that should be. People have said that I am better looking, but she soon overcame that by developing a style of her own and an immaculate taste in clothes. She is Hugh's godmother but she has never taken any interest in him; both boys find her unapproachable and, on the rare occasions she comes to visit us, she tends to ignore them. She has never married, and I think she must treat men with the same brusque disregard she treats me – I can't imagine her getting close to a man.

As I place my suitcase into the lift of the block of flats where she lives, I think I have two devils to face, the severance of my marriage and my sister. She opens the door to me and says: "Well, come in, then."

I follow her into the main room of the flat that is furnished in exquisite taste, and has an unlived-in feel about it that I rather envy, remembering the chaos at home. This is a room that has never suffered the ravages of children and a domesticated animal.

To my surprise there is someone else there, a man who rises to his feet when we come in. Monica introduces us, and I learn his name is Barry King and it is not long before it dawns on me that he lives here, in this flat, with my sister.

There are two bright spots on Monica's cheeks when she shows me to the room where I am to sleep.

"Why didn't you tell me about him?" I demand.

"I didn't think you'd be interested. You have so much on your mind at present."

When we go back into the sitting-room he tells me that he has been through the divorce courts, and knows how I must be feeling. "Four times," he says.

"Goodness."

"What time do you have to be at the court?" he asks.

"Three o'clock. I'll telephone for a taxi."

"You'll do no such thing," he replies. "I'm driving you there – it's all arranged."

"That's very kind."

He has a nice face, I decide, not handsome but presentable and he gives the impression of being well off. I'm sure that is what Monica finds attractive, his well-fitting suit and the gold watch on his wrist. I wonder what he does for a living; somehow I feel his opulent appearance is the result of his own endeavours. There are no signs of inherited wealth. He appears older than my sister, which is not surprising considering he has gone through four wives.

"What you need on an occasion like this," he says briskly, "is a stiff drink. It helped me and it would help you."

Monica and I sit opposite each other without speaking. That is part of the trouble; we can never find anything to say to each other. Our lives have become so diverse it is hard to find a common ground for conversation – it used to be that I was married and she was not, that was the big difference between us, now the difference is that I am about to be divorced and she is a career woman with a steady boyfriend. We can never meet as equals. I listen to Barry clinking glasses in the next room, and my mind turns to food. Are they going to offer me anything to eat? In my hurry to get off this morning I missed breakfast. I glance surreptitiously at my watch and see it is half past one, so perhaps they have already eaten and assume that I have too? It is a sad indication of my awkwardness with my sister that I can't just tell her I'm hungry.

Barry appears with drinks for the three of us. Whiskies – my heart sinks. I am not a whisky drinker, especially in the middle of the day like this. I start to tell him but he interrupts me. "Do you good at a time like this. Take my word for it."

It is warming, I have to admit, and I sit, clasping the glass, sinking further and further into one of Monica's incredibly soft chairs.

She begins to voice an opinion, something I have been dreading since my arrival, although knowing it was inevitable. She either says nothing to me, or too much, and I don't know which is worse.

"I hope you are not letting Dan get away with everything. You must stand up for your rights after the way he has treated you."

"Have you a good solicitor?" Barry asks. He seems to be in complete harmony with Monica's abrasive approach, so I suppose it is akin to his own.

"Not particularly," I admit, "but she is very nice and we have become good friends." To inject a little humour, and to irritate them further, I tell them how the children are often in the office when I go to see her.

"That's outrageous," he says, getting heated. "I wish I had known – I could have introduced you to a splendid fellow."

"I think I am all right as I am," I say, I hope with dignity. "She is a nice woman, just harassed, that's all, and it is not a complicated case."

"Every divorce case is complicated," Barry says sadly.

"The fact that there are two houses, and the boys and I have not been forced to move makes it easier."

"What difference does that make?" Monica demands. "Complacency is not going to get you anywhere, you know. You really must try and be a bit tougher."

"In what way, tougher?" I ask her. "I have everything I need, except my husband. Dan gives me enough money for me to pay all the bills and look after the children. He has been very generous, and it is a friendly arrangement." A friendly arrangement – I am quoting my solicitor now who marvels at the way we have worked things out for ourselves.

"Oh, really!" Monica's voice rises in indignation. "You have always let him walk over you, and at this crucial point in your life you are still doing it. I can't believe my ears when you tell me he is generous. Walking out on you and the boys and living with another woman – and you call him generous?"

It does seem a bit silly, and I sink lower into my chair.

"Where does he live with this woman of his?" asks Barry.

"Oh, nearby. A few miles away."

"If you don't mind my saying, that will lead to disaster. Why don't you sell the family home and move away?"

"It makes it easier for the children if we don't live too far apart," I say defensively.

"You must be a cool lady if you put up with that," he says. "Perhaps you don't care too deeply?"

I think of Dan and Andrea, coming to my house as if they were old friends. Dan sitting with Maeve and sharing a bottle of wine, and Hugh and Neil taking for granted the fact that their parents no longer live together, but confident, at last, that a new person in their midst, Andrea, will not affect their happiness. If I told Barry how it was at home, he would be horrified. Instead I say: "I do care. I care very much." And, as if to prove my point, I start to weep.

Instantly he is full of concern. Dabbing my eyes with a handkerchief, I do not notice he is replenishing my glass. I see they are both eying me and I bend my head to hide my tears and to avoid their gaze.

"Oh, come on," says Monica. "He isn't worth it. You are better off without him."

"No, I'm not," I shout at her. "I'm not better off without him. You don't begin to understand. Even you, Barry, with your four broken marriages, cannot begin to understand how I feel today. This is the worst day of my life."

I take a big gulp of whisky, and with that I begin to sob in earnest. I weep for the happiness Dan and I shared at the beginning of our marriage, I weep for our children who can never again experience family life with two parents, I weep for the desolate future that lies before me and, with that in mind, I weep for Tom Byrne who is lost to me forever.

Thinking of Tom, I stammer: "It's not just Dan alone – it's someone . . ." Then I see Monica's eyes widen and I say no more.

"What do you mean?" Like a cat with a mouse she waits to pounce.

Even in my confused state I am not going to give any more away. I finish the drink and slam the glass down on a low glass-topped table. I draw in my breath sharply and let it out with a shudder, like a child. I know I am in the midst of a crying jag but I can't stop myself.

I am conscious of their anxious faces – at least I have stopped them talking. They look at me silently; then at last Monica addresses Barry. "What shall we do?"

"Black coffee?" he suggests.

"No," I scream at him. "No black coffee. If I drink that I shall have to ask the Judge for permission to leave the courtroom."

I put my handkerchief to my face and weep into it until it is a sodden rag, then I press my cheek into a pristine cream cushion and weep into that.

"Well, it beats me," says Barry, a note of exasperation in his voice. "We were only trying to help."

I make a great effort to pull myself together, and I get up and run from the room. I remember where the bathroom is, and my sister does not follow me. I lock the door. I look at myself in the mirror, and I am shocked to see a stranger looking back at me, a distraught face awash with tears.

Then I notice with interest that the room is not quite steady, and I sit on the edge of the bath. It is a very sumptuous bath with gold taps, which I decide are vulgar. I find a fluffy peach-coloured flannel and I hold it under cold water and press it to my hot face. I sit doing this for several minutes, until gradually the room settles down and I begin to feel better. I can imagine the consternation of the two in the sitting-room waiting for me to emerge, wondering what to do with me. I have nothing with me to repair the damage to my face, so I can only dab at it with the cold flannel and hope for the best. I find a comb on a little table in the bathroom and I use that to comb my hair. Also on the table is a bottle of expensive scent, so I have a squirt of that.

When I come out it is obvious that Monica and Barry are immeasurably relieved to see that I look almost normal.

Barry pats my hand. "Better now? Ready for the fray?"

"Yes," I tell him. "I'm ready and, in case you are worried, I have shed my last tear for Dan."

And I mean it.

Chapter 22

Jenny thought Maeve was making the biggest mistake in her life by marrying Jack Deacon. She did everything she could to change her mind, even appealing to her lord, to whom she was now engaged, hoping he would join her in the crusade to stop the marriage from taking place. Rupert feigned interest in the affair, but he had no thoughts for anyone other than Jenny, and could only contribute by saying: "He seems a likeable fellow."

"A likeable fellow!" Jenny cried. "That is not good enough for Maeve."

Maeve was invited to stay a weekend with Jenny's nice parents, in the hope that a glimpse of comfortable middle-class family life would make her realise what she would be missing by marrying someone beneath her. For Jenny was certain Maeve had chosen someone beneath her and, as for Jack's parents, they were beyond the pale.

Even Maeve, writing to Aunt Min and Uncle Frank to tell them the news, impressed upon them not to think of coming to England for the marriage. It would be far too expensive for the four of them, she wrote, but, in reality, she could not face the prospect of introducing them to Mr and Mrs Deacon. Aunt Min and Uncle Frank were poor but genteel people, and Maeve knew they would be horrified by the vulgarity and the abrasive quality of the Deacons.

What Jenny did not realise was that Maeve was completely demoralised. She had thought herself secure being in the chorus of such a brilliant show. It was not stardom, but it was exciting and she was content with the direction her life was heading. She counted herself lucky, until suddenly it was all taken from her. She felt a failure and did not know what to do next; marrying Jack seemed the only solution. Nowadays she would be diagnosed as being on the brink of a nervous breakdown. She would receive counselling and all the traumas of her past would be brought into the open and analysed. Jenny was a sympathetic listener, but there were areas in Maeve's life she knew nothing about. There came a point when she knew she could no longer offer advice and help; Maeve would have to be left to make her own mistakes.

They were married in a registry office with only the bridegroom's parents, Jack's best mate and Jenny Graham present. When they emerged from the building as man and wife they were greeted by a group of laughing girls throwing confetti – some members of the chorus of *Buddies.*

They moved into Jack's flat at the top of the house. He had worked hard during weekends and was proud of all the innovations he had installed. There was a spanking new cooker in the kitchen and Maeve was one of the first people to own a Hoover. She liked the flat, but she could not help wishing they did not have to live in the same building as his parents.

He did not expect her to go out to work. Her fainting fit in the shoe department had worried him, and he was convinced she was delicate. As for moving, he hoped they could afford to do that one day, and he even dreamed of owning a little house, but he was practical, and argued they were better off where they were, paying a peppercorn rent.

He loved her; of that there was no doubt. He was a considerate lover and Maeve, realising she would have to put aside her inhibitions about sex, pretended to enjoy his love-making until, at last, there came a time when she did enjoy it.

She led a strange existence, wandering about on her own during the day, sitting on a park bench smoking endless cigarettes, listening to the band playing and occasionally meeting Jenny or one of the other girls for lunch.

She did not spend much time at the flat, and Mrs Deacon, who complained about everything, complained about that. "It could do with a good clean," she said, on one of the rare occasions when she climbed the stairs to the attic. It was an unfair comment because Maeve cleaned the flat every day, and did not go out until the housework was done.

She looked forward to Jack's return in the evening, and she always had a substantial meal prepared for him. She was a good cook. Aunt Min's training had seen to that, but even her cooking was criticised by her mother-in-law. "All that new-fangled stuff will make Jack fat," she said. In particular, pasta was scorned as being 'only fit for Italians'. Jack stood up for his wife, and refused to listen to his mother. "Ignore her," he told Maeve.

It was significant that Maeve could not bring herself to call Jack's mother anything but Mrs Deacon. Lily would be difficult and Mother was out of the question, Mrs Deacon she remained to the end. Maeve could not forget that avenging figure standing in her room, threatening to evict her because she could not pay the rent. That impression would stay with her always, and she could not dispel it from her mind.

It was Jenny who suggested that Maeve should get herself a job. "Anything would be better than wandering around on your own all day," she said – Jenny, who was kept busy from dawn to dusk, looking after a big house and an increasing family. Maeve took her friend's advice and did get a job, but not one that Jenny would ever have contemplated for her. She started working in the local library, and she was to work there for many years to come. Her fellow librarians were congenial companions, Mary Abbott, a married woman with no children, like Maeve, and Mr Truelove, bespectacled and dedicated to his work. The job had the added attraction for Maeve that she could take the books home to read and, when she was not busy, she could read in the quiet atmosphere of the library. When people were faced with the ticklish question of choosing a good read they started to turn to Maeve for advice.

The weeks became months and the months became years, and Maeve settled into an uneasy happiness. Somehow, she had imagined her marriage with Jack was a temporary expedient; now she began to realise it was a permanency. She wondered why there was no baby. It had happened so easily before, and she thought it must be God's judgement on her for her sinful behaviour. Although she no longer attended Mass there was enough of the Catholic girl left in her to believe this to be true.

Jack longed for a child, and Mrs Deacon was quick to exploit the situation. "It's a shame you are barren," she said to Maeve. "Why don't you go to the doctor and find out what's wrong with you?"

Maeve did go to the doctor; perhaps it was her mother-in-law's repeated use of the awful word 'barren' that made her take this step. It had an empty sound to it that reflected her feelings about herself. The doctor examined her, and said he would like to see Jack.

"There's nothing wrong with *him*," his mother

expostulated when she heard. "It's your fault, not his. You can never have a child, that's evident."

Maeve felt so angry she almost told her that she had given birth many years before but, just in time, she stopped herself. She was sensible enough to know she would never hear the end of that admission and, anyway, why should she tell Mrs Deacon something she had not even admitted to her husband, or to her best friend?

Jack did go to see the doctor on his own accord, and he was told that having German measles in his boyhood had made it unlikely that he would become a father. Man-like, and devastated by this information, he did manage to blurt it out to his wife, but he never divulged it to his mother. Therefore, Maeve continued to be blamed for their inability to conceive a child.

In the meantime, Jenny grew stouter every year and was now the mother of six children. Maeve, in her late thirties, and looking older, envied her more than she could say. It seemed to her that Jenny had everything she lacked: a beautiful house, a rich husband and (most important of all) sons and daughters. When she was asked to visit them, Jack did not accompany her. He had at the beginning, but later made the excuse that his work prevented him getting time off. It wasn't exacting work, he was a humble clerk in a government office, and Maeve knew full well the real reason for him not accepting the invitation. He felt out of place there and was tongue-tied in the presence of his host. For Maeve's sake, he tried it once but he swore to himself never again would he lay himself open to feelings of degradation and inadequacy. He was aware that Rupert and Jenny did their best to be nice to him, but he found their pleasantries patronising; better to stick to his mates in the pub, he thought.

When Maeve thought about it in later years she blamed herself for not realising the depth of Jack's despair and grief that he could not have a child. She should have been more understanding. When she went to stay with Jenny she had no idea how much he fretted until her return. "Bloody snobs," said his mother to Maeve, "I don't know why you bother with them."

She bothered because it was like stepping into a different world, the luxury of a room of her own, sinking into a soft comfortable bed and awaking in the morning to the sounds of young children in the house. It was so different to the atmosphere in the flat in 19 Primrose Road. Sometimes, she felt resentful towards Jack for not getting them out of there.

Mr Deacon died, and his passing left no impact on anyone. His widow called in painters and decorators to freshen up the basement and fill up the cracks. Mysteriously, the parrot disappeared. One day it was there, squawking as usual, the next day it had gone, and the perch as well. Jack was continually asking his mother to tell him what had happened to it, but she would not say. After the funeral, Maeve thought a great deal about Mr Deacon who had few friends and a wife who did not respect him. She supposed that at one time there must have been love between them, but it was hard to imagine. He skulked around the basement, filling the place with smoke, and his leering conniving expression was repulsive. Maeve wondered what good he was in the world and why God, in his wisdom, had sanctified his existence. After he was gone, it was as if he had never been, a man of no substance at all.

When she returned after visiting Jenny and her family it was gratifying to see Jack's evident pleasure in having her to himself again; they lay close in their big double bed and made love, and for a brief time Maeve was completely happy. Jack as a lover was a transformed person, but the next day he clamped his bowler hat on his head and set off for his dull office job, and life for him and for Maeve settled down to its usual pedestrian pace. It seemed as if nothing would alter it.

Then came 1939 and the war – and that changed everything.

*"This is a tale you will tell your grandchildren,
and mighty bored they'll be."*

LIEUTENANT-GENERAL SIR BRIAN HORROCKS,
KCB, KBE, DSO, MC

Chapter 23

Lance-Sergeant John Deacon, who had seen action in the desert, was sure that this final surge forward would bring the war to an end.

'Over by Christmas' was on everyone's lips; optimistic words because the success of the Normandy landings had put new heart into people weary of fighting. At last they thought they could see a light at the end of a very long tunnel. It was such a relief that it might soon be over and they could return to their homes. No one had doubted for a moment that we would win eventually; it had just been such a hard struggle.

Jack repeated the words to his best mate, Les Lambert, who was sitting beside him, as close as a Siamese twin. "Over by Christmas."

Les tended to look on the dark side. "We'll be lucky," he said gloomily.

"Mark my words," said Jack, "you'll be playing cricket on the village green in 1945."

Cricket was Les's main topic of conversation, that and his children, a boy and a girl. Jack listened patiently, not having experienced either of these delights. He was a little sensitive about the children, but he did not betray his feelings to Les. He would have liked to be able to say he was the father of a couple of kids, and he knew their lack was a source of sadness for Maeve.

Jack thought about Maeve a great deal in his few quiet moments, and he thought too about living in the country and playing cricket. It was a daydream he indulged in from time to time. He reckoned he was too old to learn the game, but the country sounded good and he wondered why he and Maeve and his old ma had been so hell-bent on staying in London. He was determined that after the war they would move – all three of them. He would try and get some job in a market town; he did not know if his old job was still there for him but, anyway, it was time for a change. The war had made him see things differently. They would have to rent at first but maybe, in time, they could save for a deposit on their own house and acquire a mortgage. Surely, after all they had done, the government would give them some help.

Such matters had never bothered him before; it had been easy living in his mother's house, paying her just enough rent to keep her happy. Too easy – he realised that now. His mother might be a problem but she would have to come with them, Maeve would understand that – she was a wonderful woman and he was lucky to have her. He worried about her; at one time he feared she was in more danger than he was, and he began to think she should move to Jenny's house in the country, much as he disliked the idea, but Maeve insisted on staying with her mother-in-law, now in failing health, and the two women had been together all through the Blitz. Thankfully, that was ended now, but you never know, thought Jack, anything could happen in wartime.

His brain teemed with these thoughts as he sat in the glider, crushed between two men, one of whom was Les, encumbered with equipment, a heavy harness and a parachute. The sides of the glider seemed paper-thin, which made the occupants feel very vulnerable, and there was a strange atmosphere, claustrophobic and chilly at the same time. Despite the weighty uniform and the trappings Jack felt cold, and he looked forward to leaving the aircraft. Experimentally, he wiggled his toes in the stout boots he was wearing because he felt his feet had lost their identity, and had distanced themselves from the rest of his body.

He had no fears about the descent although, drifting down to earth, he knew he was an easy target. He felt the sun on his face and it warmed him. It was a spectacular sight, hundreds of men and parachutes covering the sky. He thought he could gaze at it forever but the sharp bump to earth reminded him of what he had to do next. He had been trained for this moment, and he quickly disentangled himself from his parachute and left it lying on the ground; then he started to run. At the same time, it seemed to him, everyone around him did the same, and the ground was festooned with abandoned parachutes and the air filled with the sound of men running and the shouting of orders. Chaos ensued as Jeeps and light guns were dragged from the gliders, and green, yellow and purple smoke rose to indicate the sites of assembly points of the various units. Wireless operators were trying to establish contact, but without success, and this was a situation that would continue during the days ahead.

At last some sort of sanity prevailed, and the men began to form a group and this became bigger and bigger until, at last, the order came for them to march.

"No sign of any Jerries here," Jack said to Les. The road they marched along was narrow and sloped down on either side. The September air was fresh in their nostrils, a welcome relief after the airlessness of the aircraft they had left a while before, and they took big gulps of it as they marched. Jack felt invigorated, and the countryside around him had a reassuring familiarity about it, unlike the alien desert where he had been for so many months; this was almost like home.

They passed through a village and the inhabitants came out in droves to welcome them, pretty Dutch girls throwing flowers and kisses at them, some of them even catching hold of their rough textured khaki sleeves, calling out blessings and endearments in a strange language. It was very satisfying, and the men basked in the glory of it. Their steps grew lighter as they marched ahead, their objective eight miles distant – a place called Arnhem.

There was an unexpected skirmish on the route, sudden gunfire from a wood adjoining the road. It was returned and the German soldiers emerged, holding up their hands in surrender. Their dishevelled appearance heartened their captors; they looked like a defeated army. Many of them were wandering the countryside, having been separated from their units because of heavy casualties. They had lost their leaders and there was no one to tell them what to do – the fight had gone out of them. What they did not know, and the organisers of Market Garden (the code name given to the allied invasion) did not know was that orders from German High Command had been issued to establish detachments at bridges and ferries in Holland to intercept the remains of this tattered army and bring them under military discipline again. They were to be given new artillery so that they could become loyal subjects of the Fatherland once more. So both sides were in for a big surprise, Jack and his compatriots marching to Arnhem unaware that it had become a centre of rehabilitation for the German army, and the German leaders themselves amazed by the sight of thousands of parachutes floating to earth from the sky. They had been ordered to put new life into what seemed like a vanquished army, not face the British 1st Airborne Division.

In the gathering dusk Jack marched towards Arnhem where it was hoped they would succeed in taking over the bridge on the river Rhine. Please, God, thought Jack, it will all be as simple as this.

It was dark when they entered the streets of Arnhem, and ominously quiet. No doubt there were people behind closed curtains listening to the muffled sounds of the soldiers who had come to liberate them after four years of occupation. The men moved stealthily through the empty streets.

They took over three houses on the road facing the bridge. The Colonel and his detachment chose the house nearest the bridge, and Major Manners, Lieutenant Goode and a handful of men, including Jack and Les, were sent next door to Number Ten. The house on the other side was set up as a First Aid Post.

Major Manners beat on the door, which was opened by a smiling young woman. She was the daughter of the household, and happy to admit them. They followed her up carpeted stairs, sweaty smelly men with great clumping boots that left marks on the floor. The young Major, who had tried to look older by growing a moustache, apologised over and over again for the intrusion. The other members of the family, an old woman, her fairly elderly son and daughter, mother of the person who had let them in, looked on dispassionately. Perhaps the rigours of German occupation had blunted their emotions, and they could not look kindly on their saviours.

Orders were given for the removal of the curtains from the windows. Heavy artillery was lugged up the stairs; machine guns were set up at the windows. Already what was once a home had become a barracks. An anti-tank gun was set up close to the wall on one side of the house.

Some semblance of order was established; the family was banished to one corner of the house, the army occupied the rest. Where there had been quiet constant noise prevailed but not, as yet, the noise of gunfire – that was to come later.

That night they looked out at the bridge, shining like a giant metallic snake in the moonlight. It looked deserted and an easy target.

During the next day German mortar fire hit the house and started a fire in the upstairs section. It was speedily put out by the occupying soldiers, but it struck fear into the hearts of the owners, four years of living with food rationing, blackouts and threats from the Security Service was nothing compared to the terror that had descended into their midst. Jack heard the plaintive cries of the grandmother; she was too old to be brave, and, for some reason, he thought of his mother.

The occupants of the house next door made the first assault on the bridge, and Major Manners assembled his men at the windows of Number Ten to give them cover.

An incredibly brave officer walked slowly and nonchalantly across the bridge, followed by his men, not walking upright, as he was, but bent down and holding their guns at the ready. The watchers in Number Ten held their breath; for once there was silence. This was suddenly broken by the sound of gunfire from all sides; the men on the bridge ducked, some of them fell, never to rise again. There was nothing for it but to retreat, and this they did, dragging the wounded with them. The noise was deafening and the family in Number Ten huddled against the wall in the area they had been designated.

All the time they hoped help would arrive – they expected it, and every hour that passed was a disappointment. There was no radio communication at all, so they did not know what was happening to the other battalions. In fact, they had come across unforeseen German resistance, which prevented them from marching towards Arnhem. Although every effort had been made to get there, it had proved impossible. They were cut off by the Germans from the rest of the division, a melancholy fact that did not dawn on those unfortunates stationed by the bridge until the fourth day of the siege.

It was decided that a second attempt on the bridge would be made in the early hours of the following morning. This time Jack Deacon took part and Lieutenant Goode led the party.

Jack had the greatest admiration for Geoffrey

Goode. He was friendly and had no 'side' in spite of the fact he had been to a public school, and Jack thought he was a different character to Rupert whom, perhaps unfairly, he did not like. They had not been to Eton at the same time because Rupert was much older. Geoffrey Goode was barely twenty years old and looked as if there was no need for him to shave. Because of his smooth chin and fair hair the men called him 'Baby Face' and one of them was heard to say: "He misses his mummy." Jack thought the opposite must be true; how must a mother feel knowing all the time that her hardly grown-up son is in such danger? It didn't bear thinking about, and made him almost glad he did not have a son, for who knows what the future had in store? And yet, thought Jack, preparing for the task that lay ahead on the morrow, if he had a son he would like him to grow up like Mr Goode. Being so much older he felt sort of responsible for him, almost tenderness.

He watched his back, straight as a ramrod, walking across the bloody bridge, and Jack knew that in one second he could be with them no more. As he thought this, he felt the sharp sting of a bullet in his thigh, and he saw Geoffrey Goode fall to the ground. Jack stepped in front of the body and went on firing and went on walking, until Major Manners, from the house, ordered the withdrawal through a megaphone. Jack hoisted the inert body of Mr Goode on to his sturdy shoulders and ran with him to the side of the bridge. It felt to him as if every part of his body was being attacked by snipers' bullets and with great difficulty, for his arms were wounded, he propped the young officer against a wall. It was a sheltered bit of the bridge and he thought he might be hidden from view there.

"My leg's gone," said Geoffrey Goode, trying very hard to stay in the picture and not lapse into unconsciousness, which would have been an easy solution for him.

Jack looked and saw a blood-soaked trouser-leg, strangely flat. He knew there was no way he could get him back to the house or to the First Aid Post. The men attempting to return had been shot at from all sides, and the road was strewn with bodies. Jack wondered if one of those bodies was Les.

"I'll be back," said Jack quickly. "I'll come back and collect you later when it's quietened down a bit."

There was no reply. Jack bent his head and made a dash for the house. Miraculously, he was not hit. He did not like the idea of making his way to the First Aid Post; it seemed like tempting fate, so he allowed Les to dress his wounds. Les, who had managed to return to the house, unharmed, had taken a course in First Aid and considered himself an expert, as good as any doctor, but Jack was not a good patient; he swore at his old mate who was trying to help him.

More mortar bombs were aimed at the house. This time the area occupied by the owners was set alight and, clutching each other in a trembling mass of fear and disbelief, they scuttled to a shed at the bottom of the garden. There they remained until Jack came to collect them – the fire was extinguished and lunch was ready. They all assembled in the kitchen, and soldiers and civilians gratefully ate the meal Jack had cooked for them, fried potatoes and baked beans.

Major Manners praised him for his part in the morning's activity. "You did well," he said. Jack knew that meant his name would be put forward for a decoration, but he thought, what good is a medal to a man who has no son to pass it down to?

Anyway, his mind was not on medals, but on the man lying beside the bridge with his blood slowly seeping from his body. More than six hours had passed since he left him there. In all probability he was dead by now, but Jack felt he had to find out for certain.

During the early afternoon he wondered if he could return to the bridge, and he asked Major Manners to advise him.

"The chances of him being alive are very small."

"But even if there's a small chance . . ." Jack argued. He and the Major looked out of the window and everything seemed tranquil enough, and then there was a sound, the unmistakable sound of a tank advancing towards them. They looked at each other expectantly. Could this mean that help was arriving at last? Everyone ran to his post at the windows.

They were met with a barrage of fire, and Major Manners was hit at once. Jack in horror dragged him to the side. Then he looked at the window and saw Les standing there, and then falling to the ground. He stepped over his body and peered through the glass, being very careful to keep out of sight. It was a Tiger tank that was coming towards them.

The Tiger tank was considered by the British and Americans to be invincible. In Normandy its sweeping destruction prevented an entire division from advancing. A massive fifty-six tons in weight the Tiger had an armour 100 mm thick and was armed with the tank version of the 88 mm gun. Fascinated, Jack watched its progress, as like a primordial monster it moved forward, swaying from side to side as if in menacing fury.

It was there because two battered Panzer divisions of the German army had been sent to Arnhem to 'recuperate' and to be equipped with new tanks from a depot near Cleves. It was yet another cruel shaft of fate that impeded the Market Garden operation.

Jack went down the stairs two at a time; the blinding fury he was feeling hastened his steps. He positioned himself behind the anti-tank gun leaning against the wall by the side of the house. In the training sessions Jack had attended in England the weapon had been forced into the ground, but the hardness of the pavement made this impossible, and he had to hold it in his hands. It was weighty and the pain in his injured arms was agonising. It was difficult not to start firing right away, but he had been taught to wait. When he thought the tank was less than one hundred yards away he started to fire. He went on firing in a frenzy of rage, oblivious to the bullets being hailed upon him. In the confusion he had the thought that it was only a question of time, and it was important to achieve as much as possible in the minutes left to him.

Suddenly, to his surprise, the beast stopped in its tracks. Bodies fell out of it, rolling over and over on the hard surface of the road. There was a great explosion and the tank became a ball of fire and sparks. The dragon was dead. Jack felt a surge of exultation course through his body; it was the same feeling he had after having sex with his wife but, on this occasion, it was triggered by the fact that he has just annihilated a handful of fellow human beings. It was a strange sensation of triumph for a kind and gentle man like Jack.

He left the scene as quickly as possible and returned to the house. There, his companions, full of admiration and disbelief at what he had done, surrounded him, and slapped him on his poor wounded shoulders until he begged them to stop. Someone gave him a flask of whisky and he took a gulp from it. Even the owners of the house favoured him with smiles.

Major Manners, lying on a stretcher, managed to raise an arm in Jack's direction before he was taken to the First Aid Post. But nothing could be done for Les, and Jack felt that no amount of praise and adulation could recompense him for the loss of such a good friend.

Chapter 24

After nightfall Jack made his way back to the bridge. After the uproar of the day everything seemed quiet. No one observed a man running across the road in the moonlight.

He dreaded the idea that Geoffrey Goode might be dead. He had been lying there for the best part of a whole day with a death-threatening injury so it would be no surprise to Jack to find that he had not survived but, when he bent over his body, he thought he heard a little moan. He made no sound when Jack, with a groan of pain, hoisted him over his shoulders. A strange silhouette against the night sky, the two of them made for the First Aid Post at house Number Eight. Here there was utter confusion. Jack propped the body in a sitting position against a wall, and Geoffrey's head fell forward on his chest. By now Jack was thinking of him as Geoffrey; he was like a brother or a son, and it was imperative to save him.

A medical orderly informed him that Major Jordan, the surgeon, had been killed. He pointed with a shaking hand at all the men who needed treatment – Major Manners among them. "I can't promise anything," he said. "You can see the situation."

He wore a white coat that was spattered with blood. Although he had recently carried a man whose leg had been shot away, the sight sickened Jack; he felt all traces of civilised behaviour had been lost.

The man said; "A private house has been taken over by a Dutch surgeon. It's about ten miles away. You might try taking him there. There's a Jeep parked outside, and you can use that as long as you bring it back before morning."

"Of course," said Jack, and thought how lucky he was that this helpful man had the power to make this offer – because everyone in authority had been killed he was the only one left to make decisions. It occurred to him that he was in a similar position, now that Major Manners had gone, and it made him anxious to get going so that he could return to the men in the house before daybreak.

"Have you checked the pulse?" said the man. "You don't want to make a wasted journey."

He stepped forwards and laid his fingers on Geoffrey's neck, and then bent the head back and lifted the lid of one eye. "He's alive," he said, "just." He produced a tattered envelope and a stub of pencil from his pocket, and he drew a rough map, marking the roads. "It's in the country, at the end of a long drive – a mansion."

"Thanks."

The orderly helped lift Jack into the Jeep.

Jack drove slowly in case his passenger should slide down the seat or fall to one side.

"We'll get there," he said to the lolling head.

He had the envelope in his hand and he kept referring to it. The drive out into the countryside was undisturbed. There was a stillness in the air, and the war seemed very far away. He came to the long drive and, when he turned into it, he could see that trees flanked it, and the house, when it loomed into the headlights, was majestic. The sort of stately home Maeve had sometimes persuaded him to visit when he was at home, on a holiday or during a weekend, but he knew this one was not open to the public; it was open to the sick and maimed, by courtesy of the owners who, no doubt, still occupied a small corner of their home. Inside the carpets had been ripped up, and Jack stepped on to bare boards when he entered with Geoffrey straddled on his back.

There were signs of life here, instead of the hopeless inactivity of the First Aid Post. Someone stepped forward to help him, and together they lifted Geoffrey on to an operating table. Skilful hands started cutting through the material of the blood-sodden trousers. Jack turned away from the sight.

A man stood quietly observing the orderlies snipping away at Geoffrey's trousers. His air of authority convinced Jack that he was the Dutch surgeon. He was a short stout middle-aged man. He too wore a white coat but it was clean. It was apparent that things at this place were still running in a smooth and efficient way.

"You were lucky to get here in one piece," he said to Jack. His English was near perfect. "Where are you going now?"

"Back to the bridge."

"I don't envy you."

He escorted Jack to the door of what looked like a spacious kitchen. "Before you go," he said, "stay and have a cup of tea. That is what you like, isn't it?"

"That, and beer," said Jack.

"I'm afraid the owners of this house have no beer. A cellar full of bottles of wine, but no beer – I'm sorry."

"That's OK," said Jack awkwardly. He wished he had not mentioned the beer as a sort of joke.

"It would have pleased me to give you what you wanted," pursued the surgeon. "It was a brave thing to do, bringing your friend to this place. When you see him again, you will probably be back in your own country."

"I hope so," said Jack without conviction.

He was given two cups of tea, and he smoked two cigarettes. On the way out he stopped and chatted with some of the wounded who were sitting around in armchairs. It all looked comfortable and cosy and Jack, suffering from his own wounds, wished he could join them. As it was, he felt he had delayed leaving for long enough, but he managed to waylay one of the orderlies whose face he recognised from before, and he asked him for news of Mr Goode.

"He's in the operating theatre now," the man told him. "His leg will be amputated and he's lost a lot of blood, but he's in good hands."

"Thanks for that," Jack said.

He raised his hand in a gesture of farewell to the men in the armchairs.

"Good luck, mate," one of them called out as he left.

On the journey back to Arnhem he had time to think. In his mind he relived his encounter with the Tiger tank. He was proud of himself for having destroyed it single-handed, and he looked forward to a time when he could relate the whole episode in detail to Maeve. He could picture her sweet listening face, and she would not say a word until he had finished.

It was beginning to get light and he could see the countryside more clearly. The leaves on the trees were just beginning to assume their autumn colours, butter yellow and red, and a few leaves drifted to the ground in front of the jeep. When he reached the suburbs there was no one about, people slept behind closed curtains. Suddenly he felt full of hope; Geoffrey would live, he was sure of that now and XXX Corps would reach them somehow. Things had got to get better.

He sensed rather than heard something coming towards him.

"Don't tell me . . ." said Jack aloud, ducking his head in a desperate bid to avoid the inevitable. Everything round him disintegrated, including himself, in a massive explosion of fire, pain and blinding light.

Chapter 25

Lieutenant Goode came to see Maeve He was driven to 19 Rosemary Road in an armoured car, and Maeve and Mrs Deacon, standing behind the grimy lace curtain in the basement flat, watched him struggling down the steep steps. They thought he would never make it because he was on crutches

Jack would have noticed a change in him. The fresh-faced boy was gone and was replaced by a thin anxious-looking young man. Maeve noticed a pulse throbbing in his cheek, and she did not know whether to help him as he managed to stow his sticks while endeavouring to lower himself in a chair. She thought he might be embarrassed by assistance, so she hastened to the kitchen to make tea. When she returned she found her mother-in-law sitting in silence; Mrs Deacon could not think of anything to say to him. He looked relieved to see Maeve, and he stammered when he explained how Jack had saved his life. She tried not to look at the pinned-back empty trouser leg but, perhaps noticing her averted gaze, he told her that he was going to Roehampton to be fitted with an artificial limb.

He thought she had a sad face, with an elusive quality of beauty. He wondered whether the mean old cow with her treated her well. He remembered Jack telling him proudly that his wife had been in the chorus of *Buddies*. He had seen the film version made in Hollywood before the war. "I saw it twice," he said. "It was a wonderful show."

"I was in it a long time ago, in the stage production," she said. She had not had the heart to see the film.

He told her that operation Market Garden had not been a resounding success, and many of the men who had been with him trying to take the bridge at Arnhem, and failing, had been wounded, and had been left behind during the evacuation and subsequently taken prisoners of war by the German army. He had been more fortunate; the Dutch resistance had helped him escape.

He tried to describe the house where they had lived. "Everything went wrong when Major Manners was injured," he said, "but Jack saved the day by destroying a Tiger tank."

Of course, it meant nothing to them, although Maeve did her best to understand as much as she could. She felt she owed it to Jack to do that. She did not know anything about a man called Major Manners, or about the Tiger tank for that matter.

She had heard about Les Lambert though, and she asked about him.

"Killed," said Geoffrey Goode sadly.

He did not stay long. He tired easily, and Mrs Deacon's basement flat was oppressive. They had not asked him to attempt all the stairs to Maeve's flat, which was more welcoming.

After he had gone the two women sat in silence. Mrs Deacon spoke at last. "Well, he'll stay at home now," she said, "and his mum will be pleased about that. He'll be all right from now on, with his new leg and all." She spoke with resentment in her voice. She thought it very unfair that her Jack had been taken from her while others had survived.

Maeve tried to help her in her grief. She still clung to childish beliefs, although she seldom went to Mass, and she thought her mother-in-law should turn to God for comfort. She suggested gently that she should go to church, but Mrs Deacon said stubbornly: "His son came back, didn't He? He came back from the dead, but no one else can do that. His mother saw Him again, but us other mothers have lost their sons for good. It's not right, and I'll take no part in it."

Maeve received a letter from Major Manners. He was home again, after being in a prisoner of war camp, and later freed by the arrival of the Canadians. He wrote glowingly of Jack, and it was he, and several others, who had recommended Jack for a posthumous Victoria Cross. Maeve tried to show the letter to her mother-in-law but Mrs Deacon refused to look at it. It was doubtful at one time whether she would go to Buckingham Palace, but Maeve managed to persuade her by saying she was too nervous to attend the ceremony on her own. Reluctantly, Mrs Deacon agreed to accompany her.

It was the last investiture of the war. They sat on gilt chairs amongst an audience of mothers, fathers, wives, sisters and brothers, and while they waited, they listened to popular music in the background, mostly tunes from Ivor Novello and Noel Coward. Maeve suggested that Mrs Deacon should go up and collect the medal from King George the Sixth, but the older woman was not interested in it. It was no compensation for the loss of her son.

Afterwards, standing outside the palace, they had their photographs taken by the press, two dowdy women wearing shapeless coats, felt hats pulled over their eyes and stout low-heeled shoes on their feet.

Maeve gets awkwardly to her feet, and moves heavily to a chest of drawers in her room. She takes out a faded leather case, and hands it to Hugh. He opens it and looks inside.

"That is the Victoria Cross," I tell him. "It is the highest award for gallantry. You see what it says on it: *For Valour*. Only a very brave man would receive this, and it is very precious."

"Can I take it out of its box?" Hugh asks Maeve.

"Of course, darling."

He holds it, almost reverently, in the palm of his hand, the sombre dark cross and the unassuming maroon ribbon. For a schoolboy this medal holds all the romantic dreams of high adventure and enormous courage. He has heard of it before but he has never expected to meet someone who owns such an object. He wonders why Maeve has never mentioned it before this.

Neil sidles up to his brother and looks at it as well, but he is too young to realise its significance. His lessons at school have not encompassed World War II yet.

Hugh asks politely: "Was this given to a member of your family?"

"To my husband," says Maeve simply.

"Mr Bailey?"

"No, not Mr Bailey – he was my second husband. Before I met him I was married to someone called Jack Deacon who was killed at Arnhem – that was a big battle that took place towards the end of the war."

"I've heard of Arnhem," says Hugh, nodding, "and there is a film about it."

"That's right."

"What did he do to get this?"

She starts to get to her feet again. "No, don't move," I say. "Just tell me what you want and I'll get it for you."

"Oh, thank you, darling, there's a brown envelope in the left-hand top drawer, on the right."

I bring her the envelope that contains the Citation

describing Jack's exploits. She gives it to Hugh, and he sits on the edge of her bed and reads it very carefully. Then he hands it to me.

It begins with the words *'For supreme courage and devotion to duty.'*

It goes on to say that Lance-Sergeant John Deacon was part of a platoon ordered to assault the southern end of the bridge over the river Rhine at Arnhem. Despite incessant fire he continued to advance across the bridge and only when casualties became too heavy was he ordered to withdraw. He managed to move Lieutenant Geoffrey Goode who had been badly wounded to the comparative safety of a place beside the bridge.

The Citation explains that Lance-Sergeant Deacon and his platoon occupied a house that was vital to the defence of the bridge and he personally helped to organise the running of the house. It goes on to say: *'There is no doubt that had it not been for the bravery of the officers and men occupying the house the Arnhem bridge would not have been held for such a long time. After his commanding officer was wounded Lance-Sergeant Deacon was left in charge of the platoon and, single-handed, he destroyed one Tiger tank with a PIAT gun. Later, that same day, at great risk to himself and despite his wounds, he returned to the bridge where he had left Lieutenant Goode under cover on one side of the bridge, and he took him to a hospital some ten miles distant. It was on the journey back to rejoin the men in his platoon that Lance-Sergeant Deacon was killed.*

He was born in London in 1900 and is buried in the Commonwealth War Graves Commission Cemetery at Oosterbeek, Arnhem."

We are quiet, thinking about Jack on that momentous day so many years ago.

"Did you visit his grave?" Hugh asks Maeve.

"No, I never did."

There is a little pause, and Hugh says: "I shall go and see it one day."

"Bless you for that," says Maeve.

"You must have been very proud," I say.

"I was and I am," she says. "It was the only really worthwhile thing I did in my whole life, marrying a bloody hero!"

Both the boys laugh then, and the slightly sombre tone of the conversation is lightened at once, and the case holding the medal is closed, and it and the tattered old brown envelope containing the Citation are put back in the drawer.

Chapter 26

Many months elapsed after Jack's death before Maeve
was able to visit Jenny and her family again. She was
asked on frequent occasions, but she always refused
saying she had to stay in London to be near her mother-
in-law. Mrs. Deacon had suffered two small strokes,
and was now a sad grey little woman who managed to
potter around the basement flat making ineffectual
efforts to clean it, but mostly sat in a chair by the front
window staring sightlessly at the railings below the
street outside. Perhaps she was reliving that moment
when the boy propped his bicycle against the railings,
and descended the steps to her door, carrying the bright
yellow envelope in his hand. Despite the sad tidings
contained in those envelopes during the war years, the
vibrant colour was never changed. She never smiled,
and this alone was hard for Maeve to bear because she
was still young enough to know that life must go on.

Not for Mrs Deacon though; her life ended when her beloved Jack was killed. The death of her husband had not affected her; he was a lost cause, but the son they had conceived was the star of her universe. That was why she had felt no woman was good enough for him. And he had married a common chorus girl!

Maeve thought a great deal about the Deacons, that strange couple, the seedy little man and the aggressive hard woman who had, between them, managed to produce a heroic figure – a flower of England. She carried the Victoria Cross in its cushioned case downstairs, and suggested she put it in a place where her mother-in-law could see it, but the old woman waved it aside. She was not interested; she only wanted her boy back.

Knowing that he would never come back, she turned to Maeve who was the only person she knew who could provide her with any comfort. Maeve longed to get away but no pleas from her friend, Jenny, could persuade her to leave.

"I have to stay with her," she said.

"Why is that?" Jenny wanted to know. "She has never done anything for you, the selfish old bitch."

It was true, Mrs Deacon had never shown any kindness to Maeve, but a sort of understanding had developed between the two women; they had been through a great deal together, first the terrors of the Blitz and then their shared grief. The older woman knew only too well that she relied completely on

Maeve. She never thanked her for her help, but the look of anguished fear she assumed when Maeve had to leave the house to go to the shops for food made the younger woman realise how dependent she was on her. It would be an act of cruelty to leave her alone for any length of time.

And so she stayed, and the terrible monotony of her days engulfed her like an illness from which there was no escape. When, at the end of each long day, her tired feet took her to the bedroom at the top of the house, all she wanted to do was to sleep and forget. She did not read because the library, and the job with it, had packed up early in the war. She lay in the bed she had once shared with Jack, and the emptiness of the rooms below her filled her with fear. Miss Shaw had long ago escaped to the country, and Mr Langridge was the only lodger remaining. His lascivious smile when Maeve met him on the stairs made her hurry to get past him, and sometimes when she was lying in bed, staring into the darkness, she wondered what she would do if she heard steps on the stairs leading to the attic flat.

A sort of calm had settled over London; the Blitz was over and the only reminders of it were the gaping holes where the bombs had fallen. Everything was at a low key, people walked around at a slow pace, bemused by what had happened to them. Only the Yanks injected a spark of life into the old city and, at night, blackness settled over the rows and rows of little houses, like a suffocating blanket.

Then one day Mrs Deacon had her third and last stroke. Terrified, Maeve telephoned for an ambulance, and her mother-in-law was taken to St Bartholomew's Hospital, where she died. Maeve sat by her bed holding her hand and, before it became still in her clasp, she saw a frantic look in the old woman's eyes, the desire to say something she was unable to articulate. Maeve would never know the thoughts darting through the dying woman's mind. It was over, and she walked through the bleak corridors of the hospital and wondered what she should do next.

The ugly house in Primrose Road now belonged to her, but in wartime it was worthless. The sense of inadequacy that Maeve felt at this time was familiar to her. Jenny came to her rescue and, after the funeral, she had no difficulty in persuading Maeve to come with her to the country. The house was shut up, and it joined many abandoned houses in London, their windows blocked up, blind and unlived in; waiting to be revitalised after the war when, slowly, but surely, their value escalated until the estate agents could describe them as desirable.

Jenny's two older boys were at Eton; her three daughters were at home educated by a lady who came each day from the village, and her third son, the result of one passionate short leave, was too young to do anything else but stay at home and enchant his mother and Maeve. That was Jenny's excuse to her husband for admitting Maeve to her household; she was there to help her look after her youngest child.

Rupert was a lieutenant colonel in a Guards regiment, and his wife lived in constant fear that something would happen to him. She could relate to Maeve's suffering, and she began to think she had been wrong about Jack who had turned out to be a very special person. Rupert, when he came for a few days leave, swallowed his misgivings and made Maeve feel welcome in his home. He clasped her hand and pronounced that what Jack had done had been a 'good show' – and Maeve realised that there was something awesome, demanding respect, about the Victoria Cross. It made the distinction between an ordinary doing-his-best kind of fellow and a devil-may-care positive hero and, with one stroke, it wiped out all the differences of class. She wished she had been more understanding about Jack, had appreciated his worth during his life. She had taken him for granted, and his evident love for her she had accepted without question; now it was too late to tell him how important he was to her.

Jenny thought her friend had lost all her former bloom, and she resolved to do something about it. It gave her a respite from all her anxieties to try and reorganise Maeve's life. She felt that Maeve had been floundering in the wilderness for too long, and some stability was needed.

Stability came in the form of Theodore Bailey, who was a fairly near neighbour and had known Rupert and his parents for many years. He had been married, and the marriage had been annulled, a fact that mystified

Jenny and had never been fully explained to her. He had inherited a gun factory, producing beautifully crafted guns for the rich, which, during the war, became a munitions factory, making a huge profit. He was exempt from national service because of his importance in running the factory. He was an impressive-looking man, rather serious-minded but, nevertheless, in Jenny's view, an ideal husband for her beleaguered friend.

Maeve was not interested in the possibility of a second marriage. She wanted to get over the loss of the first, and she was happy the way she was, happier than she had been for years. Simon, aged three, Jenny's youngest child, was a delight to her, and she was given the pleasant task of looking after him while Jenny attended to the needs of the other children. He was her only godchild; Jenny gave birth to her sixth child before Rupert's family would agree to her best friend being a godmother. Maeve and Simon went for walks together, played games and it was Maeve who bathed him in the evening and kissed him goodnight when she tucked him into his little bed. She had not realised before what an affinity she had with small children; after being in the company of an old woman for so long it was absolute joy to be with someone so sweet-smelling and innocent. She never tired of listening to his childish chatter or holding his tiny hand in hers. When he put his plump arms around her neck, she felt herself truly loved by the most delightful creature in the world – she had no need in her life for the attentions of Theo Bailey.

Jenny was happy to see two people she loved so content in each other's company, but she knew the idyll could not last. When Simon attained the age of seven years he would go to boarding school, as his brothers had done. It was a tradition Rupert's family had followed for many years, and Rupert himself was adamant against change; no feminine protestations would alter his resolution. When that sad moment came, Jenny knew that, like her, Maeve would be bereft.

The two women were beginning to enjoy the war that was gradually drawing to a close. When the children were in bed they spent companionable evenings together, listening to the wireless and eating their suppers off trays on their laps. Sometimes, they talked of the old days, their time together on the stage, and the strange people they had met. Maeve was the only person Jenny could talk to about such things – much as she loved her husband she knew that he preferred to forget her stage experience. As for Jenny's mother-in-law, she would not allow it to be mentioned. The fact that her son's wife had once stood centre stage with a halo of light around her beautiful hair did not impress that lady; she considered that Jenny was in a different world now and it was as if the old world had never existed. But the two friends knew that it had existed, and they took delight in talking about it.

The big house was cold, and sometimes they wrapped themselves in eiderdowns to keep warm. Their lives were simple, concocting meals from very little for themselves and the children, living in one section of the house so that the chore of blacking out every evening was reduced to a minimum. Maeve worked in the kitchen garden, growing vegetables for the family. She had never grown anything in her life until then, but it seemed she had the magic touch. Everyone in the household thrived, and Jenny's brood, like most wartime children, were pictures of health. Maeve was completely happy, and she had no ambitions for the future other than to stay with Jenny and her family. A little doubt lingered in her mind that it was a way of life that could not last indefinitely, but she did not allow herself to think about it.

Into this existence, from time to time, came Theo Bailey. He carried in the logs for the fire and changed the washers on the dripping taps. He was useful and obviously interested in Maeve. By this time Jenny had smartened her up, persuaded her to have her hair done and spent all their combined coupons on new clothes for her. She was pleased with her endeavours; the Irish charm was still there. It had been hidden for years but she had managed to bring it back to life.

Theo took the bait. The dark-haired blue-eyed beauty captivated him, and her frailty and lack of self-esteem endeared her to him, for he too, secretly, lacked self-esteem. When the lord of the manor returned for weekend leave, Jenny excitedly told him of her success at matchmaking.

He thought it rather sweet that his worldly-wise wife had not detected a flaw in her machinations.

"Darling," he said, "remember the annulment of his marriage. Why do you think that happened? There can be only one reason."

When she thought about it, she was mortified. She tried to put things right, in her own mind at least. "That may have been the case with one wife, but surely it could be different . . ."

"I don't think so."

"You must tell Maeve," she insisted, but, of course, he refused to do that. They talked about it and argued far into the night, but it soon became apparent that it was too late for either of them to do anything. Rupert did not want to upset his old friend and he would not allow Jenny to talk to Maeve. Nothing was done, and a jubilant Theo told them that he had asked Maeve to marry him, and she had accepted. He was the happiest man on earth.

"Did you love him?" I ask.

Maeve gives a big sigh. "No, darling, I did not love him," she tells me, "but I liked him very much. He was a nice man. I knew that everything in that house, where I had been so happy, was going to change. Rupert was always kind and courteous to me, but I sensed that he did not want me there. The war was nearly over and it was a new beginning for him and thousands like him; he was returning to his family and he wanted it to be just as it was before he left. I counted myself lucky that a rich man had fallen in love with me and wanted to look after me. There was no one else to take on that task, and I had no qualifications for a life on my own. This happened a long time ago when things were different; today women can manage perfectly well without a man."

"Only some women," I say.

"Yes, well, even today, I think they are happier with a husband and children."

"But love," I say, distressed, "surely that is the most important thing of all?"

"It is desirable," Maeve says, "but I did not seem very clever at finding it. When Theo proposed marriage to me, I did not give it a second thought. At the time, it seemed to me to be the only way."

Chapter 27

They were married in church. Maeve was a widow and Theo's marriage had been annulled, so it was permissible. The fact that she had once been a Catholic seemed to have been forgotten; somewhere along the line Maeve had given up attending Mass so it could be said she had forgotten it herself. Except that she had not forgotten it, not quite, and during the rest of her life she would turn away from her faith but never completely discard it.

Theo's many friends occupied nearly all the pews of the historic church in the village where he lived. He had no family living, except for an older brother, but he knew a great many people. Maeve's representatives were Jenny and her husband (home for the occasion) and their six children, occupying a whole pew and, as representatives go, very impressive, and in the front row of the church sat Aunt Min and Beryl and Brona with their respective husbands and children. Theo had paid for them all to come from Ireland, and had managed to persuade Uncle Frank, who did not like accepting charity, that he would be doing Maeve a great favour by coming as he had been allotted the task of being at his niece's side when she walked up the aisle.

Maeve looked wonderful. Despite wartime restrictions she was elegantly dressed in a cream dress chosen, of course, by Jenny. She was pleased to put her trembling hand on Uncle Frank's arm, although she was shocked to see how much he had aged. She supported him, rather than the other way round, when they made their faltering way to the altar. When she raised her eyes and saw Theo standing there, looking so tall and distinguished, she felt very proud. When they knelt, side by side, she breathed a little prayer for Jack, hoping that, wherever he was, he did not mind too much. Up to that moment she had a niggling little doubt in her mind that, by marrying Theo, she was being disloyal to him. He had resented any man who even looked at her with admiration; she remembered how unreasonably jealous he had been of Mr Truelove, the librarian, who had nursed an unrequited passion for her. These random thoughts passed through Maeve's mind as the vicar pronounced them man and wife.

It was amazing seeing Beryl and Brona again after so many years but, after the first embraces, it became difficult, for the three women had little in common. Their children regarded her with interest. They had heard about their relation living in England, and here she was, with hardly a trace of an Irish accent to remind them that she was one of them.

At the reception, held in Jenny's house, Maeve made a point of talking to Aunt Min. She, too, had aged but not as much as Uncle Frank, and she had made a big effort to be smart for this wedding. Her hair, which Maeve remembered as a bun, was now carefully coiffured, and she wore a navy blue silk suit. She looked very different to the Aunt Min of nearly thirty years ago. Maeve wondered if she often thought of the events that happened in Orchard Street at that time. Of course she had not forgotten them, any more than Maeve had – no amount of time can make such memories fade from the mind. Even on this wedding day, the remembrance was there, unspoken, between the two women as they clasped hands.

It was time for them to leave, and Maeve hugged Jenny and thanked her for all she had done for her. Then she turned to the children and kissed each one in turn, even the two shy boys on an exeat from Eton, and then she leant down and held Simon for a minute, and he said, "Don't go, Maeve," and she felt her heart would break.

Theo and Maeve were to spend the first night of their honeymoon at the Ritz Hotel in London, and then they were going to an old hotel in Dorchester for five days. Of course, going abroad was out of the question.

The hotel was packed with servicemen, mostly

American officers, whose cavalry twill trousers and immaculate jackets festooned with medal ribbons made the RAF boys and naval officers look like poor relations. The opulent rooms of the Ritz must have been the venue for many dramas, the fulfilment of dreams or the destruction of hopes. The honeymoon of Theo and Maeve was no exception.

With disbelief, in the privacy of their bedroom, Maeve watched the total collapse of her new husband. He sat on the edge of the big double bed, clutching the bedpost as if for support, and he sobbed. The sobs wracked his body and his face was wet with tears. Maeve stood and looked at him, not knowing what to do. She had never seen a man weep before; Jack, whatever his feelings might have been, was not prone to tears. Theo wept because he was impotent, a fact he had hidden from Maeve until this poignant moment. He was deeply sorry for the deception.

When she understood what his grief was about, she hastened to assure him it was not important. She spoke sincerely for she believed that to be the case. She had enjoyed years of satisfying sex with Jack, now Jack was gone she felt it was not necessary to her any more. In some strange way she felt absolved because she would not be betraying his memory; her prayer in church had been answered. She even wondered if Jack had had a hand in this, he had not wanted her to live with Theo as a married woman, and now he had nothing to fear.

She pointed out to Theo that they had both reached

an age when such things were no longer essential for their happiness together; they were both in their forties. They slept, at last, their bodies entwined as if they had shared magical moments together. The next day they left the Ritz, driving to Dorset in Theo's Sunbeam to spend the remainder of their honeymoon. He was in a cheerful mood, the sad events of the previous night seemed to have been forgotten. They were never mentioned again during their many years together.

Maeve resolved that no one should know the truth. Not even Jenny, least of all Jenny, must know the stark reality of her marriage. There would be no children of this abnormal union, and that saddened her. Her childbearing days were coming to an end, and this had been her last chance.

As she had done with Jack, she settled for second best. She counted herself lucky that Theo was endlessly kind to her and utterly devoted. He was grateful to her for not making an issue of his inadequacy, but he put this thought to the back of his mind and did not dwell on it. He was complacently content in his ownership of such a lovely woman, and he was proud of the way Maeve blossomed during the years, becoming more self-assured and acquiring a character all her own. They settled down to an affectionate companionable life together.

Theo owned a beautiful Georgian mansion that had been taken over during the war, and was returned, when it was over, in a bad state of repair. He and Maeve tramped around the empty building, looking at the damp patches on the walls and the broken windows. For a long time the house occupied their time and thoughts, and making it a home again was a project that interested them both. When it was completed, to their mutual satisfaction, Maeve found herself at a loss.

Theo, on the other hand, had much to occupy him. He had put himself forward as a candidate for election as Member of Parliament for the area where he lived. He was much respected, the owner of a fine house and land, and well known for his wisdom and generosity. He was elected with a huge majority. He felt as if everything he had ever wanted had been presented to him, and he could not guess at the restless feelings his wife was experiencing. Maeve attended political meetings and she supported her husband in every way she could, but a sense of loss dominated her life. There must be more, she thought.

Maeve met Luke Rankin at a dinner party given by friends in the neighbouring county. Theo drove the many miles, arguing with Maeve, in an amicable way, about the reason for him accepting the invitation. She maintained, rightly, that Theo wished to be there for a snobbish reason, the people giving the party were rich and influential and, therefore worth the long journey.

When they arrived they were ushered into a room full of people. A waiter walked around with drinks on a tray that, with a wave of his hand, Theo refused because he was driving. Maeve had her own car, but when she was with her husband he did not permit her to drive. It was one of his many idiosyncrasies she had learned to tolerate, such as never allowing her to buy clothes before he had approved them, or wearing gloves (really strange, that one) and choosing the menu for a dinner party without allowing her to have a say in the matter.

Maeve, drinking champagne, knew herself to be attractive and articulate. Her deep laugh that she had cultivated over the years drew the men to her side. They found her earthy brand of humour fascinating; they thought she was a rare being, something she had never been in the early years of her life. She had always been a non-person, a nonentity; now in her middle age she was a character.

Luke Rankin was drawn to this character. Across the room he heard the distinctive laugh, and he left his wife, Ruth, sitting with a group of women at the party, and he made his way to Maeve's side. There he was to remain, as often as he practically could, for the next twelve months.

He was skilful at managing his affair with Maeve. He was able to afford a flat in London and they met there. Sometimes he took business trips abroad, and Maeve would travel separately and stay in another hotel. They were careful because they both respected the feelings of the people closest to them. Luke did not want to hurt Ruth, or jeopardise his position with his children, and Maeve was too fond of Theo to want to cause him grief.

Luke was a lawyer, the senior partner in a firm, which, ironically, dealt with divorce cases. He had been married for fifteen years, and during that time he had never been unfaithful to his wife. This was not for lack of opportunity; he was attractive to women, a tall elegant man, always impeccably dressed, clever and amusing. He had everything he desired, a devoted wife, two children who were a joy to him, and a country house where he spent every weekend. Ruth stayed there because she did not like London, and it was an arrangement that worked very well. Luke saw no reason to rock the boat, until he met and fell in love with Maeve.

Theo was so busy he did not notice his wife's frequent visits to London; he just assumed she had gone for shopping or to visit friends. It was easy for Maeve because she had no feelings of guilt. Sometimes, in their most intimate moments, she had nearly told Luke the truth about her marriage with Theo, but she stopped herself in time, knowing that the telling would make her feel guilty. She and Theo had a tacit understanding, and she could not betray that trust. And so she remained silent, even with the man she loved.

Luke was unaware that there were any secrets in their relationship. Although he was so close to Maeve he never saw her as she really was. The shy little Catholic girl who had abandoned her baby had disappeared for good and, although he knew about

Jack, he did not associate Maeve with a rather down-at-heel woman who had grieved for her husband. He loved the Maeve he knew, who was a very different person.

It seemed as if they would never be discovered. There may have been people who guessed at the liaison, but they were both so popular and charming the gossip surrounding them was not malicious. Then Maeve gambled on her increasing years; she was forty-five, and she thought she was too old to have a baby. It did not take her long to realise how wrong she was.

"Oh, no," I say, "another child? The second lost baby?"

"I'm afraid so," says Maeve sadly.

Chapter 28

"There is something important I have to tell you," said Maeve to Luke, surely the most dreaded words a man can hear from a woman, for there is an ominous quality about the phrase that catches the breath. The poor vulnerable male – what is he about to hear that will alter his life?

Maeve knew, as soon as she uttered those words, that Luke was taken aback: the fear showed in his eyes. When she told him the news she had to convey, she felt him physically and mentally move away from her. Theirs had been such an uncomplicated relationship, one-sided in respect that Maeve did not have a sexual love for her husband, a fact concealed from Luke. She had never questioned him about his love for his wife. She knew it was real love but she did not know how it was expressed, but she guessed and rejected the thought from her mind. Such imaginings were dangerous and might interfere with the happiness they shared, for it was a real and true happiness and no outside influences could affect the love they felt for each other. So far no one had been hurt, and it seemed as if this comfortable arrangement could continue for as long as they desired, at least, they sometimes told themselves, until something happened to spoil it.

Something had happened, a very substantial something that had to be faced and decided upon. Luke's immediate reaction was that Maeve should have a termination, but she still retained enough of her Catholic upbringing to reject that idea. It was not the only reason; her longing to have a child made her realise she could not face an abortion. She tried to explain this to Luke, but she could see from his expression that he was abandoning the problem; gradually easing away from it, pretending it did not exist. He considered her too old to have a child; his life at home involved teenagers, school fees, and he simply could not envisage himself taking on the responsibility of a baby. He had left babies behind him, long ago.

It was at this point that the passion they had felt for each other died, and Maeve watched its demise with fascinated horror. For the first time she realised that the love they had for each other was based on nothing more than desire and fulfilment, and without these two ingredients it was as worthless as dust.

Without Luke's support, there was nothing Maeve

could do but turn to Theo. Naively, she thought he would welcome a child. She remembered his tears when he told her they must face a barren marriage. Surely he would rejoice in this baby, maybe a son and heir, which no one would suspect was not his; it seemed an answer to all their problems.

It was not, because what Maeve did not realise was that Theo did not consider his marriage had any problems. He had forgotten long ago the anguish of his wedding night; he thought Maeve was completely happy with the companionship they shared. He could not understand why she had sought solace elsewhere. He was adamant in his refusal to accept the child of another man; his emotions fluctuated between uncontrollable sobbing and implacable determination not to change his mind. His love for her was unchanged, whereas Luke's love for her had made a rapid reversal. She found she could not longer contact him; he managed to stay out of her reach. Not for the first time in her life, she found she was alone.

Theo set out to convince her that she was not on her own. While he was living and breathing she must never feel abandoned. It was just that she must do as he decreed. She went to a modest hotel in Edinburgh, a place where it was unlikely she would see anyone she knew. The months, the weeks, the days dragged by, as they had in Orchard Street.

Theo visited her when he could. She noticed how his eyes swivelled away from the increasing girth of her stomach, and she understood, too late, that he was incapable of accepting it as a fact of life. She, who had always felt sorry for him, realised that fecundity repulsed him. The realisation made her see a new side to his character, a slightly sinister side separating him from other people. He was a sham, and all the people he worked with, who admired him for his integrity and charm, did not see the real person. She was glad he was not to be the father of her child. She started to be irritated by his solicitude during his short visits to Scotland and, although they were an interruption to the overpowering boredom of a provincial hotel, she was pleased when it was time for him to go.

She found herself looking forward to the meals, on the dot every day, the menu unvarying. After dinner she sat in the lounge watching the people, listening to the clink of the coffee cups. It was the same every evening, and a relief to go to her room, where she could loosen her clothes, and lie, stretched on the bed, watching black and white television. She walked miles, exploring every area of the city, in an attempt to tire herself so that she would be able to sleep that night.

On nights when she could not sleep, she lay staring into the darkness, thinking about that other time in her uncle's house, alone in the attic room with no entertainment, watching the changing seasons through the small window. There was only one thing in common with that time, the quickening of the entity within her body, the movements beneath her exploratory fingers on her belly. As it had been in Castlerock, all those years ago, she was not alone.

"I don't understand," I say. "Why didn't you leave Theo, have your baby, and bring it up on your own?"

"All my life has been bad timing," Maeve answers. "If this had happened to me ten years later things would have been so different. I had no money of my own, and I knew Theo was unsympathetic. Nowadays, no blame is apportioned when it comes to settlements, but at that time I would have been considered the guilty party and, therefore, Theo would have been under no obligation to pay me anything. What could I do? I had no qualifications to earn a living for us both, and no relations to help me. It was a frightening prospect."

"What about Jenny?"

"Ah, Jenny," says Maeve, "she did not know where I was, and kept telephoning Theo to try and find out where I had gone. She and Rupert guessed that I had left him – remember, she knew more about my marriage than I ever suspected. Finally, one evening, I decided to call her, and she, bless her, travelled to Edinburgh to see me. I can't tell you the joy I felt when I saw her dear face. She was astonished when she saw the size of me; it was the last thing she expected. She refused to eat in that dreary hotel, and she dragged me off to an Italian restaurant. Then we came back to my room, and I lay on the bed, propped up with pillows, and she sat in the armchair opposite me. It reminded us both of the old days in her bed-sitting-room."

Maeve told her everything, about Luke and how much she had loved him, and about Theo and his refusal to accept the baby. Her tongue was loosened, and she told her about the first birth and how she had left the child at the convent.

Jenny, the mother of six children, was horrified. "I had no idea . . ."

"No, I don't know why I never told you. For the same reason I did not tell Jack, I suppose, I felt ashamed of what I had done. He died without knowing anything about my past."

"You can't let the same thing happen again," Jenny told her.

It was wonderful to be able to discuss what she should do next. For months she had been pondering that question. Together they made plans – Maeve would travel back with her and would live in her house and have her baby in the local hospital.

"And Rupert?" she asked. "What will he have to say about this arrangement?"

"Oh, Rupert will do as I ask him," said Jenny airily. "There will be no problem there."

Maeve made one stipulation, that Jenny should return home on her own and explain to her husband what was going to happen, and she would follow later. At the time, it seemed to her only fair to Rupert who, after all, had to make the decision to accept two extra persons into his family. That was her mistake. She should have moved out of the hotel that day, and gone with Jenny. It would have been hard for Rupert to turn her away when she had one foot firmly in the door. As it was, he resisted his wife's proposal, and they had a spirited argument about it. When Jenny started to weep, Rupert walked out of the room, and at once telephoned his old friend, Theo. What Theo had to say to him only strengthened Rupert's resolve not to have Maeve come and live with them. Theo told him that Maeve had committed adultery with a married man, whose wife was a friend of theirs. He was prepared to forgive her for her behaviour but he was not prepared to accept the child of such a deceitful union. Rupert sympathised with him; he was not prepared to accept the child either.

"How could he be so callous?" I ask wonderingly.

Maeve says: "Now I can sympathise with the man – it would have been a big undertaking for him."

"What happened then?"

"A distraught Jenny telephoned me and told me what had happened. It seemed like the end of the world for me. There was no one to whom I could turn. I stayed in my room and did not venture out for food and drink. I filled a glass with water from the tap in the bathroom and that was my only sustenance."

Maeve locked the door of the hotel bedroom; the staff left her alone at first, then the manager hammered on the door.

"Are you all right, Mrs Bailey?"

"Yes, thank you."

She wanted to be alone, to be separated from outside influences. The world, and all the people in it, seemed hostile. When the telephone rang, she did not answer it, she knew it would be one of two people, Theo or Jenny, and she did not want to speak to either of them.

She knew that she would have to emerge from her hiding place eventually, it was only a question of time before the management decided to unlock the door from the outside. She was preparing to go downstairs when she experienced the first pain. The baby was not due for another three weeks, but perhaps it was facing deprivation in the womb and the environment outside offered a better chance of nourishment. Maeve packed a small case, put on her coat and telephoned a taxi to take her to the hospital.

She had many hours of waiting in a private room while the pains became more frequent. A doctor came to see her and asked if she had telephoned her husband.

"Please, will you do it?" she said.

Mystified, he called Theo and told him his wife was about to give birth.

Maeve cannot remember when everything around her became a blur. Her child, a son, was held up for her to see, but she was beyond caring. Theo arrived at last, shaken and shocked to find his wife so ill. There was a time when they thought she might not survive, and it was then that they diagnosed the precarious state of her heart.

Theo returned each evening to the room in the hotel

where Maeve had spent so many months, and it was hard to understand his state of mind. As usual, he was courteous with everyone he came in contact with, but it was as if he was in a daze. In truth, a continuous prayer occupied his thoughts, that his wife would live, and any interruptions to the prayer were unwelcome; a rumour went around the hotel that the baby had died, and so it was never mentioned.

Then, one evening, Jenny telephoned him. He was in the bedroom, and he sat on the edge of the bed, talking to her, in his hand a tie, ready to put on before descending to the dining-room, where he ate every evening.

Brokenly, he told her that Maeve was very ill indeed. She had starved herself before the birth, and that had not increased her chances. The doctors were hopeful, but they would not go further than that. Theo was constantly told 'she has a long way to go'.

"And the baby?" asked Jenny urgently.

"A boy – small but healthy."

"You will let her keep him? After all that has happened, you can't be so cruel as to part her from him?"

"At present she is too ill to know anything about him. If she lives, she will, in time, forget about his existence. He is being cared for by a foster parent, and is up for adoption."

"Theo!" There was anguish in Jenny's voice. She was in a terrible position because she felt she could not go against her husband's wishes. Everything most dear to her depended on her maintaining the status quo. She had pleaded with Rupert, wept and cajoled, but he was adamant in his refusal to have Maeve and her child to live with them, as part of their household. Perhaps there were underlying reasons for his decision, a jealousy of the close friendship between the two women or a desire, like his mother, for Jenny to forget her past – Maeve was a constant reminder of it. When the war had come to an end he had not wanted to come home and find that Maeve had become a part of his family. She had left then, and Rupert was determined it should remain that way.

"Please, please!" cried Jenny over the telephone.

But Theo stopped her from saying any more, with the words: "Nothing you can say, my dear, will make any difference." Then he put on his tie, and went downstairs to eat a hearty dinner.

A few weeks later Theo took his pale wife home. He had no difficulty in persuading her to sign the adoption papers before they left Edinburgh; she had no strength left in her to protest. She managed to regain her former strength, but not her contentment – that had gone forever. She saw Luke sometimes, at a social gathering she would catch a glimpse of him, and for a moment their eyes would meet, reflecting the sadness that something precious had been lost and could never be rekindled.

So Maeve faced an existence experienced by many

women, the devotion of a husband who could never satisfy her longings, the loss of a man who no longer loved her and, worst of all, the feeling that she had been betrayed.

Theo did everything he could to make up for the way he had treated her and, perhaps in a clumsy way to recompense her for the loss of a child, he gave her a dog, that she named Bobby. Bobby was to be her companion for sixteen years, and she loved him and spoilt him and allowed him to sleep on her bed. When he died of old age she grieved for him.

It was not an easy life but it had its compensations; at least she was comfortably well off, and that is always appreciated by someone who has suffered real poverty. She thought of her mother, eking out a miserable pittance by giving piano lessons; because of constant lack of money she had never lived. After Theo retired from politics, Maeve travelled with him to many splendid and fascinating places, and for these opportunities she was grateful.

Sometimes she looked back on her past, and wondered where she had gone wrong. From the time she first set eyes on George Palmer she had made mistakes, one after the other, all leading up to the moment when reluctantly she gave up her lovely home and moved to Riverbank to join Theo.

Chapter 29

Two events loom largely on my horizon, the marriage of Dan and Andrea and the birth of their child.

I am not in dread of either of these happenings. I have gone beyond that and, as I told Monica and Barry King, there are no more tears. I am able to talk about them freely with my children, even with anticipatory excitement, although I admit the last reaction is feigned because I know their excitement is very real and they want me to share it with them.

The marriage comes first. Because of my compliance the divorce has gone through quickly, and the wedding is to take place in a registry office as soon as the decree absolute is granted. That is today, a grey overcast day, not unlike the day I got married.

I am proud of my sons. I decide complacently that they look great, not their usual selves, but great just the same, and it is all due to my efforts. They both wear suits with long trousers and new sparkling white shirts with ties. I slick back their blond hair, and they look at themselves in the long mirror in my bedroom, and I can tell by their faces they are pleased with themselves. When Dan comes to pick them up, I come downstairs with them, and stand in the doorway to wave goodbye.

"Good luck," I call cheerfully, and Dan looks up quickly and thanks me.

When I shut the front door the house feels very empty, but I am used to this. It is always the same when the boys leave. I sit at the dining-room table and listen to small sounds, the scuttering of Flush's claws as he crosses the wooden floor in the hall, the ticking of the grandfather clock. I read the newspaper from cover to cover, and I attempt to do the crossword. I imagine the scene at the registry office, Dan and the hugely pregnant Andrea standing close together, solemnly exchanging vows before a registrar, probably a woman. It always seems to be a woman in films. Hugh and Neil watch the proceedings, slightly bemused, not quite sure what to make of it all. The only other people there are the two witnesses, Andrea's best friend who I have discovered is called Sophie, and Peter who went to school with Dan and was the best man at his first wedding. He telephoned me a few weeks ago and asked me what he should do about Dan's request for him to be a witness at the second ceremony.

"I don't know what to say to him. It's very awkward . . ."

"Say yes."

"Are you sure you don't mind?"

"I don't mind at all."

But, of course, I do mind, and I think it is very insensitive of Dan to ask him, but then, I remind myself, he is his oldest and closest male friend.

I wonder if Dan will think of me at all during this important day of his life. I think not, because he is in love with Andrea and all his thoughts are concentrated on her and his children. As far as he is concerned the parting was inevitable; after he met Andrea he felt impelled to stay by her side. He would not have understood Peter's embarrassment when he was asked to be a witness; his mind goes back to the time when they were schoolboys, long before he met me. Sometimes I think he has emptied his mind of the years we were together. It is a part of his life he does not allow himself to think about; like the chalk marks on a blackboard he has wiped away the memories with one decisive movement.

I wonder if I should go and see Jane. I have not seen her for a while. 'How can you bear it – I think you're marvellous' – those are the words she will say to me, and I decide I don't want to hear those words, so I shall go and see Maeve instead. She will understand.

As always, she is delighted to see me. She is alone in her room; for once Sheelagh is not with her. "We are free!" she says to me gleefully.

She looks at my face. "Of course, you are upset,

darling," she says. "It would be unnatural if you were not. What can we do to make this sad afternoon pass more quickly?" She glances at me hopefully. "Shopping?"

I agree because I know it is what she wants to do. I have a disabled badge on my car that I acquired when I started ferrying Maeve around the town, so we are able to park outside the main department store. We leave the wheelchair in the car; she refuses to be pushed around the shop in the cumbersome thing. We totter around very slowly and she hangs on to my arm so heavily I begin to think one of my bones will crack.

I have no interest in buying clothes this afternoon. I watch while Maeve purchases a black cashmere pullover. "It will see me out," she says cheerfully. It is what she always says when she buys an expensive item for her already overstocked wardrobe.

"Shall we go somewhere and have a cup of tea?" she suggests. She tires quickly these days, and I can tell she is flagging, although she would never admit to it.

"Do you mind terribly if we go home for tea?" I ask her. "I have to be there when Dan brings the boys back before he and Andrea go on their honeymoon."

Thankfully, Maeve lowers her large body into her special chair, and I fetch her the footstool for her swollen feet. I bring in the tea on a big tray, and we sit quietly, neither of us in the mood for conversation. Flush sits by her side, his nose on her knee, and from time to time she slips him bits of cake.

We hear the tyres scrunching on the drive, and we

look at each other. I think, now it has happened, someone else bears my name and is married to my husband. I know he has not been my legal husband for a while, but this seals the severance. There is no turning back now. I am what is termed these days a single mother, but not a single mother because my sons were born within a marriage. What should I be called then? There is no other term for me except an abandoned wife, that faceless nameless person through the ages. How many people know the name of Nelson's wife? Yet nearly everyone has heard of Emma.

They breeze in, all of them, in a jovial mood that they try, without success, to temper because of the strangeness of the situation. Peter is with them, but I am told Sophie had to return to London. Hugh and Neil have lost their pristine appearance, their shirts are hanging over their trousers, and they have stuffed their ties in their pockets. They have enjoyed themselves – the drama of the marriage service, followed by delicious eats at a local hotel. Andrea cannot disguise her radiance; the smile of pure happiness twitches her lips, however hard she tries to hide it.

I have realised for some time now that I like her. It would be hard to dislike her, although I would prefer it to be that way. It would be comforting to be able to complain about her to Maeve, to Jane, even to my children, but, maddeningly, I have not got that luxury. She is too nice. She is caring about Hugh and Neil, but she does not try to steal their affection from me, and she never appeals to their childish greed by showering them with gifts and treats. When they return from visiting her their cases are full of dirty clothes; she has not washed them and packed them neatly – I like that. She is not trying to prove anything; she is just endlessly fair and good- natured.

She loves Dan; that is certain, and he loves her back. Today, his face reflects his happiness, and I find that hard to take. There were many years when I made him happy, but I have to face reality, I never made him as happy as he is now.

Maeve, from the depths of her chair, congratulates them both. "You look well," she says to Andrea. And it's true; Andrea is blooming with that special glow that sometimes accompanies pregnancy. This is a baby much desired by her.

I have a bottle of sparkling wine in the fridge; I thought champagne was going a bit too far. Hugh walks ahead of me with a tray carrying the glasses, and the adults drink to the health of the newly married couple. I clink glasses with Andrea and then with Dan.

I notice Peter watching me closely. I know he is thinking this is a bizarre situation.

"It is great to see you again," I say.

He bends in my direction, and whispers in my ear. "You look wonderful."

I am grateful to him for that.

Maeve, clutching her glass, says to Andrea: "Having a baby seems to suit you."

She replies: "It's just my back. I have a backache."

Of course, I remember the backache during the last few weeks before the birth, and I was never as vast as she is now. No wonder she has a backache with all that weight to carry, and I assure her it will disappear as soon as the baby is born.

When they get up to leave the boys try to stop them by catching hold of their hands. "We are only going away for a few days," Dan tells them.

"They have been wonderful today," says Andrea. "I don't know what I'd have done without their support."

It is a relief when they have gone. "Do you think I laid it on a bit thick?" I ask Maeve.

I hear her gurgling laughter with the little snort at the end. "Well, let's just say, darling, you are not the archetypal wronged wife."

I protest: "I'm trying to act on your advice,"

"Then you are succeeding beyond my expectations."

The little boys snuggle up to her, tired after an exciting day.

"Will you stay for supper?" I ask, knowing what her answer will be.

I potter around the kitchen, and I hear laughter coming from the next room. I peep through the door and I see the three of them close together, watching *The Simpsons* on the box. Not two children, but three, and the sight of them lifts my spirits.

Chapter 30

Dan telephones me to say he has a third son, and they have already named him, Ian.

I don't know why I feel so surprised except that, for some reason, I was sure they would have a girl. I know that they both hoped for a daughter.

He sounds exhausted with none of the exultation of a new father, so much so that I say: "Are you all right?"

"Yes, I'm fine."

"Was it an easy birth?"

"Seems like it."

He stayed with me when the boys were born but I know it was more a duty than a pleasure. Modern men are expected to be present at the birth of their children but it doesn't mean that they enjoy the experience. They are plunged into an environment they cannot understand and they feel powerless and inadequate. I know that Dan hated it until the glorious moment when he saw his newborn child for the first time. He said afterwards that moment made up for the rest of the ordeal. After he had made sure that the baby was perfect I let him off the hook and told him to go away, and come back when I was cleaned up and smiling.

I wonder if Andrea guessed that he was squeamish, and understood. It is so difficult for me to imagine any part of the event – I can only remember myself and the exhilaration I felt when I could relax and gaze at the miraculous result of so much anxiety and pain.

Such memories pass through my mind as I drive to the hospital, with the excited children chattering in the back seat. Andrea is in a private room and we three march in. I have made her a wintry bouquet, sprigs of *Viburnum fragrans* snipped from a shrub in the garden.

"How amazing," she murmurs. "The pink flowers look like spring."

"We won't stay too long," I say. "You must be tired."

There is no sign of Dan, but I think he will be at work and will come in the evening. Andrea does look tired and not so patently fit as she appeared on her wedding day. Her face is pinched and pale, but she looks wearily happy. She waves a languid hand in the direction a crib by the side of her bed. "There he is – my hero."

I peer into the crib, and I feel my heart start to pound. Hugh was the red wrinkled conventional baby, but Neil emerged into the world looking like a Botticelli *putto*. And here I am again reliving that first moment when I set eyes on such perfection.

I manage to say: "He's beautiful."

"Yes, he is, isn't he?" says Andrea lightly. "I never stop being surprised by him. He was born looking like that, an Adonis from the start."

"Dan must be over the moon," I say. Immediately, I wish I had not said that; Dan's state of mind is nothing to do with me, and my reference to it can't help but sound begrudging.

Her reply surprises me. "Poor Dan," she says, "he's worried."

"Worried? What is he worried about?"

"Oh," she says vaguely, "being a parent brings responsibilities, and they are bound to cause anxiety." She seems to have forgotten for the moment that Dan has had other children, and I cannot remember him being worried by the arrival of either of them. In fact, it was always his intention to have a family and I was the one who was prone to doubts and fears. He never thought for a moment that the babies would not be born perfect. I imagined all sorts of horrors, and after they were born I had nightmares of cot deaths and infantile illnesses. I still find being a mother a wonderful but frightening experience.

My face must have betrayed my thoughts because Andrea is quick to change the subject. "Just look at the boys," she says.

They are silent, gazing awestruck at the baby.

"Do you like him?" Andrea asks them. "Does he pass the test?"

They answer in unison: "Oh, yes!" and then Neil says: "He's brilliant."

"I don't think they have ever seen a newborn baby before," I say, "except that I'm forgetting about Hugh. Do you remember seeing Neil when he was first born, darling? You were nearly two years old."

But he has forgotten, and that is a sadness about children. I remember the occasion so well, Hugh clambering on the bed to inspect his brother, lying in my arms. At the time, it was a big moment for him. Later, he was to resent the intrusion into his secure little existence, but in those first moments he was excited. Now, I realise he was too young to remember. It disappeared from his memory, like so many other delights of childhood.

Andrea tells me that they are keeping her in hospital for a few days. She does not give a reason. "Just routine," she says. "I'm longing to go home. And it's hard on Dan, being alone in the house." There she goes again, always fretting about Dan.

I have brought a camera with me, and I take a photograph of the three of them, Hugh and Neil standing on either side of the crib, looking down at their new brother. We start to leave then because I detect she is flagging, and I know my boys only too well. Their shyness will dissipate quickly and high spirits will return. I decide to remove them before this happens.

We say goodbye to Andrea, and I can't help thinking

that if she was a real friend of mine, and I almost feel she is, I would bend down and kiss her but, of course, there is no likelihood of my doing that. As it is, I manage to give her hand a friendly squeeze, and the boys chorus: "Goodbye, Andrea. Goodbye, Ian."

As we walk back to the car I think how wise Maeve was in the advice she gave me. If I had continued following the foolish course I was taking I would not have shared the moments we have just enjoyed, seeing Ian in the company of my sons. They would have been taken to view him, and I would have been left behind, peering from behind the curtain in my bedroom, watching their departure and, later, their return.

Now I feel confident that neither Hugh nor Neil feels strained when I am with their stepmother. They have accepted we are friends, and that must be a relief to them. The uneasiness they felt before, the challenge to their loyalties, has disappeared, and that is compensation for the feeling of loss that has never left me.

Chapter 31

Maeve has not said a word to me, but I know what she has in mind. For some time now, I have purposely refrained from mentioning the subject to her but, at last, I feel it must come out in the open, especially now I have discovered, to my surprise that Sheelagh has been let into the secret of the lost son. I suppose they spend so many hours together, it is inevitable that confidences are exchanged.

"Are you sure this is what you want?" I ask Maeve when we are alone together. "You know, it can be a very disappointing business – look at Sheelagh, for instance. I know you have grown to like her, but you must admit she did not come up to expectations."

"That is because you found the wrong baby, darling," she says triumphantly.

"Oh, come on," I reply irritably. "You know perfectly well that Sheelagh is your daughter."

"I don't know at all," she says obstinately. "I think those old nuns got into a muddle with their records."

"Sheelagh looks like you," I tell her and, it's true. As I get to know the woman better I spot the resemblances. Just little things, like the movement of the head or an inflection in the voice, but most of all, her eyes, that startling blue, are Maeve's eyes. Maeve is fond of saying that she is humourless, and I am inclined to agree with her, but she is endlessly kind and thoughtful, two attributes that are ignored by her mother.

When Maeve complains that Sheelagh's constant presence is an irritation I remind her that she asked for it. "If you find that lost boy of yours," I say, "he will probably sit on the other side of the bed and drive you mad as well."

The concept makes us both laugh. We laugh so much that Sheelagh demands to know what is funny, and the fact that we cannot tell her makes it even funnier.

Sheelagh would never speak sharply to Maeve, so she turns on me. "I hope, for Mother's sake, you'll do something about that other matter."

Why can't she do the research? I ask myself bitterly. She does nothing but sit on her bottom and knit. It is not strictly true as Sheelagh keeps her rented house as clean as a new pin, polishing the furniture, scrubbing the kitchen floor, and even tidying the garden, although a man comes to mow the patch of lawn. She does all this in the evening after she has left Riverbank or when I am with Maeve. There are times when Maeve insists that she leaves us alone, and she does not appear to resent this. She is a remarkably even-tempered woman, very little fazes her and she shows little emotion, although she is sentimental where her mother is concerned. She seems to have two important aspects to her life – the wellbeing of Maeve and her religion. Before I uprooted her from Castlerock her faith was everything to her; at least I have given her another interest in life.

I give Maeve the finished story of her life up to the time she came to Riverbank. It is neatly typed, and I have put it into a hard folder. I am pleased with the finished article.

"It's not '*Gone with the Wind*,'" she says.

It lies, untouched, on her bedside table.

"Aren't you going to look at it?" I ask.

Maeve picks it up and ruffles through the pages. "It is such a poor life," she says, "not worth recording. I asked you to do it to keep you by my side."

"You have paid me a lot of money to write it," I remind her.

"Worth every penny," she says. "Just being with you and the boys is all I want. I am sure when you were typing it, darling, you must have noticed what a sad little affair it has been up until now – one step forward and two or three back – that is how it has been all the way. I did not seem able to break the pattern."

She sees my disappointed expression. "Don't think I'm ungrateful, darling. You have made a wonderful job of it."

I hear a note of dejection in her voice, and I think I know the reason; it is true that her life has been a series of misfortunes and lack of achievement, with long periods of boredom and inactivity. The people surrounding her have made their mark, Jack Deacon, unexpectedly showing the world his true worth and Theo attaining respect in the political arena. But where have their personal victories left Maeve? A lonely figure that never managed to get what she wanted in life.

"Perhaps we should bring it up to date," I suggest encouragingly. "Bring in Sheelagh, for instance."

"No, I don't think so, darling."

"It would be a bit of light relief," I say, "and it's quite funny in its way, the picture of Sheelagh sitting at your bedside, clicking away with the old needles. I think that is what your memoirs lack, humour."

But she is in one of her implacable moods and refuses to be drawn. To get her mind of the ordinariness of the manuscript I turn to the subject of the lost son.

"The boys are going on holiday with Dan, Andrea and the baby," I tell her. Dan and I have discussed it, and he feels, at three months, Ian is too young to go abroad, so they have decided on Cornwall this year. "While they are away I'll make enquiries."

I'm glad to see her face brighten visibly. "You'll go to Edinburgh?"

"Yes, I'll go to Edinburgh."

Maeve remembers the name of the adoption society, and I write to them saying I would be grateful for an interview, and giving my reason for requesting it. In return I get a letter from a Mrs Davenport granting me an appointment, and asking me to bring with me a letter from Maeve giving me the authority to act on her behalf. I can't help remembering the secretary-nun at Castlerock who accepted me without hesitation, and did not seek any proof of identity.

Sheelagh is becoming increasingly excited about my trip to Scotland. I am always a little surprised that she knows so much; Maeve must have let her into her confidence when they are alone together for so many hours. When I am there she tends to ignore her.

"Please will you let me come with you," Sheelagh says to me. It is the last thing I want, and the idea of her trotting behind me all the time I am in Edinburgh does not appeal to me. I try to make excuses.

"I won't get in the way," she says pathetically.

Unexpectedly, Maeve comes to my rescue. "You can't think of leaving me, Sheelagh dear," she says sweetly. "How could I manage without you?"

That settles it. Sheelagh has been told she is indispensable, and it pleases her. Nothing will drag her from her mother's side now.

Later, when we are alone, I thank Maeve for her intervention.

"Yes," she says with a mischievous giggle. "I acted quickly that time, didn't I?"

We laugh, but our amusement makes us feel uncomfortable.

"She's not so bad," she says.

I agree. "She means well."

"I've got used to having her around," Maeve admits. "It's true – I would miss her if she went away."

I sit in a room where the walls are covered with photographs, so many it is like wallpaper, and all the same subject – hundreds and hundreds of babies. Some of them are on their own; some are accompanied by proud parents, brothers and sisters.

The woman sitting behind the desk opposite me explains they are the results of successful adoptions, and I'm sure she is sincere in her belief that all the adoptions her society has organised have been successful. "People are so wonderful about keeping in touch with us," she says, "and we are always interested."

Mrs Davenport is a kindly white-haired lady, very efficient. She has a file in front of her, and she says: "I had to go back a long way to find Mrs Bailey, but I did find her and the little boy who was adopted by a nice family and received a good education."

"In Scotland?"

"No, in England. Sometimes we find families living over the border. This couple lived in Yorkshire. They had been trying for years to adopt in their own country, but without success. The husband was in his fifties and that went against him. Fortunately for them, this society has a more tolerant attitude; we believe the integrity of the couple is more important than the age of

312

one of them. Just because an older man marries a younger woman there is no reason why they should not adopt a child, provided they satisfy the criteria we expect."

"And what are they?" I ask, interested.

"That they are happy together and both want the child and that they have enough money to support an addition to the family."

"And you found a couple with those advantages for Maeve's baby?"

She smiled. "Yes, I am glad to say, we did. He prospered under their love and kindness; nothing was too good for him. Of course, I was not here at that time. As you can see I am old, but not *that* old, which brings me to the fact that this 'baby', as we have been calling him, is fifty years old, and is a judge."

A judge! How pleased Maeve will be to hear that her son is a judge! I hope this fact will make her realise her life has not be wasted.

"He is happily married," Mrs Davenport continues, "and has four children: two sons and two daughters. I have been in touch with him and told him that his biological mother would like to meet him, and he is very interested in seeing her. That is all I can tell you at present. I will let you know when a meeting can be arranged. He is a busy man, as I'm sure you understand."

"Of course," I say," but have you explained to him that Maeve is in her nineties? She gave birth to him late in life. The fact that she is so old lends an urgency to the whole thing."

"Yes, I told him that, and he appreciates the significance. I am sure he will be in touch quite soon."

"You have an interesting job," I tell her, "and I'm sure you must have seen many changes in the system over the years."

"I have," she says, "and, in many ways, it is a relief that I am shortly to retire. I am finding it hard to adapt to all the new regulations. For instance, I don't wholly approve of the birth parents staying in touch with a child that has been adopted. I can't believe that is beneficial to the child. Also, I have to say, I don't think it should be so easy for an adopted child to trace its biological mother; it seldom works out happily and can lead to disaster." She added hastily, "I feel differently in the case of Mrs Bailey because she is so old, and her son is a middle-aged man. I think it is rather touching that these two people choose to meet at this time in their lives."

"Even so," I say, "it may be different to what they expect." I feel tempted to tell her about Sheelagh, but I do not because I think it puts Maeve in a bad light. It is hard to imagine how a mother could part with two babies.

"Everything is changed," she says, "since those days when girls were too ashamed or too poor to keep their babies. Of course, it is a change for the better, there is no denying that, and people have become more tolerant

314

and understanding; but something has been lost on the way. It is so hard to adopt a baby now, and I feel sorry for the parents who long for a child and have no chance of getting one. I used to get a feeling of satisfaction when I brought together a child who had no one, with a couple who wanted it more than anything else in the world."

I say: "I can imagine bringing so much happiness into people's lives must have been very rewarding."

I thank her for seeing me, and we shake hands and part. I go back to the hotel where I am staying in Edinburgh. I fill in the time before getting my train back to England by exploring this beautiful city, but sightseeing on one's own is a lonely business and makes me realise I am never going to be one of those women who enjoy travelling without a companion; I need another person to share my appreciation of something unique. I almost regret being so dismissive of Sheelagh's offer to accompany me. Tramping from one tourist attraction to another, my spirits sink lower and lower, and it is a relief to get on a train and know that soon I shall be on dear familiar ground again, where there are people who know and love me. I am returning to an empty house, but it will not be for long before the boys return, and the thought of picking up Flush, and his exuberant welcome, revives me.

When Sheelagh hears that her half-brother is a judge she says: "I think he will be too grand to be interested in me."

Maeve says nothing, but I can see the concept pleases her.

"Well . . . ?" I ask.

"It is nice of him to say he wants to meet me," she says. "He owes me nothing, so if he changes his mind, I cannot blame him."

"He won't do that."

"We'll just have to wait and see," she says.

Chapter 32

One day when Dan brings the boys home he asks to come in as he has something he wants to tell me. It is not unusual for him to come into the house and stay a while on these occasions; he often sits in his old chair and has a drink before going home. I find it strange to see him sitting there in what was once his home, but it is evident he is completely at ease with the situation. When I tell Maeve, she says: "It's a credit to you, darling, that he feels that way."

The boys too are relaxed, sometimes sitting on the floor by his feet and, when he rises to leave, clinging to his legs to try and make him stay longer.

He is here today to tell me that he and Andrea are going to employ a nanny to look after Ian. "The best," he says, "fully trained. Expensive."

I am surprised because I once asked Andrea if she was intending to return to work after the birth of her baby, and she said she had no plans to do so because she wanted to look after Ian herself. "I don't want to miss one single moment of him," she said.

I mention this to Dan, and he looks up quickly and says: "I know, but something has happened to change that."

I look closely at this face and I see he has a strained expression that was not there before. It reminds me of the look he had during the last months of our marriage, when something was not right and he had not yet told me of his involvement with Andrea.

"What has happened?" I ask with deep foreboding.

"Andrea has developed cancer of the bone, secondary to the breast cancer she had before I met her. The doctors are hopeful, but it means she has to have treatment. Of course, while that is going on she can't look after Ian full-time. He is so precious to her she wants only the best for him. She has found a young girl who has just finished her training. Her name is Margaret, and she arrives tomorrow."

"I'm so sorry," is all I can find to say. It is indeed a tragedy and, after Dan has left, Hugh and Neil question me about it.

"Cancer? That's really bad, isn't it?" Hugh wants to know.

"She is not going to die, is she?" This from Neil.

"Most people recover completely these days," I try to reassure them.

"Like Amy's mother?" asks Hugh.

"Yes, like Jane. Thankfully, she is very well now. But the treatment she had, and the treatment Andrea will have, is quite harsh so you must be especially kind and thoughtful with her. No shouting and jumping about while you are there. We must do everything we can to help."

They are subdued already by the thought of illness. Nothing like this has touched their lives before.

When I tell Maeve, I am astounded by her response. "Oh dear, that poor girl! Perhaps it is God's way of punishing her for what she has done to you."

I look at her sharply. "You can't mean that?"

Immediately she is full of remorse. "No, darling, I don't mean it. It is my Catholic upbringing that makes me speak in that dreadful way. Try as I may, I can never totally rid myself of the teachings of my childhood."

"It isn't as if it was entirely Andrea's fault," I say, surprised at myself for standing up for the woman. "Dan fell in love with her, and that was that."

"Say what you like," says Maeve, "it is the woman who decides the outcome, whether the affair will stop before the damage is done or whether she wants it to continue. However persuasive the man may be, it is she who has the last word."

When I meet Margaret I like her instantly. As Dan has told me, she is young, and has an open face and a wide smile. She looks like a country girl, with a clear complexion, rosy cheeks and a sturdy body. I think

Andrea made a wise decision choosing a well-trained girl to look after her treasured little son. Margaret strikes me as being wholly dependable; I leave my children in her care without a moment's hesitation. Although so young she has a sensible cheerful approach to everything she tackles. She drives Andrea's car carefully and well, and she delivers the boys back to me after their visits to Pollards. I ask her where she comes from, and she tells me her parents live in Devon.

Andrea has started the chemotherapy, and Margaret informs me: "It knocks her out for about a day, and then she feels fine."

"And you are getting on well with Ian?"

"Oh, he's a darling. So good, sleeps all night. I'm very lucky – this is my first job, you know, and I never expected it would be so easy. And Dan and Andrea are so good to me – they treat me like one of the family."

Dan and Andrea, it is the first time I have heard their names linked in this way. But it is right, because they are now a married couple, and not just a married couple but also a proper family with a child. There is no disputing their relationship. My own relationship with Dan is a thing of the past, has faded into nothingness, and I recognise that Margaret must hardly be aware that it ever existed.

"Have you seen Ian lately?" she asks.

"No, not lately."

"Shall I bring him over next time I come?"

"I'd like that," I say.

Hugh and Neil are enthusiastic about Margaret. "She plays cricket with us," they tell me.

True to her word, she brings Ian with her on her next visit. She removes him gently from the car seat where he is lolling in an ungainly fashion – so far no one has invented a suitable car seat for a very small baby. She hands him over to me while she takes the carrycot and the wheels from the boot of the car. He is awake and he gazes at me with Neil's big eyes. When he makes a puzzled little grimace, a contortion of his undefined features, I hold him against my shoulder. I can't resist kissing the top of his silken head.

Margaret puts the pram under a big tree in the garden. Without being told, she has placed it in the exact spot where my babies used to sleep in the morning. I look at Ian, nearly asleep with his hand near his face.

"He is so like Neil at that age," I say. I put my finger in his miniscule hand and his fingers tighten on it.

"Yes," says Margaret, looking at me. "Dan said the same thing, and I've seen photographs."

We go into the house and I make coffee. Hugh and Neil are at school. "It's very quiet without them," I say.

"They are amazingly good when they are with Andrea," Margaret tells me, "like little mice. I take them outside into the garden so that they can let off steam."

"They've told me about the cricket."

"I learnt to play with my two brothers," Margaret explains. "I'm used to boys."

We sit opposite each other at the kitchen table with mugs of steaming coffee and the biscuit tin between us

"I don't think I should have a biscuit," she says. "I'm fat enough already." It's true, she is quite plump, but it suits her. I ask her if she feels lonely so far away from home, and she tells me she misses her boyfriend who is a farmer living near her parents' house. "He writes a lot," she says, "and he telephones once a week. We were at school together."

"Do you think you will marry him one day?"

She colours slightly. "One day perhaps. At present I'm concentrating on my career. It could take me anywhere in the world, so I'm not thinking of settling in one place yet."

"I think you are very wise," I tell her. "You have all the time in the world to make up your mind."

"I'm not lonely," says Margaret, reverting to my original question, "but I think Andrea is sometimes, when Dan is not there. That is why I'll take Ian home as soon as he wakes up. She misses him dreadfully when he is not there." She pauses. "It is a strange house," she says, "and I don't like to be alone there myself. For some reason it hasn't got a very friendly feel."

She looks around her. "Not like here," she says.

Andrea finishes her treatment and seems better. Dan tells me the chemotherapy took it out of her and she is taking it easy, resting every afternoon on her bed while Margaret takes Ian in his pram for long walks. I believe

Margaret makes excuses for getting out of the house, either walking or shopping at the supermarket, and she takes the baby with her wherever she goes. She is young and active and has not been brought up to spend hours indoors. I can't help wondering how Andrea feels when they have both left her and she is alone in the house; in her predicament I think it might lead to gloomy thoughts.

On impulse, I invite them to come and sit in my garden. It is the most perfect warm summer, and the chairs remain permanently outside as there is little likelihood of rain. The boys are home for the holidays, and normally they would be with Dan and Andrea, but this year is different because of her illness. It is wonderful for me, and wonderful for them also, and I love hearing their cries of delight as they splash in the pool on the far side of the garden – their father's last gift to the family before he want away. I have my swim every day before breakfast, and Margaret joins the boys in the pool during the afternoon. Day follows day of glorious sunshine, and I impress upon Andrea how foolish it would be not to make the most of the garden, and soon it is understood that they will come every day while the good weather lasts.

A tacit arrangement is made whereby Margaret brings Andrea and the baby at noon. That is my cue to get in my car and go and collect Maeve and Sheelagh. By the time we get back Ian is asleep in his pram under a canopy of leaves, and Andrea and Margaret are ensconced in garden chairs under a big umbrella. It is important that Andrea stays in the shade.

When she sees me Margaret leaps to her feet and goes inside to start preparations for lunch, while I help Maeve into her chair and Sheelagh plumps herself down in another. It is always a simple lunch, a big bowl of salad, sometimes with cold meat or fish, and Maeve usually brings with her a punnet of raspberries or strawberries. I have found a recipe for homemade lemonade that I keep in bottles in the refrigerator, and I fill a jug, clinking with ice cubes, and I carry it to the table in the garden.

When Ian gets restless, one of us moves to lift him out of the pram, and he is placed on a rug on the lawn. He is very active now, waving his fat legs in the air, smiling his broad toothless smile and chortling with glee when the boys play with him. He is a substantial being now, and Hugh and Neil are no longer afraid of hurting him. They can't wait until he is old enough to join in with their games.

One afternoon, he starts to crawl. His bottom lifts up, and in no time he has left the rug behind. He makes the mistake of looking back to receive our cries of admiration, and this makes him topple over, and he has to be righted again. There is much rejoicing and exclamations of delight from his adult audience, and then Hugh and Neil are called to witness the miracle. They race across the lawn, droplets of water falling from their lithe young bodies and their bare feet making marks on the parched grass. They are suitably impressed, and kneel down so as to get a better view of Ian's progress.

I know I shall never forget this happy time, and the feeling of astonishment that it should be so happy when there are so many reasons for it being the opposite. I want to hold on to these moments, to work some magic so that the sky remains a cloudless blue and I can go on hearing the shouts of the boys and go on seeing Maeve lying in the long chair under the tree, positioned so that she can keep an eye on Ian when he is in his pram. Even Sheelagh, sitting upright on a canvas seat, has abandoned her wintry pastime of knitting gloves and socks, and leans her head back to get the sun on her face. It is hard for me to believe that it could be like this; that I could sit in harmony with Dan's wife, derive pleasure in watching her delight in her little son and find myself giving little surreptitious glances to reassure myself of her continuing good health.

When Dan arrives in the evening to collect his family, my heart no longer contracts when I see him walking across the lawn. I am over him, I think, and the realisation gives me strength and a certain satisfaction.

When we are alone I tell Maeve this and she says: "Loving someone is a great burden. It's a loss but you will be happier without it."

He brings with him a tray covered with glasses that he has fetched from the house (he knows where everything is kept) and a bottle of wine that he has purchased on the way from the office.

Maeve says: "Darling, you're a marvel!"

He looks hot and crumpled, and he bends down to kiss his wife, and then takes Ian from Margaret. Hugh and Neil gather around him, and they implore him to have a swim, but he says he has nothing to change into and he will remedy that tomorrow by bringing with him summery clothes and bathing trunks. Everything is falling into place, like a jigsaw that was missing pieces for so long, and I feel like the person in the middle, the one upon whom they all rely, the puppeteer who pulls the strings that will make the show a success.

I think Dan looks tired, but he has had a tiring day, while we have been doing very little except luxuriate in the sun and attend to the wants of the three boys. Everyone is getting older. Dan, I note, has a few grey hairs, which make him look distinguished, and Hugh and Neil are tall now, sturdy children seeming to grow in stature and robust good health during the long school holidays. Maeve has aged since I first met her. She finds is increasingly hard to move around, and sometimes I fear she has lost some of her old zest for life. Only Hugh and Neil can bring back the sparkle, and when she is with them she disguises her impatience with old age. She has now reached the age she told me she was at when I first met her, and I remind her of this, and she says: "I thought it sounded good then, but I don't like it any more. I have nothing to look forward to except gradual decay."

"Oh, really!" I get exasperated with this sort of talk.

It seems selfish to me, especially when there is someone in our midst who must have fears about what lies ahead.

I look at Andrea and I think she has acquired maturity with motherhood.

"*She* does not complain," I say to Maeve.

"I know, darling. You have succeeded in making me feel an ungrateful old woman, and I'm ashamed. Of all of us, only Margaret and the children have the glorious glow of the very young, and isn't that a beautiful thing to see? My poor Sheelagh, I think she has been this way for a very long time, and I can't imagine her ever being anything but old, but she was a pretty baby so she wasn't born that way."

We no longer mention the lost son. There has been no communication from Edinburgh. Tentatively, I suggest that we telephone Mrs Davenport and ask if she has heard from the judge again. Maeve says: "No, let it be. If he wants to see me he will do something about it. I have no right to try and persuade him."

It seems curious to me that a judge should make a decision and then go back on it – I thought that was the last thing judges were supposed to do. Mrs Davenport told me that he was anxious to meet his biological mother, and I am wondering why he changed his mind about something so important.

Sheelagh expresses her feelings about him in no uncertain terms. "I can't forgive him for disappointing my dear mother. He must be an unfeeling man."

"Perhaps he has good reason."

"Well then, he can tell us what it is."

Each day is very like the last – it seems as if the hot weather will go on forever. The boys and Margaret have healthy tans, the result of being in and out of the pool so much. Even Sheelagh's face has the pinkish tinge redheaded people get when they are out in the sun. We try to protect Ian by making him wear a white cotton hat on his head, which he pulls off at every opportunity. Only Andrea and Maeve, under the umbrella and the canopy of leaves manage to retain their pale complexions.

Dan comes every evening now carrying a holdall containing a change of clothes and swimming trunks. I think the evening swim relaxes him after a stuffy day in the office, and I can't help wondering what my sister and her lover would make of it. One evening he arrives to find his youngest son standing on his plump wobbly legs, holding tightly to Maeve's finger for support. The cries of admiration are too much for Ian and, with a broad smile, he collapses into a sitting position.

The magical summer comes to an end when a strange greenish light settles over the garden, and a crash of thunder heralds the coming storm. We watch it happening from the dining-room window, the lightning zigzagging across a leaden sky, and then the rain descending on a lawn browned from weeks of relentless sun.

Through the wet windows we see Dan's car turning into the darkening drive. He has the lights on, and it is as if the summer has been snatched away from us. I fetch a bath towel and Margaret wraps it around the baby, and together they make a dash for the car. Then I find an umbrella, and Dan holds it over their heads as he and his delicate wife head for the car door that Margaret holds open for them.

Chapter 33

It seems to me, looking back on that summer, that everything has changed for us with the advent of the great storm. The rain does not diminish and the wind increases in volume. It blows down trees and dislodges tiles from the roofs. Driving the boys and Amy to school in the morning I find the road is blocked by a stricken branch, and delivering Maeve back to Riverbank the door of my car resists my efforts to shut it. I manage to muster all my strength to close it, and Maeve and I, buffeted by the wind and clinging to each other, slowly make our way to the front door. An anxious Moira is there to open it for us.

"What weather! And after such an amazing summer!"

It is before Christmas when Dan comes to tell me that Andrea is ill. I am in the process of stringing Christmas cards in their usual place across a beam in the sitting-room. He brings Ian with him, now walking unsteadily but with great determination, teetering across the room from one piece of furniture to another. He spies the cards on the string, and I let him play with them while his father imparts the sad news.

Dan says he is employing a nurse. This salary, together with Margaret's, will make great inroads into his financial expenditure, and I wonder how he will manage. He pays me maintenance and the school fees for the boys, and my heart goes out to him at this worrying time when despair is reflected in his face.

I don't know what to say to him. I wonder if I should offer him a drink, but I know he will refuse it because he is driving and carrying a precious passenger. The awkward moment is diverted because Ian has tired of the cards, having pulled most of them off the string, and he is now staggering around the room again. I leap to my feet to save him from falling.

"I am so sorry . . ." It sounds so banal; something else is needed at such a poignant moment. "You know, the boys and I will do everything we can to help."

He is sitting on the edge of his old chair, head down, staring at the carpet; then he looks up suddenly and says: "I know. Thank you."

I telephone Andrea and ask if she would like me to come and see her.

"I'm in bed today," she tells me, "as I have not been so well. It is very boring, lying here, and I would love to see you. Please can you bring Flush?" She loves Flush, and Ian dotes on him, almost strangling him with a neck hug as soon as he sees him, testing the dog's good nature to the limit. But Flush never lets me down, and now, here he is happily assuming his old role of comforter to the less fortunate.

It is strange that, although Andrea has been to my house so many times, this is the first time I have set foot in hers. The inside of Pollards is like the exterior, solid and with little charm. It is dark, and vast pieces of furniture squat in places they must have occupied for years. I don't think Andrea can have made any effort to change the curtains and covers since her parents lived here. It occurs to me that it must be a mixed blessing inheriting a house that you have known since childhood; perhaps she thought it was disrespectful to their memory to make changes. It smells of years of polish, and a woman is buffing a table in the hall with a duster as I go through. I think that soon they will be employing three people, a nanny, a cleaning lady and the trained nurse who is to arrive shortly. Then through the tall window on the stairs I spy a man sweeping the leaves on the lawn, and I have the sobering thought that Dan will have to meet the expenses of four people working for them.

Margaret has met me at the front door, and I follow her up a staircase carpeted with a red patterned carpet, the walls on one side adorned with lithographs of great composers. I reflect that it is a ponderous, rather depressing house and I can't help wondering what Dan, with his architect's passion for light and space and his great sense of style, makes of it.

Andrea lies in bed in a large room with windows looking out on to the garden. Unlike the rest of the house it is a charming bright room; the blinds are half down and the sun filters through the bottom halves of the window. This is the room she shares with the man who was once my husband.

I am shocked by her appearance, but I do my best to hide it. I have brought with me a bunch of freesias, shop bought as my garden is bare of flowers at this time of the year, and I have put them in a little pottery jug that I place on the table by her bed.

"They are lovely. Thank you so much."

"They smell sweet . . ." For some reason, I am suddenly transported to a hotel in Castlerock, pressing my nose into a bunch of stocks.

"The jug," says Andrea. "Do you want . . . ?"

"No, keep it until the next time I see you."

She stretches out a thin arm and pats Flush on the top of his soft head. "I'm so glad you brought him," she says.

She asks me about the boys, and I tell her that they are fine. We are polite with each other, and I realise this is my first encounter with Andrea on her own; during the summer that has passed I saw a great deal of her, but always in the company of other people. Sheelagh and Margaret were there to support me; it was my house, my garden, and I was in control of the situation, Even at that first meeting with her, Dan was there, and Hugh and Neil, standing close to me, protecting me.

I am relieved when Margaret coming into the room interrupts the slight awkwardness. She is holding the hand of Ian who I see, since our last meeting, has almost mastered the art of walking unaided. He pulls away from Margaret because he no longer likes his hand being held while he is on the move. He manages to break away and scrambles on to his mother's bed. I wonder if I should restrain him, for she looks so frail and I fear his robust exuberance will hurt her.

She hugs his wriggling little body but I can see it is a strain for her. Margaret comes to the rescue and lifts Ian in her strong arms. "We'll come back soon," she says with false cheerfulness.

Ian attempts to squirm from Margaret's hold, stretching his plump arms and screaming: "'Lush," which is his version of Flush. He is protesting as they leave the room, and we can hear his loud cries as she carries him down the passage.

"Oh, dear!" says Andrea.

The cries stop and there is silence. The silence is so poignant I am at a loss for words. Eventually, Andrea says: "You will keep an eye on Ian, won't you? Always? It's important to me that he keeps in touch with Hugh and Neil."

"Of course."

She heaves herself up a little with a tiny grimace and, glad to have something to do, I plump up the pillows and put them at her back. "Is that better?"

"Much better," she says.

I sit back in my chair, and I'm ashamed to say I am wondering when it will be tactful for me to leave. I am very conscious that her eyes are fixed on my face. I begin to feel distinctly uncomfortable, and what she says next justifies the feeling.

"I'm so sorry for what I did to you," she says. "It was unforgivable. It was just that I loved Dan so much it seemed as if I lost all sense of integrity. Nothing mattered as long as I could be with him."

I do not like the way the conversation is heading and in normal circumstances would retort: 'And I suppose you managed to persuade Dan to feel the same way?' – but the circumstances are anything but normal, and I hear myself saying: "It is over now. Done. You must not dwell on it." I long to leave her, breathe the sweet air outside the sick room, be allowed to carry on my life without having to shoulder this additional burden.

But she is determined to make me listen. "I have wanted to say it," she says, "so often I have wanted to say it. Now seems the right moment." She stares down at her hands, folded on the white sheet, as if she is hiding her tears.

"You must not feel depressed. . ." I start to say clumsily.

"Oh, I have every reason to feel depressed," she says, looking up and staring at me so that now I can see the tears in her eyes. "I am a doctor, you see – I know what is happening to me."

It would be foolish to protest, to mumble something

about new treatments, miracles, so I just tell her I am sorry.

"Dan will feel it so much," she says. "I think about him all the time. He will be so alone." She pauses. "Sometimes I wonder. . ."

I know exactly what she is trying to say, and this time I reply with spirit, a slight irritation taking over my sympathy with her predicament. "He is not a parcel," I say, "like the children's party game, where it is passed from one to another."

She smiles then, a small sad smile. "I know. Of course, you are right. It is just an idea I have when I am lying here thinking about the future."

"Try not to think too much," I tell her. "Oh, I know it's easy for me to say that, and I can't imagine how I would feel if I were lying there instead of you. If the very worst happens I promise I will support Dan as much as I can, and you can rest assured I will see that Ian stays in touch with his brothers. They love him, as I do, and they will want to see as much of him as possible."

"Thank you."

I ask: "What can I do to help? Perhaps you would like me to collect Ian sometime during the weekend so that the boys can be together?" It is all I can offer. Hugh and Neil have not been going to Pollards since Andrea became ill.

"Yes, please, but bring him back for the night, won't you? I like to think of him under the same roof as me. Margaret can go with him. She will help you, and I'm sure it will be a relief for the poor girl to get away from the doom and gloom here."

She is right because Margaret's face lights up when I tell her that she and Ian will be coming to see us on Saturday. We are standing by my car, and the little boy is pushing a miniature wheelbarrow, a recent present from his father, round and round the circular drive in front of the house.

"She will be all right, won't she?" Margaret asks, her hand on the handle of the car door, as if wishing to restrain me for a few more moments, anxious for reassurance.

I decide it is best to be truthful.

"No," I tell her, "I'm afraid she will not be all right. You must prepare yourself for that."

"Oh!" There is a note of anguish in her voice. She may have already half guessed what the outcome will be, but she is too young to accept the finality. We both look sadly at Ian; now busy filling his wheelbarrow with stones from the gravel.

"I'm sorry," I say, "but I didn't want to lie to you."

"I'm so glad you didn't," she says. "Of course, I can see Andrea is very ill, but it is a shock to know that she will not recover."

She breaks away and fetches Ian. He turns his attention to Flush, and Margaret holds him near the dog so that he can stroke him.

"Nice Flush," she says. "Nice dog," and he repeats after her, "nice".

"I'll see you both on Saturday," I say, trying to be normal and cheerful.

"Thank you," Margaret replies. "We'll look forward to that, won't we, Ian?"

As I drive away, I look at them both through the mirror in my car. Everything about them is so fresh, so vibrant with good health and vitality; it is hard to imagine either of them connected with the spectre of death. I think that one will be too young and the other too busy with living to take it in.

Chapter 34

The next time I see Andrea the nurse is in residence. She wears a uniform and is quietly efficient. Unlike Margaret, who adopted Christian names from the onset, she refers to Dan and Andrea as Mr and Mrs Maitland. She is older than Margaret, and I hope her presence will be a comfort; at least her arrival has taken some of the responsibility from the younger girl's shoulders. It must have seemed a long day to her before Dan's return.

I keep my visits short because Andrea is no longer inclined to talk. Her breathing is poor and from time to time she drifts into sleep. I am there most days, sitting quietly beside her bed. When she was able to be more communicative I asked her if she liked having me there, and she said: "Yes" – and I felt she meant it. I hope my presence is helpful, and I feel it is when she opens her eyes and smiles at me. Today is different. She seems restless, and her hands flutter on the white sheet like trapped birds. I catch one of them in mine, and she looks straight at me as if she doesn't know who I am.

I whisper to her: "Goodbye."

Outside the bedroom door I am met by the nurse who says; "I think oxygen would help Mrs Maitland. The doctor left me a prescription for a cylinder. Please, could you collect it from Boots in Melford?"

"Of course."

"Are you sure it is not too much trouble?"

"No, it is no trouble."

When I hand in the prescription a girl asks me to wait, and I sit on a chair by the counter until a young man appears carrying a bulky cylinder.

"Have you seen one of these before?" he asks me.

"No."

He goes into a lengthy description of how it operates and how it must be set up for the patient. I have always been bad at taking in verbal instructions, and this is no exception – less than halfway through his little lecture I am lost. I cannot concentrate on what he is saying, and yet I know how important it is that I know how the thing works. My head is swimming with the horror of what is happening to us now and what has happened to us in the past, a normal little family, cruelly dislocated in a comparatively short period of time. I find my heart is hammering and my hands are shaking. I follow the kind young man when he carries the cylinder to my car.

"Thank you so much," I manage to say.

"Are you all right?" He sounds concerned. I feel sick, and I'm sure the colour has drained from my face.

"Yes, yes, I'm fine."

I sit quietly for a few moments, trying to steady myself before I start the car. Now I have to return to Pollards, the house I have grown to dislike. Nothing good seems to emanate from that cold austere dwelling. I tell myself I am being fanciful, that Andrea's parents, the kindly doctor and his wife, lived there happily and brought up a daughter there.

Panicky, I try to remember the instructions the young man give me but I can't remember one word of them. I dread being inadequate in an emergency, and I pray that the nurse will understand how it works.

She does, and between us we carry the cylinder to the bedroom. Andrea seems to have shrunk to a little ball somewhere in the middle of the big bed, and the nurse crawls across it to fix the mask over her face. I don't want to see any more, and I leave.

There is no one around to see me go. I think Margaret will have taken Ian to the local playground. My feet echo on the wooden floor of the entrance hall of what seems like an empty house. I get in my car and drive away.

Maeve, always a good listener, says: "It's awful for you, darling," when I tell her of the events of the morning.

"It isn't really awful for me," I reply unhappily. "It's awful for *her*. I'm healthy, as far as I know, and lead a normal life. After I leave you I'll go to the school to collect my two wonderful sons – I'm so lucky. How could I ever think I was unlucky?"

I feel guilty, guilty for having so much going for me, guilty for a transient feeling of resentment this morning when I felt I should not be involved in Andrea's troubles, guilty at this moment because I have just given Maeve a graphic description of my difficulties collecting the oxygen cylinder, selfishly making out it was such a terrible experience for me. Me – that's all I think about.

"It's a tragedy that's bound to affect everyone," Maeve says.

"Margaret and Ian are coming to me on Saturday. You'll come, won't you? Sheelagh as well, of course."

"I think I should give it a miss," she says.

"The boys will be there."

"I'm so useless. I can't help you. I'm afraid I'll be a burden."

"You know you can never be that," I tell her. "Please come."

When Margaret arrives on Saturday morning, I hold the ladder and she clambers into the loft to fetch the old high chair, not used since Neil grew out of it. Between us, we scrub it for Ian's use. He sits in it for lunch, next to Maeve.

Maeve dotes on Ian. Her laughter can be heard when he stretches out a little hand and snatches a potato from her plate. After the meal she sits in her usual chair by a bright fire, protected by a guard, and he clings to her knee and plays with her pearls. Somehow, she manages to haul him on to one of her knees, and she jiggles him up and down, singing 'The Grand Old Duke of York'. There is complete rapport between them, and it doesn't pass unnoticed by Neil, who says reprovingly: "He's only a baby."

"Yes, I know," says Maeve, understanding at once, "and rather silly. Not like you, I'm glad to say."

Later in the afternoon we go for a walk. Margaret, stronger than I, pushes the wheelchair, and I am in charge of Ian in his pushchair. He sleeps, his face rosy in the crisp air. Sheelagh wrapped in a thick coat with a woolly hat on her head and gloves on her hands, strides stoically. I get the impression that she does not really like the country. The boys and Flush race ahead, disturbing fallen leaves with their feet. I mourn the passing of a beautiful summer but the change in the seasons is the thing I appreciate most about England. Winter has its compensations and I welcome the sharp cold air on my face. I wonder how I should feel if I knew I would never see another spring? Although I try hard to suppress them, my mind is prey to gloomy thoughts.

When we get home Ian is awake, and we all feel invigorated by fresh air and exercise, and ready for tea.

Getting everyone organised is an undertaking; collecting the coats, hats, gloves and scarves and stowing them away. Folding Maeve's wheelchair and

Ian's pushchair, and getting Maeve settled into her chair. And all the time, Sheelagh fussing around, and getting in the way. I know that in a moment Margaret will come and help me in the kitchen but, in the meantime, Hugh and Neil are showing off and I am shouting at them. Ian, who is unused to a raised voice, starts to cry, and it is at this moment that I glance through the window and see Dan walking up the path.

I know what he has come to tell us, and I open the door.

"Yes," he says, "early this afternoon." His face is wooden. "Will you fetch Margaret?"

I go back into the room that is suddenly quiet. The boys are silenced by the realisation that something has happened, and Ian is in Margaret's arms and has stopped crying. Maeve, Sheelagh by her side, looks on.

I nod to Margaret and, still holding Ian, she follows me into the hall. Dan speaks quietly to her, as if he thinks the baby might hear and understand him, and she bursts into tears. He looks at her in silent amazement, no pity, no sympathy, as if he is in a dream. He takes his little son from her, and Ian wraps his fat arms around his father's neck. Dan walks ahead, and Margaret, still weeping, follows him to the car. Nothing more is said.

"Should I have suggested that Margaret and Ian stay here?" I have the old feeling of inadequacy – that somehow I should have done more.

"No," says Maeve firmly, "I think Dan wanted them to be at home."

Sheelagh says: "God in his wisdom has released her from her suffering."

We have all forgotten about the boys.

"Is Andrea dead?" Hugh asks urgently.

He and his brother stand and regard us, eyes wide open and questioning.

"Yes," I answer, "you must have known she was very ill."

"We knew she was ill but we didn't know she was going to die."

I see Neil looking at me with fear in his eyes. I know he is wondering if I am going to die as well. He thought I was safe; death is for old people and animals.

"Sometimes young people like Andrea get ill and die," I tell him kneeling and hugging him to my breast. "It does not happen very often, and when it does it is especially sad."

"What will Ian do without a mummy?" he wants to know, and I do not know how to answer him.

Chapter 35

Of course, I do not go to the funeral; it would be inappropriate for me to be there, and Maeve stays away because it is difficult to get her wheelchair through the church door. Sheelagh insists on going, and Margaret, driving the car, picks her up at her cottage before coming to my house to collect the boys. They are dressed in the same clothes they wore for their father's marriage ceremony. I wondered if Neil was a bit too young and sensitive to go but Dan wanted them both to be there.

I am left at home with Ian. We dress up warm and go into the garden and play in the plastic sandpit I have recently bought for him. He fills his little bucket with sand and solemnly scatters it around the garden, returning to refill it. I feel the same little twinge of irritation I remember sensing when Hugh and Neil, in turn, did the same thing and, to divert him, I show him how to make a sandcastle. This occupies us for some time before I take him indoors for a cup of milk and a biscuit.

Margaret appears, without Sheelagh or the boys, and she explains she has dropped Sheelagh off at her cottage, and Hugh and Neil are with their father. She is anxious to talk and I am ready to listen. She tells me the church was packed. Apparently, Andrea had many local friends, having lived in the same place all her life. There was a group of young women, schoolfriends, who sat in a disconsolate line; Margaret's voice breaks when she tells me about them.

Later, I hear Sheelagh's version of the event. "Dan behaved with such dignity," she tells me. She admires him greatly, and never remembers that he deserted me and his children to be with another woman. It is such a classic case of infidelity one would imagine someone like Sheelagh would be shocked by it. Not her. Sometimes I think she has convinced herself that I was responsible for the breakdown of the marriage and the subsequent divorce – she has managed to reconcile her religious views on morality with the approval of the man. Maeve takes an amused cynical stand, and maintains that Sheelagh is in love with Dan. "All devout Catholic women are the same," she says. "Religious fervour is just sex that has no outlet."

Andrea's death occurs just before Christmas, a festival very hard to disregard. It has to be faced whatever the circumstances. I am aware of Dan, Margaret and Ian in that house of mourning, and it is inevitable that they should come to me on Christmas Day. For the sake of Hugh and Neil who look forward to the event, and for Ian who does not understand it, we all make a tremendous effort to be cheerful. And, surprisingly, we succeed. Maeve buys the Christmas tree and Dan purchases the turkey. Everyone helps so there is no question of me playing the martyr; Sheelagh sets the table and Margaret prepares the vegetables. When it is suggested she go to her family in Devon she opts to stay with us. "I think I'm needed here," she says.

In the midst of all this activity the telephone rings and it is Monica.

"I thought you might feel lonely."

"Well, no, as a matter of fact . . ."

"I just thought I'd give you a ring." She has never done so before on Christmas Day.

"It's very nice of you. How is Barry?"

"He's fine." There is a little pause. "We're getting married."

"Monica! I'm so happy for you. When is that going to happen?"

"Sometime in the new year – I'll let you know. You like him, don't you?"

"I do, very much. He was so kind to me. Please tell him how pleased I am that he is going to be my brother-in-law."

"I'll tell him. He likes you too. We often speak of you."

During that short phone call I feel closer to my sister

than I have for a very long time. When I return to the table, laden with food and strewn with remnants of crackers, I say: "That was my sister – she is going to get married."

Dan looks up and says: "How do you feel about that?"

"Pleased," I say.

I am glad that Christmas worked for everyone; it could so easily have been a disaster. In no time at all we are plunged into a new year, and our lives continue in the same pattern as before, except that I am aware that Dan is alone in that unfriendly house. Not strictly alone because Margaret and Ian are with him, and Margaret tells me that he comes home early so that he can see his little son before he goes to bed.

Ian starts going to nursery school, mornings only, and Margaret has got in to the habit of coming to see me before she collects him in the car. I see a lot of Ian, on the days when Margaret is free to do as she likes and always during the weekends. She tells me that her romance with the young farmer in Devon is over; the distance between them finished it. She has a new boyfriend, a vet who lives locally. He has a little house, and enough money to support a wife, so it is serious.

The boys spend most weekends with their father. Dan brings them home early on Sunday evenings, and he usually stays to have a drink. A routine is established, and one evening before the end of the summer I ask him if he would like to stay for supper.

"Yes," he says, "I would like that very much."

"What about Ian?"

"Margaret is with him. She has her boyfriend there, so I expect I'd be in the way."

"What's he like?"

"A nice bloke, I like him. He spends a lot of time at Pollards, but he is so pleasant I can't object. I can see it's a bit of an out-of-the-way place for a girl like Margaret. I don't want her to leave so I'm glad she's met him."

"Do you think they are lovers?" He laughs. "Of course, they are! It would be unusual if they were not, these days, wouldn't it? But nothing like that happens in my house because he has a place of his own."

Every Sunday when he brings the boys home the same thing happens. I ask him if he wants to stay for supper, he hesitates and then accepts. It is apparent that Hugh and Neil like him to be here. I sense they are not so sure about their visits to Pollards. Perhaps, like me, they find it oppressive, but, with the years, they have acquired sensitivity, and they would never let on that they would prefer to be at home.

The Sunday suppers are easy and relaxed. I wonder if they would be if the boys were not present. Sometimes Maeve joins us, and he drives her back to Riverbank. I know she is fond of him.

One day she asks me the question that I know is inevitable. "Have you thought of taking him back?"

The possibility has crossed my mind from time to time, but I don't want to think about it. The months, the weeks, the days pass so quickly; I can't believe it is nearly a year since Andrea died. I know Dan still grieves, but the strained look has left his face. He looks younger than he did when Andrea was so ill.

"It's far too soon to think of anything like that," I say to Maeve, "and anyway, it wouldn't work. We are better off as we are."

Chapter 36

It is a year and a half since Andrea's death. Margaret, who comes to my house as often as she can, tells me that the vet, David Abbott, to whom she is now engaged, does not like her staying in the house with Dan.

"It's unreasonable," she says, "and I keep telling him that, but he won't listen. Dan has never touched me. He isn't interested – Andrea was the love of his life."

She realises what she has said, and I watch the colour suffuse her face. "I'm so sorry," she mumbles.

I ignore her embarrassment, and ask: "Are you and David going to get married soon?"

"We are saving up for it," she tells me, "but weddings are so expensive. My parents are poor people, so we would have to pay for it ourselves."

I wonder why so many young people think that a full-blown wedding is an important beginning to a marriage. "Couldn't you have a quiet wedding," I say, "without all the trimmings?"

"We could," she admits reluctantly, "but it's supposed to be the best day of a girl's life, isn't it?"

"What are you going to do about David's objections? It seems an insoluble problem. If you get another job, and I know that would upset Dan and Ian, you will be moved away from here, and surely that wouldn't suit David either? I agree with you, he is being very unreasonable."

"I don't know what to do," says Margaret unhappily. "I suppose I shall have to mention it to Dan, but that is so awkward."

"I'll talk to him, if you like."

"Would you?" she says eagerly. "I would be so grateful."

Sometimes when Dan gets away from the office early during the week, he telephones me and suggests that he picks the boys up from school. Today he says: "If I bring the food, may I stay for supper this evening?"

I reply: "Of course," and I think, this will be a good opportunity to talk to him about Margaret's problem.

Three cheerful males burst in, the oldest one holding a fish pie that he has cooked himself; fish pie was always Dan's speciality. As usual, he brings with him a bottle of wine. He is always careful to restrict himself to one glass as he is driving home, and I try to do the same. This evening is different because there is a feeling of festivity in the air, which has been sadly lacking for many months. When Hugh and Neil go to bed Dan does not get up to leave, but sits down in his chair and refills his glass.

I tell him what Margaret has told me, and I see at once his mood changes. I have presented him with a difficulty, and his life during the last two years has been besieged with difficulties. Perhaps this evening, the light-hearted chatter of the boys and the good food and wine, has made him forget his troubles, but I have given him something else to worry about, and I feel mortified about it.

"I'm sorry," I say. "She asked me to mention it to you."

"I don't understand," he says. "What is she worried about?"

"It is not Margaret who is worried. It is David, and I agree it is quite unreasonable of him. Poor Margaret does not know how to deal with it."

"She could tell him to get his act together."

"I think she loves him."

"What difference does that make?"

I begin to feel slightly irritated by his reaction. "I am only passing on what she has told me. What you do about it is your own business."

Immediately, I am sorry to have spoken harshly. He looks so dejected. "I don't have the slightest idea what to do about it," he admits. "I can't imagine what I would do without Margaret. She is a splendid girl, and Ian loves her. I suppose she will leave, and I will have to start looking for someone else. It is not a pleasant prospect."

We sit, holding our glasses of wine, looking at each other. He is preoccupied by thoughts of Margaret's departure and a stranger entering his house. I am certain he has no inking of what I am about to say and, for that matter, I could not have foretold it myself. The words came out without my planning them, and now they are in the open there is no recalling them.

"Do you want to come back here?"

Maeve and I have talked endlessly about the situation. Sometimes I think we hardly talk of anything else when we are alone, without Sheelagh who we have been careful to leave out of our discussions.

Maeve says: "He would never ask you himself. His pride would stop him from doing that."

We weigh up the pros and cons. The pros consist of advantages to the boys, especially Ian, now nearly three years old, who would benefit from having a proper family, and the shelving of the access weekends and the holiday arrangements would be a great relief. Lately, I asked Dan:"What about the holidays this summer? Have you made plans for you and the children?" Last year, when everything was so raw and he had to attune himself to a completely new way of life, the holidays were not mentioned, and Hugh and Neil spent most of the time in my garden.

He looked harassed. "No. Should I have?"

Getting rid of the annual token holiday, when I am miserable until their return, would be a welcome change from my point of view.

The cons are more difficult to analyse.

"You have to think of yourself," says Maeve. "Are you happy as you are?"

"I am no longer unhappy."

"Do you still have feelings for him?"

"Not as I did. I feel differently. I don't love him in the same way."

"Perhaps that is a good thing." But I can tell she is uncertain.

As soon as the words were uttered, I wish they had never been spoken. "Do you want to come back here?" sounds like a plea. I remember, so many years ago, saying: "Please don't leave me," and how, on that occasion, Dan had purposely misconstrued my appeal. This time, I do not want him to think I am begging.

"Is it the wine talking?" Dan asks. "You don't usually drink so much."

"Maybe, but answer me, just the same, and we will think about it again in the sober light of day."

"Do you want me to stay here tonight?"

It is the last thing I want. "No, I don't want that. I know you should not drive, so leave the car and I will ring for a taxi."

I feel my heart hammering and my hands are clammy because he has not answered my question.

Perhaps I have presumed too much, and returning is the last thing he wants to do.

"Yes," he says firmly. "I'd like to do that. Come back, I mean."

"It is not going to be easy for either of us," I tell him. It is Maeve talking. "We have to be kind with ourselves because we have been through a great deal. All we can do is take it day by day. There are rules I think we should agree upon before we embark on such a venture."

"You have the right to make the rules," he says.

"The most important one is sleeping – no double bed."

"Oh?"

"Singles. Better than separate rooms, which the boys would notice. Children are very perceptive about such things and, in that way, we would not lose the delight of them coming to us in the morning."

I pause. It is the first time I have thought of it, but I wonder if Hugh and Neil invaded Dan and Andrea's bedroom when they stayed with them. Suddenly, I have a picture in my mind of two little boys bursting into the room and hurling themselves on to the bed, with much laughter from everyone.

"What is the matter?" Dan asks.

"Nothing."

"Is it going to work?" I ask Maeve. She never advises me, one way or another, on this issue. She tells me that

I must make up my own mind, but I sense her doubts and they worry me.

"Something important is lost forever," I say. "Can we make anything of what is left?"

I ask the same question to Dan, and he answers seriously, "I believe we can. I want it to work."

He does not waste any time after I ask him that question. The following day he puts Pollards on the market at a price lower than recommended by the estate agent. He wants to sell it quickly.

Decorators come to my house and completely change what was once our marital bedroom. The double bed is put into the spare room, and this is to be Margaret's room. I give her a television and an armchair and I tell her that David can come and stay whenever she wants. After all, I reason, the boys are used to unmarried people sleeping together.

I planned for Hugh and Neil to have separate rooms now that they are getting so grown-up, but this plan has been scrapped because the little room has to be delegated to Ian. Dan and I discuss the possibility of building on when Pollards has been sold. He will have money to spend on improvements then. We make many plans, and he comes most evenings and we sit and talk about the future. We skim the surface, both of us too afraid to explore the tricky subject of how we will face life together again. Andrea's name is never mentioned, and I wish he would speak of her. I hope a time will come when we can talk about her quite naturally.

I think he has more confidence about what lies ahead of us than I have – I feel an intense excitement in him, an enthusiasm that has been missing for a very long time. I welcome it, but I find the responsibility overwhelming. He relies on me not to have a change of heart. I am aware of his anxiety and it should gladden me, but I am strangely unmoved.

I am busy creating a bedroom for Ian, and I scour the shops for original curtain material to replace the old hat soldiers the boys still have in their room. All this activity reminds me of the days when we first moved into our house, when every new acquisition was a thrill. I am so preoccupied I tend to forget the mind-blowing change that is about to take place in my well-ordered life. For my life has become ordered; somehow, at some stage, it changed from being chaotically unfulfilled to being comfortably organised. Now, everything will be different, and I am not sure I want it that way.

My thoughts often turn to Ian. Instead of two boys I shall have three. Because of his startling resemblance to Neil he has always seemed like my child, but I don't want to lose sight of the fact that he is not wholly mine. By showing him photographs and talking to him about his mother I hope to instil in him an interest in someone he cannot remember. It is the least I can do for her.

Chapter 37

I get a telephone call from Edinburgh, for a young woman called Emma Banks who has replaced Mrs Davenport, now retired. She says she has heard from the judge who apologises for the delay and says he would like to meet Maeve, as planned.

It is so unexpected, I am lost for words for a moment; and then I ask: "Does he give a reason for taking so long?"

"He has been very preoccupied with his daughter's wedding."

I think it is a pretty feeble excuse and, when I tell her, Maeve agrees with me. "Cold feet," she says. "It's understandable."

Sheelagh is incensed. "He must be completely heartless! Don't waste your thoughts on him, Mother dear. We have each other – we don't need him."

"No, I don't need him," Maeve says slowly. I feel she has lost interest in so many things. Not in my family, not in the three boys whom she adores, but in some of the things she enjoyed so much, eating in restaurants, shopping, they have lost their allure, and public places and crowds of people daunt her. It has been a gradual process, and one that I suppose is inevitable now she is approaching ninety-eight. I think she is in pain most of the time, but she does not complain. Her kindly doctor prescribes drugs to help her, but she takes them for a couple of days and then forgets. The drawer of her dressing-table at Riverbank is crowded with discarded pill bottles. The nurses at the Home try to persuade her to take her medication, but she gets tetchy with them. Advancing years have made her querulous.

"He would not think much of me," she says.

"Do you want to see him?"

She can't make up her mind. "Let's leave it for the present, darling," she says wearily.

But the judge insists, and Emma asks me to give a date when I can meet him at the station. "Perhaps he could stay overnight with you?"

"No," I say firmly. "There is no room. The house is full of workmen. I'll arrange for him to stay at a local hotel."

"What do you think?" I ask Dan. I have got into the habit, once more, of consulting him about almost everything.

"I think Maeve should meet him," he says. "You

know what's she's like, she'll rise to the occasion, and it can't be more disappointing than Sheelagh, and look how's she turned out. Quite helpful, in fact, and Maeve has grown fond of her. However, you must warn her he's coming. Don't let it be a surprise. She might never forgive you."

An unforgiving Maeve is too awful to contemplate. I break the news to her gently. "If you agree, he can come next week. I'll meet him at the station and bring him straight here."

She smiles at me sweetly. "All right, darling. That's good of you." She leans back in her chair and closes her eyes, as if she is tired of the whole thing.

With so little enthusiasm I find it hard to make the arrangements, but after many telephone calls to Edinburgh it is finally settled; I will meet him at noon, and we three will have lunch at Riverbank. I suggest that Maeve lunches with him alone, but she will not hear of it.

"What would we find to talk about? It would be too awkward."

Sheelagh is not included. Maeve, who is now very considerate of Sheelagh's feelings, says to her: "You don't mind, do you, dear? You will have lots of time to talk to him during the afternoon."

Sheelagh does not mind, or pretends she does not mind. She has taken it into her head that she will dislike the judge.

On the morning of his impending arrival I go to

Riverbank. Something impels me to call at the Home on the way back from taking the children to school. I tell myself that I want assurance that Maeve is prepared for this important day, that she has no last-minute qualms. It is strange, because I know that she is not good in the mornings; she never wants company until after eleven o'clock. I have always respected her wishes, no telephone calls, and no unexpected visits. And yet that is exactly what I am doing this morning, making an unexpected visit; it is as if an unseen hand is pointing me in Maeve's direction. I park the car and walk thoughtfully into the hall.

I see Moira, already behind her desk, and her face betrays her.

"Early this morning," she says. "She rang her bell, and the night nurse went to her at once. She had a heart attack, a bad one this time. I called the doctor and Father Donovan. The priest arrived in time, but the doctor came too late."

Even at such a moment, I am doubtful. "Would she want a priest there?"

"Oh, yes," said Moira decidedly. "She wanted him there all right. I've seen it over and over again. Once a Catholic, always a Catholic I say. He gave her the last rites and we could both see she was pleased." She looks into my stricken face. "I'm so sorry," she says. "I know how fond you were of her."

It is hard to believe, but not really. The death of a very old lady whose life has been fading away for some time; I recognise that fact but it does not make it any easier to bear. I can't think of anything to say to Moira.

"And her friend was coming to lunch," she says, and illogically, "so disappointing for them both."

"Her son," I tell her. Even at this moment of grief I can't resist uttering those words.

"Really?" Moira looks satisfyingly mystified. "I didn't know she had a son."

"I must let him know at once, stop him from coming. Please forgive me for not staying any longer." I drive home and telephone Emma straight away. For reasons best known to themselves the adoption agency have never revealed the judge's address, nor, of course, his telephone number, but various clues have led me to believe he lives in London, so it is not far to come. I do know his name, Stephen Hollingsworth, Hollingsworth being the name of his adoptive parents. Somehow, we have never called him anything but the judge.

Emma says: "Of course, I will let him know at once. He will be devastated."

I do not believe her. He will not be devastated by the death of someone unknown to him. Perhaps a little disconcerted that his plan for the day has been scotched.

Next, I have the onerous task of telling Sheelagh. I drive to her little rented cottage and break the news as kindly as I can. She sobs uncontrollably, and I put my arms around her. When she can speak, she says: "I have to thank you for bringing us together."

I wait until we are at home, after the school collection, before I tell the boys. Hugh and Neil look at me in total disbelief. Like me, they can't imagine life without Maeve. It seems to them that she has always been there; she has been part of the fabric of their childhood, reading aloud to them long past the time when they could read for themselves, talking to them at their own level in a language they can understand, swearing in her inimitable way, inoffensive but causing them great delight. Ian watches their faces, and bursts into tears, as if he has decided it is the right thing to do. I think how strange that he weeps for Maeve, and yet was too young to weep for his mother. He is a sensitive child and picks up the moods of others very quickly. Dan and I are careful not to speak sharply to him because he gets upset. Now he has detected a change in the normal routine of his childish existence, and it frightens him. Margaret appears, and I tell her quickly what has happened, and she takes him off to divert him by playing with his cars and garage. Presently I hear them chatting happily, and I put my arms around my two sons, who are not so easily diverted.

"Does Daddy know?" asks Hugh, and I am instantly aware that Dan does not know. I telephone him at his office, and I hear a little groan at the end of the line.

"Oh, God," he says. I know at once that this is something we share, our love for Maeve.

"I'm coming home," he says, "right away." This is, and always has been, his home, and I rejoice to hear him acknowledge it. After a lot of uncertainty, broken chains and restarts, Pollards has at last been sold, and he can call this house, the place we found together so many years ago, his home.

Chapter 38

Emma telephones me from Edinburgh and tells me the judge has expressed a desire to attend Maeve's funeral.

And so it is, I am standing on the platform watching the train draw into the station, studying the passengers as they disembark. I see him walking towards me. I know it must be the person I am waiting for because he is a man travelling alone and because he looks what he is, a judge. He is wearing a long black coat, very elegant, and no doubt his funeral coat. His head is uncovered and I see grey hair. He is tall and thickset. I move towards him, and he says: "Mrs Maitland?"

I nod. We smile at each other uncertainly as people do when they have not met before. His handshake is cool and firm, and I look into the familiar blue eyes and a face with a slightly quizzical almost amused expression.

I know at once that Maeve would have loved him.

When we are in the car and I am driving to the crematorium, he says: "I'm sorry it is like this, and I am entirely to blame. If only I had come sooner."

"You were busy with your daughter's wedding," I say generously. "It is not your fault."

"It was not just that," he says. "I was not sure . . ."

I think for a judge to admit uncertainty must be unusual. I stare at the road ahead of me.

He goes on: "I thought my motive for coming was between curiosity and commitment, and I could not decide which was the stronger reason. Curiosity is base and I had doubts about commitment."

"There would have been no need for commitment," I reply coldly.

"No." His voice is faintly reproving, and I can see his opinions are rarely questioned. "Without commitment the meeting would have had no meaning."

I drive in silence. I am at a loss for words. I want to say something caustic about his non-appearance at Riverbank having said he wanted to come, about Maeve being a very old lady who had suffered a disappointment, although I am not sure about the last bit. Perhaps Maeve had been secretly relieved at not having to endure the awkwardness of meeting him. The man sitting stolidly by my side is slightly formidable, so I say nothing.

He speaks again, this time rather sadly. "I'm afraid I'm inclined to be too cautious."

I find my voice to say: "Well, it's a failing Maeve did not possess."

There are only a few people at the service. Dan and I discussed whether Hugh and Neil should go but then decided against it. We both felt that Maeve would not want them to be at her funeral. I want them to have memories of her, as she was, an everlastingly good-natured friend. I am glad they are not here, sitting beside me, looking at the coffin covered with flowers, disturbed by wild imaginings of the cumbersome form lying within. Dan is collecting them from school, having taken off time from the office to do so. He takes more time off work than he used to. I remember thinking when we were first married that work came top in his order of priorities; now I am sure it is much further down the line, and the family takes first place.

I nod at Moira, looking smart, and some of the staff at Riverbank, and I can't help thinking how tired they must get of attending funerals. I sit on a hard chair in this rather ornate room between the judge on my left and Sheelagh on my right. Sheelagh was here when we arrived, and there was no time to make introductions. She is wracked with sobs, and I notice the judge gives her a puzzled glance. He does not know of her existence, and I fear she will blurt out the truth of her identity after the service. This would be acutely embarrassing, and I sit wondering how I shall deal with such a contingency.

There is a planned efficiency about the procedure that makes it seem rather impersonal. I compare it to marrying in a registry office as opposed to marrying in church, and I remember that we are in a slot and there are people waiting in the wings to take over from us. Father Donovan wanted Maeve to have a funeral in the Catholic church with a Catholic burial, but I remembered her expressing a wish to be cremated. After a great deal of discussion I won. Now, remembering Moira's comments (once a Catholic always a Catholic) I wonder if I did the right thing. Father Donovan is here, hovering around the man taking the service, and he gives a small homily, depicting Maeve as a deeply religious lady with an unblemished character.

My thoughts wander and I think of Dan collecting the boys from school. I think they will be unusually quiet. Margaret and Ian will be at home waiting for them, and they will all sit down at the kitchen table to have their tea (about now). Tomorrow is the end of term, and the day after we go abroad on our summer holiday. Dan has made himself responsible for all the planning, and I know he is anxious to make it a success. I am looking forward to it. Much as I love our house I can't wait to turn my back on the workmen and the endless negotiations with the council for permission to build an extension. That is to start soon after our return and it will coincide with the completion date on Pollards and Dan's departure from that house. In the meantime, we will be able to relax on a beach, eat food that I have not prepared, and Margaret is coming with us so she will be there to help me with the children. When we return she is taking another holiday with David.

I am thinking of all these things throughout the service and, when it is over, I feel ashamed that I have hardly thought of Maeve at all, but I don't think she would mind. To my relief, Sheelagh does not move when we all get up to leave, and she remains, kneeling in prayer.

"Are you coming with us?" I whisper.

"No, thank you, dear. Father Donovan is giving me a lift."

"I'm afraid that service gave you no idea of Maeve," I say to the judge as we walk back to my car.

He nods. "Funerals can be like that. I find some memorial services give a flavour of the person involved, reminiscences of friends and family make for more understanding."

He is so pedantic, but there is charm there as well.

He takes my hand. "I have enjoyed meeting you," he says. For a moment he looks rather forlorn, more human than at any time during our time together. "Please can you tell me where I can get a taxi back to the station?"

"No," I say firmly, taking his arm, "you can get a later train, and I will see that you get it. In the meantime, Stephen, I would like to take you home so that you can meet my family." It is the first time I have called him by his name, Stephen, and marks the beginning of my forgetting about him being a judge, and remembering only that he is Maeve's son.

"I'd like that," he says, smiling.

In the car he says: "The lady who sat next to us, and was so upset – is she a friend or a relative?"

I explain Sheelagh's part in Maeve's life. He is amazed. "Good heavens," he says, "is there no end to what I am going to discover? I wish I had known. I would like to have met her."

"I'm sorry you did not."

There is a silence while I think about Sheelagh, and an idea I have in my mind comes to the surface. "Now I am beginning to understand what you meant by commitment – when you told me that a meeting with Maeve would be meaningless without it. Of course, you were right when you said that, and from the moment Sheelagh discovered about her real mother she was committed. Every moment of her life from then on was devoted to Maeve. I did not appreciate it until now, but it's true – she is a wonderful woman."

He says: "You make me feel ashamed for the sorry part I played."

"No, there is no reason for you to feel ashamed. I was just a little late in finding you, and by that time Maeve had lost her hold on life – she was beyond taking on another relationship."

They are all there to greet us when we arrive. Dan grasps Stephen's hand, the boys are polite and interested, Margaret is introduced and Ian races around the room being silly.

I catch Stephen's eye, and he give me his whimsical little smile. I see in his face relief for this oasis in all the complications that have faced him today. We are, as he sees us at this moment, refreshingly ordinary, a nice straightforward middle-class family, no doubt similar to the one he has left at home.

Chapter 39

Dan and I have been back in our house for about a week when I receive a letter from Maeve's solicitor asking me to come and see him. I hand it over the breakfast table to Dan who is sitting opposite me. For a few moments only we are alone, and I can hear the boys upstairs, banging and shouting while they get their belongings ready for school. Margaret is on holiday with David; otherwise she would have quietened them down by now. In a minute they will all three come clattering down the stairs, and Dan will hustle them into his car. This morning it is his turn to take them to school. We take it in turns, he takes them in the morning and I collect them, Ian at noon and Hugh and Neil in the afternoon. Tomorrow the arrangement will be reversed, and it is a plan, like so many of our recently made plans, that works well.

Since the family holiday, I know, without doubt, that my decision to ask him to return was the right one. On the first night in the hotel we sat on the terrace, listening to the sea quietly lapping on to the beach, and we talked. As I hoped, he was open with me about his love for Andrea. It had been very real, and that is a fact of life I must learn to accept and understand. I can never forget that he was prepared to give up his home, his children and his life with me to be with her. If, miraculously, she was alive again I know he would be with her and not with me. But, at last, I have learnt to realise that life is not about perfection, it is about getting on with things, and appreciating what one has. And I know, and somehow I have always known, that Dan did not stop loving me; he just loved Andrea more.

It helps me to feel that I shared Andrea with him, a small part of Andrea. Hugh, Neil and I shared her – we felt grief when she died, not like Dan, of course, but it touched us. I cannot think of her as a vengeful fury, intent of my destruction, but more as a young woman, vulnerable after a traumatic experience, who happened to fall in love with my husband.

I remember that night in Castlerock, and I think I begin to understand. Sitting, with our glasses of wine, surrounded by the warmth of a Spanish summer evening, I could so easily have told him about that night in Ireland. But I did not, because Dan is a man, and men do not understand about such things unless they are happening to themselves. I told Maeve, but now she is gone, the secret is mine alone, and I can think about it whenever I please, and no one can ask me questions about it, or make it seem insignificant and tawdry. Instinctively, I know that, with the best will in the world, Dan would diminish its importance, and he would be wrong. Only Tom Byrne and I know how wrong he would be. I think of him often, and I am sure he thinks of me, and that is a comfort. We are both getting on with our lives, making as many people contented as we can, and yet knowing, at the same time, we had those brief moments of complete happiness that set us apart from everyone else. That must be a blessing to carry into old age.

Dan hands me back the letter across the table. "She has left you something in her Will," he says.

It is hard to believe that I have never thought of the disposition of Maeve's wealth, for wealth I am sure she possessed. She mentioned it enough, goodness knows, when she was making excuses for extravagances – but that may have been one of her exaggerations. Now it has been brought to my notice I feel slightly tainted, as if I am suddenly made aware that there are other aspects to her death, other than that I miss her and would give anything to have her back with us again.

The solicitor's name is Mr Andrews. He tells me that Theo's parents were friends of his parents. "I knew him all my life," he says. "Of course, he was a great deal older than me." It is hard to imagine anyone older than Mr Andrews, and I can't imagine why he has not retired years ago. He must just enjoy pottering around his sumptuous office.

I take the chair opposite him, and he sits behind an imposing desk on which reposes a file containing, I surmise, the Will.

He extracts it with a slightly shaking hand, straightens his spectacles on his nose, and says: "Mrs Bailey left several bequests . . ." There is a long pause, and then he begins to read very slowly. "To each of the children of her friend Jennifer, Countess of Durlington, now deceased, she leaves the sum of five thousand pounds, with the exception of Simon, her godson, who receives ten thousand pounds." He then proceeds to read out a list of people who are to get five thousand pounds, many of the names I do not recognise and I assume they are friends in Shropshire or servants who worked for her, then I hear names that are familiar to me, members of the staff at Riverbank who cared for her during her final years, and to Moira Adamson (strange that I never knew her full name) a pearl and diamond brooch she once admired. Margaret too has not been forgotten, she has been left five thousand pounds, and I have the fleeting thought she will now be able to afford her wedding, so she will be leaving us.

Mr Andrews continues reading in his flat emotionless voice: "Her daughter, Sheelagh Devane has been left all her furniture and effects stored in a depository in Wolverhampton. Her portfolio of investments is bequeathed in equal shares to three minors, Hugh, Neil and Ian Maitland. The Victoria Cross awarded to Mrs Bailey's first husband, Sergeant John Deacon, is left to

Hugh Maitland because he showed such interest in it."

Mr Andrews removes his spectacles and looks at me. He speaks in a dispassionate voice. "Mrs Bailey's jewellery and the residue of her estate are left to you."

I am speechless. He says: "I cannot give you a definite figure at present, but after the bequests, death duties, payment of money owing to Riverbank and various shops, funeral expenses and my firm's fees I think it will be in the region of. . ."

He names a figure that is hard to take in. I find myself clutching the arms of the chair. "Goodness!" is all I can say.

He continues in a kinder tone: "After Theo's death Maeve put a lot of money into various building societies. I don't think she had much faith in stocks and shares; she never touched them and she was quite happy to leave the administration of them to a firm dealing in financial management. She received a pension from the company Theo owned, and that was paid into her bank account, and she drew upon that for incidental expenses and payments to Riverbank."

The idea of inheriting so much money makes me feel unreasonably guilty. I have enough already and a husband who earns enough to keep us all in comfort. And then I remember I do not have a husband, for Dan and I have decided not to remarry. We are independent people. I wonder how much Mr Andrews knows about Maeve and her background. Did he, as Theo's friend, recognise that the marriage was a charade? Theo lived nearly all his life in the same place, and Mr Andrews told me he lived in that county also, and perhaps heard the gossip about Maeve. Maeve herself told me there was gossip about her affair with Luke Rankin.

And now, what is his opinion of me, a stranger to him, about to receive a great inheritance? The thought passes through my mind that he must think I befriended Maeve with an ulterior motive, and I cannot bear him to think that. Suddenly I have a picture of Maeve lying in the spare room bed and saying: "I am completely happy," a sentiment she often expressed when she was with us, and, to my dismay, I feel the tears welling in my eyes.

"I loved her," I say.

His reply is gentle: "I can see that." He hands me a letter with my name on the front, written in Maeve's spidery handwriting. "She wrote to you," he said, "and you can read it in private."

I take it from him and get to my feet. I shake his frail liver-spotted hand. He volunteers a scrap of information difficult to envisage. "Theo was a rugger player," he says, "one of the best."

I do not open the letter until I am settled in the corner seat of the train carriage returning to Melford.

'Dearest girl,

By the time you read this you will have seen old Bob Andrews and he will have told you about my Will. However, I thought I'd explain it to you in my own way.

I have left my portfolio to the boys; Theo was a dab hand at investments so I hope they will be all right. I don't know the first thing about them myself, and I prefer to have money at hand rather than locked up where you can't touch it. As they are all minors, Bob has suggested he will open a trust fund for them, of which you, of course, will be a trustee, so you can put the dividends into their post office accounts, if you like, and take out some money, from time to time for treats.

The stuff in storage has worried me for years, and I think it is a real brainwave to leave it to Sheelagh. That woman needs a project, and this is it. It will give her something to think about instead of that bloody knitting. I would not dream of handing the responsibility to you, darling, you are much too busy, but Sheelagh has all the time in the world. The furniture is all antique, but most of it vast and hideous. Dan would not touch it with a bargepole. Let Sheelagh deal with it she can keep what she wants and sell the rest. The task will keep her occupied for years, and then she can give the proceeds to the church, if that is her wish. Please give her anything she wants from my effects; I did not think she would appreciate an item of jewellery, but I may be wrong about that. I'd like her to have the photograph of my mother – her grandmother. Tell her how glad I am to have found my daughter at last; she is endlessly good to me, and every day I appreciate it more.

I admire the step you are taking in setting up home with Dan again. It is a brave thing to do, and I wish you all the luck in the world. I hope the money will help in a small way. To my mind there is nothing like money to boost confidence, and it is there in case you become uneasy with the life you have chosen. I did not get independence until after Theo's death, and by then it was too late. Do you know, he would not allow me to buy any garment until he had vetted it? Men can be so domineering in many ways, but money has a magical effect on them. It makes them think twice before becoming overbearing. I know if I had been a woman of means, and not reliant on Theo for every penny, my life would have been very different. Women have power over men, but money gives them extra power and is more potent in the long run than personal attraction. Do what you want to do, and be happy, that is all I want for you.

Among my effects will be the life story, and please burn it in one of those lovely bonfires you have at the bottom of the garden. It is a life not worth recording, a series of mistakes and lost opportunities, but good moments just the same.

And one last thing — try to forget Andrea in your relationship with Dan. As I said before, women have power over men, but the power starts diminishing when the last breath is taken, whatever foolish people say to the contrary. He will remember her, of course, but the memory will become less clear every day of his life, until one day it has faded to almost nothing. It is sad for that poor girl, but we are all sad, we lost people who are gone forever.

You have been like a daughter to me (don't let Sheelagh see this, it might upset her and I would not do that for the world) and I love you and those precious boys of yours more than I can say.

Maeve.'

Postscript

One late afternoon in autumn I collect the fallen leaves and stack them on the bonfire. Then I tear the pages from Maeve's book and press them into the pile so that they form a basis for the fire. Ian is with me, stumping around in his Wellington boots. I tell him to stand clear while I light the paper with a match. The fire is sluggish at first, and then it suddenly comes to life and the flames and smoke rise towards the sky.

I stand holding Ian's hand while we watch it. I feel this is more of a thanksgiving for Maeve than I witnessed in the crematorium. The wind changes and the ashes blow in our direction.

Some of the leaves I have not managed to gather up are blowing around the lawn, and Flush starts chasing them – although a mature dog, on occasions he behaves like a puppy, and Ian joins in and they run around the garden together.

I stoke the fire with more paper until it has all gone, then I wait for the fire to subside.

Darkness is descending, and I say to Ian: "We'll go in now." He is well wrapped up, but even so it is cold, and I glance at my watch because I have to collect his brothers from school. In the house I can see Margaret moving about upstairs, drawing the curtains. Soon she will be downstairs, closing off the light from the windows.

Hand-in-hand we walk towards the house.

"Do you remember Maeve?" I ask.

He does not reply. He is thinking. Dan and I have decided he is a very thoughtful child. "I think I remember her," he says at last, but I suspect he is trying to please me.

He gives a little skip, letting go of my hand, and he runs, with all the abandoned grace of childhood, towards the lighted windows and the warmth within.

THE END

Published by Poolbeg.com

STILL WATERS RUN DEEP

NANCY ROSS

A scandal has broken – the secret mistress of Roderick Macauley, MP, has just sold her diary to the newspapers. He may have to resign.

Bridget, Macauley's daughter, sets off for Pondings, the family home. Her only thought is to be with her mother Duibhne in this crisis. But the political scandal is just the tip of the iceberg. Other secrets are lurking that will rock the family to the core.

Delphine Blake, reporter on *The Daily Graphic*, stumbles upon an even more startling story – the truth about the cool, beautiful Duibhne Macauley – or Lady Duibhne Shannon, as she was formerly known.

As Duibhne's extraordinary story unfolds, we learn that her serenity is like the polished, unruffled surface of a lake, hiding powerful currents and sinister secrets in its depths.

ISBN 1-84223-106-5

Published by Poolbeg.com

THE
ENCHANTED
ISLAND

NANCY ROSS

'It seemed to her that this short episode in her life had the substance of a dream – a dream from which she feared she must now awaken.'

Christabel first meets Ambrose Silveridge at a dinner party. The Silveridge name is synonymous with immense wealth and generosity. But Christabel is attracted to his striking good looks and how he overshadows everyone else at the table.

After a whirlwind romance, Ambrose proposes, but the forceful Lady Silveridge shows her displeasure at her son's choice of wife. By marrying Christabel he will lose his birthright. Christabel is enraged and her angered response drives the couple apart.

Hurt and confused, she goes to stay with her Aunt Bell on the tiny island, La Isla de la Fuga, the Island of Escape. Among its inhabitants she finds friendship and understanding and learns an intriguing tale of love which endures against all odds.

Can the love between Christabel and Ambrose overcome the obstacles in its path?

ISBN 1-84223-132-4